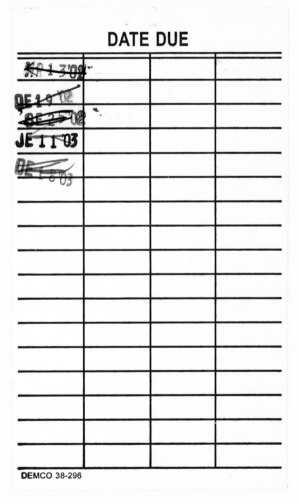

DATE DUE

~~JA 13'01~~		
~~DE 19'02~~		
~~SE 2 02~~		
JE 11 03		
~~DE 18 03~~		

DEMCO 38-296

BEST DETECTIVE STORIES
OF THE YEAR–1974

28th Annual Collection

BEST
DETECTIVE STORIES
OF THE YEAR
1974

28th Annual Collection

Edited by
ALLEN J. HUBIN

E. P. DUTTON & CO., INC. / NEW YORK / 1974

Published simultaneously in Canada
by Clarke, Irwin & Company Limited, Toronto and Vancouver

ISBN: 0-525-06433-8

Library of Congress Catalog Card Number: 46-5872

Contents

Introduction

Dark and boding have been the laments in recent years for the short story, particularly the mystery/detective short story—and this, it must be admitted, not without some justification. Gravestones have been erected over short crime fiction, as in the sepulchral implications of science-fiction writer Brian Aldiss' pronouncement in London's *The Bookseller* for July 14, 1973: "Science fiction is one of the remaining bastions of a strongly-told narrative . . . and certainly is the last stronghold of the short story."

Perhaps—just perhaps, these reports of moldering death have been grossly exaggerated; perhaps the pallbearers have turned out prematurely. Let's have a look at a few bits of evidence.

In 1972 the London *Times* had a happy idea: a contest for detective short stories. Expecting a modest harvest, the *Times* and the judges (a panel of five including Agatha Christie) were inundated with over 1000 entries. Out of this came a fine anthology, issued in 1973 in the U.S. (see the "Yearbook" section at the end of this volume), with the almost unique credentials of containing only hitherto unpublished stories.

(A publisher willing to chance untested detective stories, largely by unknown authors, in a dead art form? exclaimed the incredulous pallbearers. But then, of course, they recalled that the prestige of the *Times* was involved. *That* must be the explanation.)

Perhaps. But there's more.

The 1973 Yearbook also records *Men & Malice,* another an-

he 17 stories in this excellent volume, 13 were
en appearances.

. . .

on to an expansion of the number of general maga-
ishing fiction (and occasionally crime fiction), the
ng eyes of the pallbearers saw the launching of two new
st new) related magazines in 1973.

ne first is the quarterly *Weird Tales,* actually a revival, in
the pulp format of yore, of a magazine which vanished from the
scenes 19 years ago. Although generally directed to horror and
the supernatural, under the brilliant editorship of Sam Mosko-
witz it strays not infrequently into crime fiction as well. Most of
its tales are selected expertly from years past, but as its success
hopefully grows, so should its content of new stories.

The second new publication, from the same enterprising publisher, is *Charlie Chan Mystery Magazine.* Two quarterly issues
have appeared on newsstands as of this writing. CCMM is not
likely to wrest away EQMM's crown on first evidence, but all its
stories are new and it is certain to warm the criminous cockles of
not a few readers' (and writers') hearts.

The permanence of neither new magazine is assured, it is true,
but blessed be an expansion of the marketplace . . .

Possibly I'm immoderately encouraged. We (and the lurking
pallbearers) shall see. In the meantime, good times to you in a
selection of the tales published in 1973 that gave me most
pleasure.

ALLEN J. HUBIN
January 11, 1974

BEST DETECTIVE STORIES OF THE YEAR–1974

28th Annual Collection

I have argued before that the mystery story is the most versatile form in which to accomplish the widest diversity of literary objectives. For example, Arthur W. Upfield used it to explore a subculture (Australian aborigines) in fascinating depth and detail; Tony Hillerman studied the modern Navajo in similar fashion; and such is but one of the captivating elements of Chelsea Quinn Yarbro's MWA scroll-winning story. Here are the Iron River Indians of Canada, the Royal Canadian Mounted Police, and the unexpected in a sacred burial ground.

CHELSEA QUINN YARBRO

The Ghosts at Iron River

"Damn it, Nicholson, not over there!" James Raven Feathers yelled at the soccer players as the ball rolled between the staked mounds. "That's sacred ground! Cut it out!"

"Sorry, chief," came the call as Ian Nicholson retrieved the ball.

"Yeah. Just make sure you keep it away from here. Understand?"

The young man waved good-naturedly, jogging away across the dry grass. Nine other students in soccer togs followed him as James turned back to the RCMP Captain who stood with him in the staked enclosure at the end of the wide meadow.

"Aren't you being a little hard on them?" Captain Grey asked with a wink. "Should have thought you'd be out there yourself."

James Raven Feathers shook his head. "Not for me. Doctor's orders. And this is more important." He nodded toward the burial mounds.

"Right. I assume you've got it all cleared with the chief? There isn't going to be any nastiness over this." From the way he said it, Captain Grey was doing more than hoping. He straightened his rangy six feet and pulled on his gloves. "We got to stay around while you get the bodies moved, but after that, if you want to do anything special over them. . . ." He left his thought open.

"Thank you," James said quickly. His dark, intense eyes were out of place in his young face. He scowled at the mounds. "First we'll have to open them. My grandfather will oversee that. Then we'll have to make sure all the skeletons are complete. They were buried wrapped in leather, but once that rots, there might be some drift. It's very important, a complete skeleton. My students are all set for that. When we're through, your men can come in and take care of the hauling."

"A lot of trouble for a . . ."

"A bunch of dead Indians?" demanded James fiercely. "You bet it is. But no one will move from here unless those dead Indians go with the live ones. And if we don't go, you don't get your hydroelectric dam."

Captain Grey shrugged. He liked young Wilson (Raven Feathers, he reminded himself) and trusted him to make the Iron River Indians' move as uncomplicated as possible. He knew that the younger men were touchy about being Indians, and he tried to go easy around them. But the habits of thirty years died hard and occasionally he blundered.

"We *do* value our dead," James said forcefully.

Grey sensed more irritation than usual in the Indian. "Has Chief Jackson tried to interfere?"

"No. It's not that. There was an article in the *Globe & Mail.* Davidson was kind enough to mail me a copy. One of their reporters had talked with Yngvessen."

"Oh? Who?"

"That muck-peddler Choffe." James fairly spat the name.

"What did he have to say?" Grey kicked a rock out of the path as he asked.

"The usual garbage. That we're a child-like, simple people, lacking culture and civilization, and that it's the responsibility of intelligent, progressive Teutons to look after the poor, incompetent Red Man." He snorted. "Predigested to words of two syllables."

"As bad as all that?"

"Yes, and we have to take it. Sometimes I wish Berenet had lived long enough to publish that bloody book of his. At least he had a different point of view. As it is we're saddled with that *dreck* of Yngvessen's."

"I see," Grey said, involuntarily looking at the bleak setting of the Iron River village.

James followed his glance. "Grandfather wants to talk to you. Today, before you leave. He told me to tell you."

Grey nodded. "Good. I'll go now. Always like seeing William. He's been a lot of help over the years. He sure knows how to handle people." The praise was genuine and it won him a wintery smile from the sullen young man at his side.

"Yes, grandfather has always been a peaceful Indian. A real model of failing culture." There was just enough resentment in his voice to make Liam Grey say sharply: "Now, you look here, James, being peaceful kept your people together more than once. Back in the '20s the tribe almost got broken up and William fixed it. Even when Berenet disappeared, your grandfather kept everyone here out of hot water, in spite of Yngvessen. You've got no call to speak of him that way." He had begun walking back through the mounds toward the few, plain houses that were the homes of the Iron River Indians.

"Grey, he's my grandfather. I know what keeping us all together has cost him. Lots." The straight dark brows drew down over his eyes. "And we're still getting moved."

"The tribe voted to move," Grey reminded him.

"With half the province looking over their shoulders. And with the experts in Regina and Calgary quoting that damned book of Yngvessen's. A lot of choice we had."

Although Grey secretly agreed with the young man, he had had enough. "You stop being a professional Indian, James. If you want to do that to your students at McGill, fine, but don't try it around me. I'm trying every bit as hard as you to keep this tribe together." Abruptly he stopped talking.

"I'll take you to my grandfather," James said stiffly. "Follow me." Without looking at the Captain he moved ahead of him. At the door of the largest house he stopped. "He's inside. He hasn't been well. It's his eyes."

"I won't be long." Grey smiled with what he hoped was warm assurance, and went into the house.

The room was a fugitive from sunshine. The curtains had been marshaled against the windows, the colors vague and dim. Even the big-bellied stove showed only a faint ruddiness at the grille.

In the corner between the stove and the bookcase was an old leather chair, made so comfortable with use that it was nearly shapeless. At the moment William Wilson sat in it, his near-blind eyes trained on Grey.

"Good afternoon, Liam," he said.

"Good afternoon to you, William," Grey answered.

"My grandson been giving you a piece of his mind?"

"No more than usual."

The old man chuckled. With his white hair braided neatly down his back and his high-necked robe he looked more like a venerable Korean scholar than the medicine man of the Iron River Indians. "He has even lectured me. Wants me to change my name to Raven Feathers. That was his father's name, of course. Mine is Hand-of-Water." He pointed to a chair. "Sit down, Liam."

"They're ready to start digging out there tomorrow, William," Grey said gently.

Wilson simply nodded. He pulled the blanket on his knees higher up his chest. "Watch out for John Yellow Sky. He wants to turn this into an incident." He shook his head. "An Indian informing against an Indian. A thing James deplores."

Grey tugged at his gloves. "What kind of incident?"

Wilson shook his head again, this time with disgust. "Yellow Sky wants headlines, and with Maxwell Choffe, he'll get them. Aaron Jackson almost called a tribal council over it."

"But he didn't." Grey wondered how much pressure had been put on the chief from both sides to bring things this far.

"No. I stopped him. He's left the running of the tribe to me for the last fifteen years, anyway. He knew he couldn't handle it. Well, I can. I suggested James have a little chat with Yellow Sky." He reached out to the stove and the pot of coffee. "Don't think James understands Yellow Sky. John wants the blood." He poured himself a cup, returning the pot to the stove with the handle toward Grey. "James wants justice. John wants vengeance."

Grey rose and poured himself a cup of coffee. He had learned that this was the simplest form of hospitality, and that if he had been offered the drink, then the endless ritual of repaying would begin.

"Better be on the alert, Liam."

Grey sipped the coffee. "Who else is in with Yellow Sky?"

"Eddie Two Foxes. Both of the Harris boys . . . calling themselves Hare-in-the-Snow these days. David Lynx. Henry Running Bear was with them, but shied off a while back."

"As far as you know?"

"As far as I know," he admitted. "Talked to Aaron about it. I hoped he'd take a hand for once, but he's sitting on this. I think he wants it to go away."

Captain Grey did not like Chief Jackson the way he liked William. To him, the old chief was evading the issues, letting the tribe grow dangerously polarized. He said: "Is he planning to be here for the disinterring?"

"Don't think so. Told me he thought it would be better if we all kept away. Let the university people handle it."

After a moment Grey said cautiously, "He's asking for trouble."

William nodded. "Yes," he said.

James was waiting for him when Grey left the old man. His Indian calm had returned and he looked at Grey with remote severity. "My students are waiting for you. We want to discuss the arrangements for tomorrow."

Grey considered his answer. "Good," he said at last.

"They're waiting at the trailers."

"Right." Grey started toward the four small house trailers that hid behind the wooden buildings as if ashamed of their shiny aluminum bodies. "Coming?"

James did not answer but fell into step beside the Captain.

The students were gathered around the ashes of a campfire in the circle of the trailers. They had changed from their soccer togs into more practical camping clothes, and now they were getting ready for the long northern twilight of summer. Grey thought them all very young, especially the tawny giant who was laying the fire.

"A little early for that, isn't it?" James asked sharply.

"The sun's down," said the short stocky one. James introduced him as Sandenny.

"And that's Nicholson, Adams, Kepple, Feyette, Alyoisu, Stuart, McCloud, Whiting, and over there is Bates."

Grey nodded to each and hoped he could keep them straight. Nicholson was easy, the blond giant; Adams, wiry; Kepple, lean and lantern-jawed; Feyette, unremarkable; Alyoisu, absurdly handsome; Stuart, carrot hair, no freckles; McCloud, nothing noticeable; Whiting, big-chested and sturdy; Bates, retiring and unfriendly. So long as he could keep Feyette and McCloud straight he would be fine.

"Go ahead, Captain," James said.

He stepped forward. "About your project tomorrow: we'll be here to help you, and to keep publicity at a minimum. You aren't old enough to remember the trouble when Berenet turned up missing fifteen, sixteen years ago. Yngvessen took advantage of that incident in his book, as you probably know. We're going to try to keep that from happening again. Now, some of the young men of the tribe might try to force our hand here. If that happens, you're to stay well out of it. Let the RCMP handle it." Grey hated this kind of talk and knew he did it badly. Doggedly he continued: "For the rest you take orders from Professor Raven Feathers—he's in charge of the whole operation, even the police. We rely on his judgment. Are there any questions?" He hoped for a response just to show that they'd been listening.

"Captain Grey?" Stuart, red hair. "What should we do about reporters? Chief Jackson said we might have some around."

"Do as Dr. Raven Feathers tells you. He'll know best what the press should cover and what is private to Iron River. Any more questions? Mr. Kepple?" This last was in response to Richard Kepple's hand tentatively in the air.

"Suppose the press is pushy? And we can't manage them? Should we call you?" He was obviously referring to Choffe.

"If a reporter won't be referred to Dr. Raven Feathers, and is not respecting the barriers you've set up, all you have to do is ask for our help."

Ian Nicholson put his huge paw into the air. "What if John Yellow Sky and his bunch try to make trouble? They've said they would. What are you prepared to do to stop them?"

This was a question Grey had dreaded. He thought about his answer very carefully. "I know what John Yellow Sky has been saying about the moving of the tribe. I've read his statements about the obligations of the white man to Indians and the restitutions he feels are due. I will not debate that question now or later. But I know that he wants to create some particular reaction here for the moving of the burial grounds. The whole project is supposed to take a week, and his group could cause trouble at any time throughout the week. We know that he will certainly be present most of the time. But until he has actually done something, leave well enough alone. My men have handled John and his"—he almost said boys—"bunch before. We can do it again. If we have to, keep out of the way."

"Any more questions for the Captain?" James asked briskly. When none were forthcoming, he turned to Grey. "That does it. But just one more thing: a couple of Yngvessen's students might show up with Choffe. What are you going to do about them?"

Grey shrugged. "What can I do? Lock them up? Toss them in the river? They've got a right to be here if Chief Jackson gives them permission. If they don't have his permission, then they get sent out. That's all I can do. Sorry, James."

"Aaron Jackson will let them in," James said with certainty. "Yngvessen scared him gutless with that book." He frowned. "All right. Thank you for speaking with my students." On cue there was a ragged bit of applause. "We start tomorrow, and work for a week."

"Yes," said Grey. "I'm glad you're in charge, Jamie. You're a good man."

Reeling mentally between the insult of his childhood nickname and the compliment of being called a good man by someone who had known him most of his life, James Raven Feathers found himself stammering for the first time in years. "I . . . I'll . . . walk you back to your car," he said lamely.

"I'll be glad of your company." He turned to the group around the fire. "Tomorrow morning, then. Thank you for your co-operation."

The young men at the campfire waved before they turned back to their projects.

As they walked away from the trailers, Grey said to James, "We do know that there will be reporters from Calgary and Regina here to cover the moving, not just Choffe. And a sports writer is coming from Winnipeg to get a story on you for his magazine."

"Shit!" James said through clenched teeth.

"Wants a story on what a famous la crosse player does in his spare time," Grey added apologetically.

"I'm not even playing any more. What makes them think that the only thing I do is play la crosse?" he demanded of the air.

"You were doing pretty well until that accident. You're still headline material in sports."

James was about to speak and then thought better of it. Finally he said, "Well, it paid for my Ph.D. even if I got a chunk of steel in my arm that tells when it's going to rain." He glanced shyly at Grey. "It felt good, all that fame. For the first year I thought I was king of the world."

They walked on in silence, letting the understanding slip away. Then, "Was it hard to give up, James?"

The young man laughed abruptly. "Yes. I thought that they'd fix me up like new. *Really* like new." He pushed out with his hands before jamming them into his pockets. "Well, they didn't. They couldn't."

With a sympathetic smile Grey said, "I know how I felt when I read about the accident. Dreadful."

"Another poor Red Boy proved he couldn't take care of himself, huh?" James asked bitterly.

He had not understood. Grey looked at him with a certain shock on his weathered face. "No. I thought that William's grandson was pretty bad hurt."

Unable to express either shame or contrition, James took refuge in petulance. "And hoped there wouldn't be a fuss. How did we get on this, anyhow?" he went on in a different voice. "This is too depressing."

They had reached the Land-Rover that Grey drove in the rugged country of Iron River. It was equipped with every extra that was available. The Captain had once used the winch to pull four stranded cows out of a mudbank. Grey put his hand on the door but made no move to open it. "About tomorrow," he began awkwardly. "We might be in for more trouble than we counted on."

The dark eyes that looked into his blue ones were flinty. "Yes?"

"I can have guards if you think it necessary. Now, don't fly off the handle, James," he added quickly. "I know that gets your back up. But there's going to be reporters and everything here tomorrow. You know that John Yellow Sky isn't going to let an opportunity like this slip by. And some of Yngvessen's people are bound to be here with Choffe. He's trouble all by himself. So think it over. I'll do what you think best." He opened the door. "Don't make me any speeches, just think it over. I want you to be sure." He stepped into the car, fumbling for the keys as he moved.

"What if I don't want any guards, after all?" This was a challenge.

"It's your decision, James. If you think it's better without guards, all right. That's the way we'll do it."

"What about stand-by?" James shifted uneasily as he looked beyond the Captain to the burial mounds.

"Certainly. As many men as you want. I'll check with you first thing in the morning." He slammed the door before James could say anything more. He started the motor, gave it a minute to warm up, then drove off down the rutted dirt road of the Iron River reservation.

James watched him go, then walked thoughtfully back toward the circle of trailers.

The signs were all over, the next morning. Written in clumsy block letters, terse, simple, they framed the burial mounds.

THIS IS THE WHITE MAN'S LEGACY . . . THE ONLY GOOD INDIAN IS A DEAD INDIAN . . . WE HAVE A RIGHT TO OUR WAY OF LIFE . . . ELECTRICITY IS MORE IMPORTANT THAN RED DIGNITY . . . SING-ING LOON BETRAYS US and cryptically, *JACKSON'S FOLLY.*

James Raven Feathers stood looking at the signs for a few minutes, his eyes hooded. "Yellow Sky, damn him." That was said softly. The next was not. "Sandenny! Nicholson! Whiting! Get out here!" He started purposefully toward the trailers.

"Something wrong?" Bert Adams bounced out of the trailer first, an eager smile on his face. "Are we late?"

"Go look," James said stonily as he walked to the trailers and began to pound on the doors.

The first grumblings and stirrings were heard inside the trailers as Bert Adams ran back from the mounds. "That's going to have to come down, sir, isn't it? They're in awful deep."

"Yes. It's going to have to come down. Feyette, get out here!" he bellowed as Bates, McCloud, and Stuart stumbled into the morning.

"What's the matter?" asked a sleepy Richard Kepple as he opened his door.

"Yellow Sky is playing games," James said violently. His hands clenched at his side. "That bloody fool. He's going to turn this into a grandstand play if it kills him." He took three deep breaths, saying more calmly: "I want one of you to get my grandfather. We need him here."

"Right," one of the young men said.

"And I'll want to talk to Henry Running Bear. He ought to know about this, and he's cowed. He'll tell us what Yellow Sky is up to."

"I'll do it," McCloud volunteered.

"Good. Thank you." He nodded. McCloud took this for an authorization and trotted off toward the houses. "The rest of you, get some hatchets and come with me. We've got to get those signs down before Captain Grey gets back here with the observers." He stood while the others went for their tools, muttering, "Damn Yellow Sky. He makes Yngvessen look right."

"I've got the hatchets. And Dave's bringing the shovels," Nicholson said as he came up to James. "Where do we start?"

"Come along," James said coolly, taking a hatchet from Ian and heading back toward the mounds.

"Is there going to be trouble?" Ian asked amiably as he trotted beside James. "I'll do my bit, if you want, Dr. Raven Feathers."

James stopped in his tracks. "Ian, don't. You try anything and you'll be playing right into John's hands. And Choffe's. He wants headlines, dirt, savages. He thrives on ugliness." He looked up into the wide blond face. "Don't let this get out of hand."

"Okay. I just thought you wanted Yellow Sky's head on a pole."

It was a terrible admission for James to make. Here was a Nordic giant beside him asking about a fellow Indian. Inside, James allowed that Nicholson was right, but he could not say so. "We've got work to do," he said and resumed walking toward the burial grounds.

McCloud was waiting for them. "Your grandfather will be along shortly. He wasn't up yet. He sent Charlie to find Running Bear for you. Looks terrible, doesn't it?"

"Yes." James glanced back toward the trailers and saw that his students were following him. He waited for them to catch up, then he said, "We've got about forty-five minutes to get all that crap down. Chop 'em down or dig 'em out, I don't give a damn which. Just don't disturb any of the mounds. The ones close to the mounds, use hatchets on them. Anything beyond the stakes, those you can dig out, if you're careful."

"We'll be careful," Michael Whiting assured him as he started toward the signs. "Boy, they really set those things up." He grabbed one of the poles and shook it. "That's in deep," he said and started to dig.

The others selected poles and began either to dig or chop while James anxiously watched in case the burial mounds should be disturbed. The first of the signs had come down when William Wilson joined his grandson by the signs.

"I am not surprised," he said when he had had the signs read to him. "John Yellow Sky wants to make trouble here. He is just getting started. Watch. This is so."

James shook his head at his grandfather. "This is a grandstand play. If we handle it right, he'll leave us alone."

The old man wagged his finger at James. "He is a dangerous man, Jamie. You will not contain him so easily."

"I've sent for Running Bear. Between us we should get some sense out of Henry." There was a stubborn set to his mouth, so William did not press him further.

"There is not much time," he said.

Then, "Doctor. . . ." Mark Alyoisu said from where he was digging. His eyes were frightened in his handsome face. "There's something down here. I thought this was safe. I didn't know that there were other mounds. . . ."

"What is it?" James went to him, puzzled. "You're outside the area. . . ."

"But I've hit some . . . one. . . ." He was quite pale now, white around the mouth. "There's a body down there. I didn't mean to do anything. Honest. I thought it was safe."

James pushed him aside and looked into the small hole Alyoisu had dug. He knelt, and scooped the dirt away with his hands. Then he stopped. "You're right." He said it quietly, but they all heard it.

Old William stumbled toward James. His fading eyes tried vainly to see what was in the hole. "This is not the sacred ground. It is too far to the north. This is not right."

James rose. "There is someone down there, grandfather. I had my hands on the ribs."

"Yellow Sky!" William said in a terrible rage. "He has desecrated the graves of his ancestors. For his futile posturing he has done this! I am ashamed." The leathery old man stopped shouting quite suddenly. He turned to his grandson. "Call Liam. Tell him what has happened. See if he can stop the visitors until we can find out how far his sacrilege has gone."

"Yes, Grandfather."

"And call Aaron. No. I will call him. I want him to know what his vacillation has done to us." And feeling his way he stalked off to his house.

The rest stood, looking into the hole.

Finally Edgar Bates asked, "Should we go on digging?"

"Better not," James said slowly. "Not with this." He looked over the burial mounds. "But you'd better clear away around that one. Make sure you don't disturb the skeleton. Keep it intact if you can. I'll have to talk to Grey and see what he wants done. We might just need those guards after all."

As he walked off the young men began, reluctantly, to dig.

Twenty minutes later Grey came barreling down to the houses. His face was set and his shoulders were tense.

"And I thought Berenet used to take chances on this road," James greeted him as he slammed out of the Land-Rover. "We don't need another accident on our hands."

"What's this all about?" Grey demanded without preamble.

James hesitated. "It's pretty awkward." Then, as Grey strode angrily toward him: "We found an extra body. The boys are digging it up now."

"What do you mean, an extra body?"

"Just that. It was beyond the mounds, oh, about ten feet. We thought it was safe."

Grey clamped his hands to his hips. "What the hell were you doing digging, anyway? That wasn't supposed to start until we all got here."

Realization dawned on James's face. "That's right. You don't know about the signs, do you?"

"What bloody signs?" So as they walked toward the mounds and the extra skeleton, James explained about the morning. "And now we have this extra body to deal with. I don't even know who it was. I was hoping that grandfather might tell us."

"Yellow Sky," Grey said as James finished. They were next to the staked mounds and James's students were taking down the last of the signs with their hatchets.

"I've told them not to dig any more out. There might be more."

"You haven't brought this one up yet?" Grey cocked his head toward the hole. He did not want to get too close to the stakes.

"No. I don't want to disturb more than I have to."

"Good. What about Yellow Sky? Seen him about this morning?" Grey pulled out a small notebook and began to sketch the sign and the hole. "Go on; I'm listening."

"Well, I've sent for Henry Running Bear. Probably won't do any good, but I hope he might be able to fill us in on what John is planning to do next. This may only be a warm-up," he said grimly.

Grey snorted in agreement. "How is William taking it?" He toed the sign that lay in the dirt at his feet. "He sounded very upset on the phone."

"He is. He thinks that John opened the mounds or moved the staking so that the graves could be desecrated." James paused as he thought it over. "Does that make any sense to you, Grey?"

It was Grey's turn to think about it. "No," he said at last. "Not John Yellow Sky. This isn't his style. He wanted this for publicity, for a soapbox, not to shut the place down. This isn't flamboyant enough for him, not this way. Unless he's got something more in mind, other than a skeleton." He looked around again, squinting against the sun. "This is going to be real trouble if Choffe gets ahold of it."

James said nothing. He sighed unhappily. "But it would have worked," he said wistfully.

"I know."

Then James shook off his mood. "Do you want that body brought out of the ground?" he asked briskly. "I've told them to start, but this might be in your sphere, not mine."

"No, not yet. There are some other questions to take care of first. I'm going to talk to William now. Keep Henry around wherever you are. I don't want him wandering off until we have a little chat. Who's picking him up?"

"Charlie Moon." James gave a half-smile at the mention of his lawyer cousin. "Ogilvie, Tallant, and Moon decided they could spare him, so he flew in last night. He said he had a feeling we might need a good attorney. We turned Henry over to him. Charlie will take care of him."

Flipping his notebook closed Grey said, "I don't doubt it." He started walking toward William's house. He went slowly, reluctant to disturb his old friend again. He turned over all the questions that faced him in his mind. He was fully aware of the trouble this would bring to the tribe. With one Indian agent disappearing, followed so closely by that ruinous book of Yngvessen's, this might well be the final disaster for the Iron River Tribe. More than either James or William, he knew the ambivalence most people had for Indians. A thing like this, well, it was a great excuse to scatter the tribe. Even Yngvessen had suggested it; it would be a way for them to upgrade their culture. He was deeply afraid that this would be the end. His heels bit more deeply into the pathway. He did not know how to influence the reporters who were coming to cover the disinterring, especially Choffe, who was armed with Yngvessen's opinions. He hoped that they could all be held back, if only for a few hours. Otherwise it would be difficult.

"Come in," said the old voice in response to the knock. Grey pulled the door open.

"Come in, come in," William ordered. "Want to talk to you. Don't want those foolish heads outside to hear us." He grunted impatiently as Grey secured the door.

"Now then," he continued as Grey walked forward, "we have got a proper mess now. There's a body out there in the wrong place. John Yellow Sky put it there. . . ."

"I'm not sure he did," Grey said quietly. He was silent, waiting for William to go on.

"What do you mean?" The old man rose and came toward Grey. He was a head shorter than the Captain, but he seemed taller. "What do you mean, Liam? What is that body there for? Who put it there?"

Grey shook his head. "I don't know. I don't think Yellow Sky did it. There's no point to it. I think that either the stakes were moved or the old mound was flattened in the '43 flood. You remember? You said some of the old graves were lost."

"That was thirty years ago. Even before Berenet came. It could be." The old man shuffled back to his leather chair. "What if Yellow Sky found out about the body and planned this?"

Grey shook his head reluctantly. "It doesn't fit the pattern, William. What publicity would he gain?"

"You're as bad as Berenet with the endless history of the tribe he was writing." William paused, then reached for his coffee mug. "I don't know. That's puzzled me, too. Yellow Sky is usually direct."

When the coffee pot was returned to the stove Grey helped himself. "Can you get Aaron to keep the reservation closed for a few more hours?"

"I will try." He drank half the coffee in silence, then went into the other room where the tribe's one telephone was kept. Chief Jackson lived in town, visiting the reservation only when necessary.

Grey waited while the call was made, meditatively sipping his coffee. He could hear William's voice raised in anger, but could not make out the words. He refilled his mug and sat down.

"The old fool," William was muttering as he came back into the room. "He told me to shut the thing up. Choffe is flying in from Saskatoon in two hours, and I'm supposed to shut it up. How do you shut up a body? Told me to have them bury it again and leave it. And he's an Indian." The scorn in his voice almost choked him.

"May I make a suggestion, William?" Grey asked, as soon as the old man had stopped talking.

"Go ahead. Won't hurt anything more. He's keeping the other reporters at the gatehouse for an hour so that George Snake Killer can give them a lecture on the history of the tribe. Without Yngvessen's theories. That's all he's willing to do. More than that would look suspicious, he says."

Mentally Grey damned Chief Jackson for a fool, but he said, "Let's take the body out. Remove it to the hall, get it out of the way. Then we can dig up the others, and claim that the sign poles were part of the preparation for the disinterment. We can tell them that only Indians were allowed to attend that ceremony."

For a moment William was silent. Then he chuckled, *"We* do this for *us* Indians?" He grinned at his friend. "All right. It is not what I would want to do, but there is no time for that. I will order the body to be removed from the area and placed in the meeting hall so that I can set to work finding out who it was." He hesitated for a bit, folding his hands across his chest. "There is no need for you to support us. That was your decision. I am proud to have you my friend." Which was as close as he could come to saying thanks.

"There is still going to be the devil to pay. I just brought you a suggestion. All we've got is very little time." Grey said this hastily as he rose from his chair, determination back in his manner. "I'll get the boys on it. Guess James will go along with us?"

With a steely smile, William said, "Oh, yes."

The students were standing uncertainly outside of the staked area when Liam Grey returned to them. "All right," he told them, "it's back on. Dig him out. Put him in the hall when you've got him out. You've got about half an hour." He looked around as he heard his name called, and saw Charlie Moon coming toward him, a wolfish grin on his pointed face.

"I've got a surprise package for you, Grey. He's waiting in the trailer. A nice little teddy bear." He waved offhandedly to the students. "James is keeping him company, but I think you'd better come along. James can be pretty rough on toys."

Promising the students that he'd be back shortly, Grey strode off with Charlie Moon to the trailers.

"What has he said?" he asked the young attorney at his side.

"Denies all knowledge of the skeleton. He said that they only put the signs up to annoy James. I get the feeling that John is saving the main event for later."

They turned into the circle of trailers. "Any idea what?"

"No," Charlie said as he opened the door of the second trailer.

James was seated backward in a chair, his arms folded across the back, chin resting on his arms. In front of him was a sturdy young man trying very hard not to look frightened. He was saying ". . . and all your talk about reconciliation with the White Man. Look what it's got us. We have to move and. . . ." His voice trailed off.

"Hello, Grey," James said without turning. "Glad you could make it. Henry here was telling me about how you've abused us. Do you think you've abused us, Grey? Do you think Berenet abused us?"

Quickly Grey took over. He feared that otherwise it would degenerate into a name-calling contest. "Hello, Henry. You know about our find out there?"

"I don't know anything," was the fast sullen answer.

"Not even about the signs," Grey assumed incredulity. "I thought you were in on that."

"Well, on that. . . ."

"And I thought you might know if John Yellow Sky had any clever ideas about planting skeletons? No?"

"I don't know what you're . . ."

"Forgetting for the moment that you broke the law when you put up those signs. . . ."

"I didn't. . . ."

"Yes, you did, Henry. Unless I say otherwise, you did. Now, where are John Yellow Sky and the Harris brothers?" He waited. "Well?"

"I don't know."

"Make a guess," said Charlie Moon gently.

"You can't make me. . . ."

"I can't," Grey agreed cordially. "But James and Charlie might want to." He let that sink in. "I don't have time for any more nonsense, Henry. We've got a hell of a mess on our hands right now. If you're going to play Martyred Indian, then off you go to jail until I find out what's happened."

"You're trying to bully me," Henry Running Bear lurched to his feet. "You stinking, genocidal White Man!"

"That's enough!" James's voice cut like a whip. "Let us talk to him, Liam. We can find out."

"Give him a chance," Charlie smiled. "He's read Yngvessen's book. He knows we're not civilized. He knows that our hard lives have made us brutal, stupid and violent. Right, Henry?"

"Hey, Captain, they can't do this." Henry looked beseechingly at Grey. "Can they?"

"If I know about it, they can't. But I told you, I don't have much time. If you haven't given us an answer I'll have to leave you with them." He managed to sound sorry.

"But that's not fair. You lousy cop!" He took two steps toward Grey. "It's not. They don't understand. They've already talked to John and he told them he. . . ." Henry looked around uncertainly. "He told them how he felt about the move," he ended defiantly.

"Do you think he'd tell me?" Grey asked. "I haven't got much time, Henry. Remember that."

"I don't know. I don't," he said desperately. "He went back into the woods last night, after we put up the signs. I don't know where he is. I don't know if he'd talk to you."

"But he is planning more . . . entertainment?" Charlie suggested.

"He didn't tell me. Really." He was certainly scared now. "I asked him what he was going to do. He just said he had a real surprise for them. But it wasn't for today. It wasn't." He looked from one man to the next, pleading with his eyes. "I didn't think he'd do a thing like . . . that. . . ."

"Right," Grey said firmly. "Tell us where he is."

"In the woods. That's all I know. Back in the woods on the North Fork. He and Lynx and Two Foxes are up there. The others are off in Calgary. They left last night. They're going to get supplies. So you see, they can't do anything until they get back." He spoke in a rush.

"Anything more?" James asked.

"I don't know any more!" Henry yelled. "I don't! At least. . . ." He glanced uneasily at Charlie Moon. "You're a lawyer, Charlie. You got to protect me."

"Oh, I will," he said pleasantly as a grin split his face.

"No, Charlie. Really. You got to help me. . . ." He stopped for a moment. "John might show up sometime while the press is here. But that's all I know. Honest, it is. Tell him, Charlie."

"All right, Henry. We believe you," Grey smiled down at him, taking full advantage of his height. "But let's suppose we get it all on paper, just on the chance you're wrong?" He pulled out his notebook and pen.

There was a knock on the door and Jerry Feyette stuck his head in the door.

"It's McCloud, James," Liam Grey said.

"Feyette, sir," he corrected. Then: "Sorry to bother you, Doctor, but there's something you should see before we move the body." He was uncomfortable, rubbing his hands on his overall as he spoke.

"Is it urgent? Can't it wait?"

"No, sir, I don't think so." He pulled his earlobe. "There's something you'd better see."

James shrugged. "Oh, all right, if it's important." He rose from the chair and turned to the other two men. "Keep Henry company until I get back." With that, he slung his jacket over his shoulder and went out the door.

"What did you find?" he asked Feyette is they walked back toward the mounds.

"There's something strange about the skeleton. I figured you might know. . . ."

"Well, what is it?" he demanded.

But Feyette shook his head. "Better wait until we get there." He did not speak again until they had reached the gathering around the pile of bones on the ground.

"Now what is it?" James demanded as he came up to them.

Michael Whiting stepped aside for him as he pointed to the skeleton. "Take a look. The right arm, just above the elbow." James twinged, but knelt next to the skeleton.

"There, Right there," Lincoln McCloud said, touching the bone with the toe of his boot. "Look at it."

Puzzled, James picked up the humerus and turned it over in his hands. There, imbedded in the bone, slightly above the elbow, holding an old fracture together was a pin of stainless steel.

"One of you go get Grey," he said softly. "Tell him it's urgent." Gingerly he moved around the rest of the skeleton. When he got to the skull he stopped.

"That's the other thing we wanted you to see, Doctor," Leon Sandenny said cautiously. "That sure got bashed, didn't it?"

James picked up the ruined skull, trying to keep the fragments together. "This isn't anyone I know," he murmured.

"Did that happen after he was buried?" Bert Adams asked, a little frightened.

"I don't know. The break is in the back. I don't think so . . . I doubt it," James said dubiously. Somehow all the objectivity he had felt in Peru vanished now that his own tribe was involved. He put the skull down carefully. "Don't disturb that, all right?" he said to his students. "I want Grey to see it this way." He fingered the head of the pin in the bone. "No Indian I know has one of these. Except me." He studied the bone around the pin. "That was one hell of a fracture."

"What caused it?" asked Leon Sandenny as he squatted next to James.

James shook his head. "Some kind of accident. It put his arm out of commission for months, by the look. . . ." Suddenly he remembered back. When he was ten? eleven? Berenet had had an accident while driving at his usual murderous speeds on an icy road. He had worn his arm in a cast for quite a while . . .

"What is it *now?*" Grey demanded from above him.

James snapped out of his reverie. "You'd better take a look at this skeleton." He rose and stepped back. "Take a good look."

With a grunt and a perfunctory obscenity Grey dropped to his knees. "Pretty tall, wasn't he?" he asked of no one in particular.

"The skull and the right arm," James prompted.

"Right." He picked up the skull, handling it with great care. "He really got his, didn't he?"

"With metal."

"The proverbial blunt instrument," Grey said drily. He looked up at James. "You're the anthropologist. You should be able to tell me what did this."

James knelt again, taking the skull from Grey. He turned it over slowly, checking the splintering of the bone. "I don't know, but I'd put my money on a hammer from the side. You see how this angle here. . . ." He touched the edge of the hole in the skull. "I think it's a hammer."

"And the arm." Grey had picked up the bone and touched it with some worry. "This. . . ."

But James tugged at his arm. "Yes. I want to talk to you about that, but not just here." He stood and drew Grey aside. "Do you remember the way Berenet drove? Didn't he have a bad accident about fifteen years ago, say a couple of years before he turned up missing?"

"His arm was in a cast. The right one," he said reflectively. "You think that's Berenet?" he asked suddenly.

"It's not an Indian."

Grey sighed. "I'll check it out. I'll have to phone out. It might make it worse, if this isn't Berenet and Choffe or Yngvessen gets wind of it." He looked evenly at James.

The look was returned. "We've got to do this, no matter what. The body's got to be identified. There's a little time yet."

"Right." He stood, his weight slung into his hip, thinking. "You've got tools for sifting?"

"Sure. We were going to use them to be certain we got all of the effects in the mounds. Taken out with the bones and re-buried in the new site—that's what we planned."

"So you're going to refute Yngvessen?"

"Not a chance," James said bitterly. "He's like Moby Dick. I'm not up to him."

"Gadfly?" Grey asked with a twinkle. "You can use those sieves now, to find out if there was anything else in the hole with that poor bastard."

"We'll get on it right away." He paused. "Can Grandfather buy us any more time?"

"I don't think so."

"Well," said James. "We can try. About half an hour, you'd say?"

"About that. Maybe William can hold them at the houses for a little while, but half an hour is the best I can guarantee." He shook hands with James and went off to the houses.

Twenty minutes later he had his answer, all the way from Regina. Yes, Agent Claud Berenet had had a bad accident; yes, it had resulted in a multiple fracture of the right humerus; yes, it had required surgery. Yes, a pin had been used. Grey fingered his notebook, lost in thought. If the skeleton were Berenet, then who killed him? Why did the whole tribe deny knowledge of it? Grey thought that he knew William well enough that he could trust the old man to leak information like that to him. True, this case was fifteen years old, but he hoped that William had been sure of him even then . . .

He left the house, walking slowly back toward the mounds. Nicholson and Alyoisu were waiting for him, triumph in their eyes. "What have you found?" he asked.

Nicholson held out his hand. On his palm lay a tarnished silver crucifix and a St. Christopher's medal. "The chain was almost completely corroded. We found this under the head."

Grey touched the crucifix. "I see. Catholic." He stood still for a moment. "Where is Dr. Raven Feathers?"

Alyoisu cocked his head in the direction of the trailers. "He and Leon are processing a couple more things we found. It's all lab work for them."

"What things?" Grey asked, frowning deeply at the hole and then at his watch. There was very little time left.

"We found a few items that might have been caught in his clothes. Of course, they might be his, but they might be his murderer's too. Dr. Raven Feathers is waiting for you." Nicholson smiled benignly at him. "Should we fill the hole in, Captain?"

"Hum. Oh, certainly. Go ahead. The press should be along any minute now. Which trailer is Dr. Raven Feathers in?"

"The green one. You'd better knock before you go in. They're using some ruddy awful chemicals in there," Nicholson said happily. "Tell Dr. Raven Feathers we'll finish this up out here. And Mike Whiting will pitch them some guff about anthropology until he's free to talk."

"Good idea. Thanks for thinking of it." He kicked at the moist earth with his boot. "Make it neat, will you?" Before they could answer he had moved on toward the trailers.

Whatever chemicals James was using, they stank. Grey paused in the doorway as his lungs objected, then he went into the trailer, closing the door behind him.

James and Leon Sandenny were bent over the sink, each working with jeweler's pliers and small shards of metal. "Hi, Grey. I think we've found something."

"Yes?" He peered over their shoulders. "What is it?"

"Part of it," James said enthusiastically. "The rest is on the table over there. Be very careful with it."

Grey maneuvered to the table and saw there, on a strip of muslin, four or five tiny bits of metal like an incomplete jigsaw puzzle. "What is it? It looks like it had a chain."

"Right on the first try. It had a chain. It was under the left hand."

"Could it have been *in* the hand?" Grey held his breath as he bent over the table.

"Yes, it could have. There's a magnifying glass on the seat there. Have a look at that bottom line." James had not taken his eyes from the bits of metal in the sink.

As he picked up the glass, Grey asked, "What's on it? What am I looking for?"

"Look at it."

Curiously Grey moved the muslin into clearer light. As he did he could make out the lower halves of numerals. It was either 1936 or 1956.

"I'm betting on '36, myself." He managed a tight smile.

Leon Sandenny, hunched over a sliver of metal murmured, *"Mehr Licht."*

"Macht doch den zweiten Fensterladen auch auf," James said promptly. He remembered Yngvessen's fondness for the truncated version of Goethe's last words, and his anger at having the full quotation rendered, in quite acceptable German, by a poor Indian boy not yet in his teens. Then he realized. "What did you say?" he demanded.

"Look," Sandenny offered the scrap of metal to James. "That's what it says."

James let out a whoop of pure joy. "The watch fob. We've found the watch fob."

"So what?" Grey said. "It could have been planted. It might be Berenet's, if this is Berenet."

James scowled. "It might have been planted," he allowed. "But why? It's been in the ground quite a while. If it is a plant, who planted it; Yellow Sky? No, I'll bet this is a souvenir of Nils Christian Yngvessen." He leaned on the table, bright intensity lighting his face. "This could almost make up for the book."

Grey put a restraining arm on James's shoulder. "If the tests prove you wrong, Jamie. . . ." He didn't finish. He, too, wanted the guilty party to be Yngvessen. "It's not a lot."

"It's enough. He'll have to answer one hell of a lot of questions about this." He looked over his shoulder at his assistant. "How soon can you have this ready, Leon?"

"About an hour?"

"Good. Choffe will be here by then. Grey," he turned impulsively to the Captain. "Suppose Choffe finds out that Yngvessen did this. What will he do then?"

Grey answered drily, "He'll ruin Yngvessen."

James drummed his fingers on the table, smiling.

At this Grey was genuinely alarmed. "You can't accuse him, Jamie, not with so little proof. Especially in your position. If it turns out you're wrong it will look like a put-up job from the first. Yngvessen will pounce all over you. He'll destroy you. He can do it, too."

There was mockery in James's eyes. "I'm not going to accuse anybody. I am simply going to tell those nice gentlemen of the press what we found while digging in our own graveyard. They might not respect me as an anthropologist, but you said yourself they respect me as a la crosse player. They'll pay attention for that reason alone. I'll remind them that we do not allow digging within twenty feet of our burial mounds, and that whoever buried that man knew it. Then I'll have Leon produce these little displays, and put a few words in about the probable identity of the skeleton. . . ."

Grey relented. "It's Berenet. He had the fracture and the pin."

"Oh, we've got enough of a jaw to send along for dentals. That should take care of any doubting Thomases. Lincoln McCloud has taken some very interesting photographs, on Charlie's advice. And we've sent Henry off to meet Yellow Sky at the gates. So long as he is going to harangue the press we might as well get a statement from him. Without him, we'd never have found Berenet. I never thought I'd be happy for John's mischief, but I am now. I'll give him full credit for the find, if he likes. Publicly."

"But you can't be sure."

James smiled serenely. "That watch fob was a thing Yngvessen was very proud of. All the time he was here he boasted of it. It was a graduation remembrance from his family."

Grey nodded. "All right, Doctor, why did he kill Berenet?" Then, as he said it, he thought he knew the answer. "Berenet was writing a book, wasn't he? About the tribe."

James's smile deepened. "And Berenet didn't want Yngvessen's book published. He said Yngvessen was wrong. Talk about academic rivalry. Poor Berenet worked on that book of his for years. Grandfather said it was dreadful, but his history was right."

"There's the rest of it," Leon Sandenny said from the sink. "All we need is the bits around the edges and we've got it." He passed it over to James. "There you are, Doctor. 'Uppsala' and the date is 1936."

As his smile broke into a grin, "Great. Thanks," he said to Leon. "Well, Grey, care to wager what year Yngvessen graduated?" He put the missing sliver into the fob. "Aren't those nice reporters due here about now? It would be a crime to keep them waiting." He straightened up. "Coming, Grey?"

"You don't have a case yet."

"Oh, I'll leave it to you and Charlie to do that for me. There's certainly enough evidence to warrant a preliminary investigation."

"So you dump a case like this in my lap without so much as a by-your-leave?" He glanced at the watch fob and heaved a sigh of resignation. "Right. Lead on, James."

"Oh, no." Dr. Raven Feathers paused in the door. "After you, Liam."

They went out together.

Another reason for optimism about the future of the crime short story is the number of impressive debuts in 1973, several of which are found in this anthology. Mollie Pearce McKibbon is in her twenties, and will, I suspect, be heard from again to the further enrichment of crime fiction.

MOLLIE PEARCE MCKIBBON
Beyond the Last House

If only I could sleep. This coffee certainly didn't help but then neither did my new Agatha Christie book nor the third rerun on TV of *Arsenic and Old Lace*. I have tried the other channels with the same results. On each one either Queen Elizabeth or President Nixon has waved goodbye and disappeared abruptly into that small white dot. Now even the dot has vanished, pulling with it the familiar outlines of my living room. Only the cheshire leer of my luminous clock remains, suspended somewhere above the cold fireplace. It is three o'clock.

The outside world is almost as invisible to me now as the inside one. There is fog to disguise everything.

I pull Joe's bathrobe, dear old thing, closer to me as if it were Joe himself and peer out my front window. Any minute now his headlights will be visible and I'll hear that short impatient toot. I tell myself that, but I really know better. Of course it won't happen. Joe is dead.

A lump rises in my throat but no, I will not give in. Instead, I keep my eyes fixed on the distant end of the street and avoid looking toward Joe's favorite easy chair. From the direction of the highway I can hear the hum of an approaching car. I shall concentrate on that.

A dark shape advances slowly and I wonder who frequents dead-end streets at this early-morning hour. This unlighted portion of the street is a local haunt for eager lovers.

I'm glad the last streetlight is not directly in front of the house. My curiosity thus has the anonymity of darkness. The dark shape, moving cautiously without lights, has now taken on a definite contour. It is a four-door sedan, I think.

Why am I standing here and staring out at a strange car?

The car has paused just beyond the house but I can see no movement. It is difficult to see through the fog, but a form is emerging—yes, I can just make out a man who is coatless and has his shirt sleeves rolled up. He closes the front car door very carefully and moves toward the back of the car. He now has a flashlight in his hand.

We live in the last house on this street—at least, I do now. Joe always liked this location. The lot has a large treed backyard and there is a grove of tall poplars between the barrier at the end of the street and the children's playground. Plenty of privacy, Joe used to say, no noisy motorbikes or fast cars. But I have always felt uneasy living here in this last house.

The man is acting very oddly, considering that he is alone on the sleeping street. Then so am I alone. Joe and I are usually in bed by ten thirty. I turn to look at the clock. It is 3:15.

By this time the man has unlocked and lifted the door of the trunk compartment. Straining through the fog, I can discern only that he is tugging on something heavy inside the car. It looks at this moment to my startled eyes very much like a body.

I shiver as the hair on my neck begins to prickle. I can hear my heart pounding as I shrink behind the curtains. The man is looking toward this house. I inhale until it pains; but apparently reassured somehow, the man and his burden melt gradually into the fog.

I am stunned. The import of this occurrence is overwhelming, but I must think. The trunk compartment is still open. Will I have time?

I hear the sound of dirt on a shovel coming from the playground. The job is very quietly and carefully done—I can tell because there are long pauses between shovelfuls.

I have formulated a plan but I must waste no time carrying it out. The idea is preposterous, impossible, but even as I'm saying this I am working at it. The effort to get to the front steps is tremendous, but I am desperate and amazingly strong for my small frame.

It is not so easy from the front lawn to the car. The lawn is wet and I keep slipping. Finally, with a last great effort, I manage it and close the trunk compartment noiselessly.

There are only seconds to spare before I hear the man's returning steps. I am back inside at the window trying to regain my breath when, lurching out of the disintegrating grayness, the man appears, now minus his burden. He is unsteady and unsure. He goes to the trunk compartment to replace his shovel and pauses to stare at the closed door.

I hold my breath, shuddering, but suddenly he bends over, his back to me. I can't see his face, yet I know the man is throwing up. Disgusting! I'm about to turn away but now he has straightened up and looks in this direction. I freeze, one hand clutching the curtain. His flashlight has spotlighted me, barefoot in Joe's soiled robe, standing between the drapes. I can't see his features though I know his eyes have me in focus and I feel naked in panic.

The phone, if I can just reach the phone! It's an arm's length away. I can just manage.

Oh, my God, darkness. He's turned off the flashlight! Momentarily blinded. I can see nothing, not even the clock. My hand is on the receiver now, but whom do I call? I am dialing without a number in mind. Any number. Then I replace the phone receiver. It's no use. I don't really want anyone.

Somehow, unbelievably, my decision is not necessary. The man throws the shovel onto the back seat of the car and speeds away. Thank God for Joe's chair. My legs are shaking so badly I must sit down.

Think, woman! He will be back. You are safe now—but for how long?

Sergeant Clark was incredulous. He and Officer Ramey exchanged looks over the top of the car. In the back of their squad car sat a hysterical man.

"All I did was hit my dog. It was late and I backed into the driveway in the fog. I didn't hear him bark until . . . Oh, my God, the kids will never understand."

He was almost incoherent, trying to explain to both policemen what he obviously couldn't comprehend himself.

"All right, sir, so where did you bury the dog?"

"At the end of a one-way street, in among some trees. I mean, what could I say? George was their dog and the kids. . . . Anyway, when I got home I remembered I hadn't put the shovel in the trunk compartment. So I did and there was that body. I don't even know who he is!"

Urban crime statistics, these perilous days, are no cause for rejoicing. The twisted and brutal are abroad in our streets; suspicion and fear come to rule contacts between strangers, even between neighbors, until we cannot discern whom we may trust . . .

ROBERT MCNEAR
Neighbors

He was watering the avocado plant when he saw her. The girl was standing behind a sliding glass door, one hand on the mechanism for opening it, and she was peering out in a gingerly manner, presumably leary of the strong wind that was blowing. Apparently satisfied that the air currents would not pitch her from the balcony, she opened the door wide enough to let herself through and stepped outside.

Her costume, he thought, was most appealing, a long-sleeved gingham dress blood red in color, which contrasted nicely with the blonde hair straight and falling in the most natural style. Leaning into the wind, she walked with purpose to the point on the balcony where the railing met from south to west. With the wind snapping at clothes and hair, with the clouds rolling ominously from the southwest, she resembled the figurehead of some noble ship about to meet the storm head on.

Being a longtime student of high-rise life, he reached for that one accouterment necessary to the vertically glassed-in male species such as himself—binoculars. To the unaided eye, she had appeared tall, well formed and perhaps pretty around the face. Magnified seven times, the matter of height and build was confirmed, though the face did give pause—a squat nose, eyes set too widely apart, a thin mouth that seemed frivolous, a little chin that seemed pointless. Studying this, he decided that the ingredients did not work individually, for each feature was out of whack with the next one, but collectively the parts meshed very well, indeed, and he let the glasses linger on this most promising neighborly discovery.

For several long minutes she remained motionless, giving the impression of toying with the wind, vamping the gusty outriders of the approaching storm. Then when all hell was about to invade her balcony, she began to turn in his direction, a graceful whirl in preparation for going inside, but at that precise instant when head and body faced him directly, she aborted the swinging movement and froze completely, as if upon command.

She sees me, he thought in panic. A distance of 50 feet at most, so how could she miss? But did she? In part, he was shielded by the avocado plant, the lights in his apartment were not turned on and the gloom outside was increasing as the storm approached. Yet with the binoculars, he could clearly see the color of her eyes, a soft brown that blended nicely with the blonde hair.

If the girl had caught him in the act, she was behaving as no one ever had. Upon rare occasions when the object of his viewing had in turn viewed him, the person had simply left the balcony or, if inside, pulled the drapes. Never had one stared him down like the girl in the red gingham dress.

A single raindrop on his window skittered across the binocular's field of vision, a peal of thunder clapped around the buildings. Forewarned in earnest, the girl nimbly dashed for the sliding glass door and a moment later vanished inside.

Terrible timing for him to be heading out on a date, of that there was no doubt, but already he was late, so he put on a raincoat and left. All in all, the evening was not bad—dinner, movie, a walk back to the girl's apartment with the smell of the recent storm all around them. Later, back at his place, and with the lights off, he took up station by the avocado plant.

Where are you, you smashing thing in red gingham and blonde hair? Where are you, Marian Taylor? He had already learned her name and the thought of this caused him to smirk to himself.

Undoubtedly, the layout of the apartment across the way was identical to that of his own, for the builders of this apartment-house complex were not known for originality among buildings. The living-room drapes were drawn, as were the shades in the one bedroom, leaving visible to him only a small corner of a room certain to be the kitchen and a portion of the hall leading to the living room.

His wait was not long. Apparently, she had gone into that part of the kitchen he could not see and raided the refrigerator there, because she showed up in the portion of the kitchen he could see with a glass of milk in her hand. The girl drank slowly from the glass. Her red gingham dress appeared mussed, and so did her hair. Who was the guy? he wondered. Whose hands had explored the dress and rummaged around the hair? The mild disarray suggested that he had been slightly rough on the girl, though perhaps the experience had not been entirely unpleasant. On her face: a trace of what could be annoyance, a measure of excitement. When she finished the milk and left, he went off and lay awake in his own dark bedroom, knowing that he had witnessed the beginning of an affair.

The next evening, however, she stayed home alone. Obligingly, she left the drapes open. Dressed in blue jeans and a plaid shirt not tucked in, she took to the ironing board, doubtlessly sprucing up for the pending rounds. The red gingham dress was ironed, as were other dresses, and even put to the iron was a blue nightgown, transparent, he noticed, when she held it in front of her.

The following week, the girl went out three times. The bed-drapes were always pulled shut, so the first he knew of the inent date was her grand entrance into the living room. ...cipating her date's arrival, she would empty an ashtray here, smooth a pillow there, all the while moving with that lithe grace that he was beginning to love.

Upon each of these three occasions, he would abandon his watching post beside the avocado plant to go out before her date arrived and would return home after she was home, and alone, at that; so, curiously enough, that week he never caught so much as a glimpse of the other guy.

The other guy. Whoever he was, he was managing to pull off two neat little tricks at the same time—one good, one bad. He excited her, to be sure, as he had noticed after the first date, when she was drinking milk in the kitchen. And judging from her face, this emotion increased after each of the next three dates. But from the very first, he had seen what he took to be annoyance, and this grew in tandem with the excitement until it was no longer annoyance. Make it read fear, he thought. Pure, undiluted fear. Even terror. Was he viewing the beginning of an affair or the prelude to murder?

Don't be so dramatic, he observed to himself. It was Saturday morning. A week to the day had passed since he had first seen the girl in the red gingham dress. And, like the previous Saturday, the air was heavy with storm, for it is axiomatic that fine Chicago summer days are not reserved for weekends.

In the apartment across the way, 17 floors above the street, the living-room drapes were unexpectedly drawn, and so were the bedroom shades, shielding the lovely girl from his inquisitive gaze. Well, he had nothing to do tonight. Likely, in time, she would pull the drapes and he would take up his post. Perhaps he would even see her date, although he somehow doubted this. The guy, he felt, was all through. He had something going for him and something going against him, but whatever it was that inspired the negative factor surely was adequate to mark finis to the matter.

Which raised an interesting point. Suppose she was in some danger. Suppose the guy was a threat to her. Ah, he would ride to the rescue. You dreamer, you, and he put on his raincoat and went to the supermarket. Returning with the fixings for dinner, he noticed the two thunderheads over the lake. Nigrescent like bruises against the summer sky, they lurked above the water, motionless, pointing menacingly at the sweltering city. Other passers-by, also noticing them, hurried on their way.

He unloaded the groceries and made sure that the air conditioning was turned up high. Several afternoon hours passed with the twin thunderheads stationed over the lake and the girl's drapes shut tight. Marian Taylor, what are you doing behind those curtains?

The time was nearly five o'clock when suddenly the sky became quite dark. Since sunset was some hours off, he went to the window and looked lakeward, knowing what he would see. In front of him was a wall of black; the thunderheads were on the move. Suspecting that he was not witnessing an ordinary summer storm, he turned on the radio. The weather bureau, the announcer said, had just issued a tornado watch. A moment later, the watch was escalated. Tornado warning!

Outside, all traces of day receded until the building next door was in evidence only by a scattering of light showing. The wind increased its vicious tugs at the windows, and on the quivering glass, raindrops hammered in fury. The first lightning flash was tentative, brief in length, arching over the lake-front sky, but following the exploratory electronics, the air was shattered by a trio of simultaneous zigzag bolts, each grotesquely seeking and finding the earth. The resulting thunderclaps were immense to the ears, and when the buildings had tossed back their last echoes, the silence was absolute. In his apartment, the radio announcer's voice was still, the air conditioning silent. The power had failed in the glass-and-concrete complex.

The fickle lightning moved north toward Milwaukee, leaving in its path trailings like fireflies on a summer night. With the lightning gone, the complex was plunged into darkness, although he could see through the pelting rain the flickering of candles and the beams from flashlights. Which do you use behind your curtains, Marian Taylor? If only I could help you.

This pleasant fancy had no sooner passed than he was startled to see her balcony door slide open and the girl appear outside. With several large steps suggesting urgency, she went to the corner of the balcony nearest him and waved frantically in his direction. Impossible, he thought, she can't see me, for it's as dark as moonless midnight. Nevertheless, there was terror in the wild waving and he opened his own balcony door and went outside.

"Help!" she yelled, her voice diluted by the wind.

"What's the matter?" he shouted. Leaning forward at the balcony, he tried to see more of her, but all he could make out in the gloom were the white of her shorts, the blonde of her hair.

"Please help me!"

"What's the matter?"

"He's going to kill me."

"I'm coming, Marian."

Resembling tennis balls bouncing about a court, the wind-propelled clouds tumbled toward the group of high-rise apartment buildings. In a few minutes, she thought, the storm will be upon us with lightning and rain. Still, there was time before it hit and, opening the sliding glass door all the way, she stepped out onto the balcony. To her feet, the floor of the concrete balcony was hot from the late-afternoon sun now rendered invisible by the coming storm. At that place on the balcony where the view was directly toward Old Town, she placed both hands on the railing.

Go to church, her mother had said, and you will surely meet some nice young men. In a big city, the advice had proceeded, you must be careful where you meet people. Church is a good place. Well, she had tried church, the Episcopal one over on

Neighbors

Dearborn Street, and no thanks, Mother. Not her type, or typ[
but what was her type? He was . . . maybe. The guy on t[
number-151 bus and her date tonight. Mother, you'll never gue[
where I met him. On the bus. On a Michigan Avenue number-
151 bus. His name is Don Moretel, but that wouldn't mean
anything to you.

The wind played with her dress and long blonde hair and,
leaning into the wind, she could feel the temperature of the air
descend. Nearly time to go in, she thought, since it appeared that
date and storm would arrive almost simultaneously. She was
starting to turn, to head back into the apartment, when she
noticed the man in the next building. Not more than a shadow
in the failing light; nevertheless, he was visible: standing next to
a plant (avocado?), holding binoculars pointed directly at her.
Of all the nerve, you creep! she shrieked to herself.

No more than 50 feet away and there he was, devouring me
with those big powerful glasses, eating me alive at close range.
Strongly tempted to bolt inside and escape those invading eyes,
nevertheless, she remained motionless and met the gaze head on.
Obviously, he must know that he was caught in the act, yet he
stayed still and frozen. Or did he believe the fading light
rendered him invisible? Anyway. . . . A scattering of raindrops
smacked her in the face and she went inside.

Some hours later, she critiqued the first date, mulling it over in
the kitchen with a glass of milk for an audience. Don Moretel
was an interesting guy, a strange one, too. Possessive and moody,
though entertaining and amusing. Contradictions galore. She
looked into the glass as if for the answer. Speak, glass. It spoke:
The creep's looking at you again. Without glancing his way, she
knew it for a fact. Good night, creep, she thought. After finishing
the milk, she went to bed.

Next evening came and, with it, the call of a girl who suspects
that romance may lurk nearby—a session with a hot iron. The
red gingham dress and other possible dating apparel fell to the
steaming metal, and she even touched up her blue nightgown.

After ironing the nightgown, she held it to the light, approvingly noticing its patent transparency, wistfully musing whether or not Don would ever see her draped in such. While temporarily suspended in this reverie, she became aware that her solitude was an illusion, that the guy across the way was nocturnally scanning, and by turning slightly, she confirmed it. By the potted plant, there was a vague shape in the darkened apartment. One thing, creep, she mused, you'll never see me in this nightgown.

Events of the following week called forth a mixed bag of emotions: pleasure, puzzlement, annoyance. Don Moretel was solicitous, polite, generous with his dating cash.

He was also somewhat of a mystery man concerning where he lived. "Nearby" was his only reply. And he was suspicious, jealous, even threatening.

"What do you do when I don't see you?" he asked at one point.

"Right now, I'm seeing *you,* Don."

"But when I'm not around?"

"Just you, Don."

"Better keep it that way."

"What do you mean?"

"I have this picture of you in my mind, Marian. It's like I monitor you with some kind of ESP." She remembered that one of their early conversations had been about thought transference. It was one of his peculiar interests—but she hadn't been able to tell whether he'd been joking about it or whether he really believed in it.

Six short days had passed since the first date, and in six days and four dates it was all over, ending far short of any scene starring the blue nightgown. Saturday morning and dressed in white shorts and dark T-shirt, she chainsmoked behind closed drapes, hardly aware of the humming of the air conditioning, completely oblivious to the weather outside.

Last night had seen the proverbial final straw. Following an expensive and well-turned-out meal in a French restaurant, they had gone to a Near North bar popular with the young set. Before she had finished her first drink, he had pulled the possessive act with such force that she had taken refuge in the ladies' room and there she reached the final decision. She was returning to the table, threading her way through massed humanity, when she noticed that Don had opened her purse and with one hand was rummaging around inside.

"Don, what are you doing in my purse?"

"Looking for a match. What took you so long?"

"Take me home, please."

In the cab on the way back, she owned the conversation. In precise language, without attempting to keep the heat out of her voice, she delivered the nonnegotiable.

"You don't own me," she concluded.

"Good night," he replied sweetly, not bothering to get out of the cab. And as she was walking away from the cab, he tossed her a kind of throwaway line, one that exploded around her head like a bomb.

"Marian, I'm going to kill you. That's a promise."

She had rushed into her building's lobby, mentally urged the elevator on to greater speed and, once inside the apartment, she slammed the door. Turning the double lock at the top, she felt satisfaction at the solid, metallic click.

"No way," the building superintendent had said when she moved in, "for anyone to get through that double lock without a key. Of course, they could always take the door off," and he laughed at this, since the neighbors would be bound to hear or notice.

Saturday morning passed into afternoon and she sat there behind closed drapes, smoked, commiserated with herself. The principal reassuring thought: Thank God for the double lock. And there was always the phone and the police. And, as a last resort, the gun in the bedroom.

She went into the bedroom. Nestled beneath a maroon wool sweater was a Ruger Mark I automatic target pistol. Great on tin cans and for just fooling around, it wasn't an unusual gun for a city girl to have, especially for a former downstate tomboy. A box of .22-caliber ammunition was kept under another sweater, and she placed both pistol and bullets on top of the bureau.

The world's full of kooks, she thought, returning to the living room. Like Don Moretel from the 151 bus. Well, her mother would say, what would you expect? Now, I suggest. . . . OK, Mother, I get the picture. Kooks. An ocean full of them. And not to mention my little friend with the binoculars across the way.

That week she had been aware of his watching her when tidying up before Don came over, after Don had brought her home and had left, and the time she had done the ironing. But oddly enough, she had not believed her apartment under surveillance when Don was with her there, although there was no reason to doubt that even creeps have their own social life and go out, too. What do you suppose he's up to now? she wondered. To be sure, the drawn curtains did not offer a tempting view for him; she went to the curtain and drew it back a slit so she could see into the next apartment.

Looking out, she was surprised how dark it was. There could only be a storm on the way, she knew, for it was not quite five o'clock. And, yes, he was there, not by the avocado plant but back in the apartment with binoculars hanging from his neck, the glasses flat on his chest, his head facing the lake, no doubt eying the coming storm. To Marian, he was an indistinct figure in the false dusk.

With the first flash of lightning, she let the drapes return to their normal state and stepped back into her living room. Putting a hand to her chest, she could clearly feel the beat of her heart, strong, increasing in tempo, reflecting anxiety about to overflow to the grounds of panic. Several things were wrong, dead wrong, yet their essences eluded her. She glanced around the room, as if the room itself held an answer—any answer. The double-locked door. Newspapers on the floor. An overflowing ashtray. The lamp burning on the coffee table. The purse on the couch.

"The purse!" she said out loud, fingers tearing at the zipper.

Turning it upside down, she let the contents fall to the couch, and then she got down on her knees to better inspect. Suddenly, the little pile of feminine effects seemed to glow not once but three times, localized evidence of three monstrous thunderbolts ripping the sky; but even before the coffee-table lamp went out and the air conditioning ceased to whoosh, she knew that the extra set of keys was gone.

"Marian, I'm going to kill you."

At any moment, entirely at his discretion, Don Moretel could come through the door. The police, she thought: but from the lifted phone, she was insulted by the lack of a hum, isolated by absolute silence. The word escape rang in her brain and, in a trifling, she was in the hall and running for the stairs. With the power failure, surely the elevators were out of action, but 17 flights down she would be in the lobby, with the street outside and a police car soon to pass.

Normally, an electric sign indicated STAIRS in the hall, but this also had been extinguished by the storm. Four doors toward the elevators were the stairs, she reckoned on the run, and she was right on target, opening the door as the building shook with an outrageous rumble of thunder. She started down the stairs but had not traveled a flight in the dark when a noise brought her to a stop: from below, the heavy tread of a man ascending the stairs.

The rational part of her mind suggested that an occupant of the building had elected to hoof it up home, while the other part shouted that Don Moretel was on the way. It was impossible to meet anyone in the elevator, so what better place for murder than in a glass house without electricity? She fled back to her apartment, stopping in her dash to bang on two doors, hitting them hard with a doubled fist, striking them with force enough to send the little brass knockers into crazy metallic dances. Thunder answered her desperation.

Back in her own place, she did not bother to lock the door, for what good would it do with Don having the key? She did light a candle, however, to afford some light for the apartment, and placed it on the coffee table. She had a plan now and this made her feel calmer. To her, the use of the gun was repugnant and a last desperate remedy. But there was someone to whom she could call for help. The creep across the way. To be a creep was one thing, to be a possible murderer, another. He was probably safe enough and, at least, better than no one. She rushed for the balcony door.

He must see me waving, she prayed. He does see me. He's coming. Still no more than a blur in the murk, he stood across from her on his balcony, leaning over the railing, trying to catch her plea.

"Help!" she yelled.

"What's the matter?" he shouted.

"Please help me!"

"What's the matter?"

"He's going to kill me."

"I'm coming. Marian."

He knows my name, she thought, both relieved and perplexed. The lightning was very distant now, barely illuminating the dark skies north along the lake. She closed the sliding glass door and returned to the living room. He knows my name. When concentrating hard, Marian had a stance that was, in effect, a characteristic gesture of deep contemplation, legs stiff, with the right foot at a right angle to the left. Standing in such a way, staring at the undulating wave of the candlelight, she grabbed for what was loose and brought it down.

"Oh, my God!" she said, speaking out loud in her solitude for the second time that day. The graceful position evaporated into a huddled figure on the sofa, one hand behind the other and both pressed tightly to her eyes.

"I have this picture of you in my mind, Marian." Don had boasted. But now she guessed the picture came from something more tangible than ESP.

Squarely she must face one ghastly, inescapable truth: Don Moretel and the creep were one and the same.

Surely this was the reason the man in the next building had never snooped when Don was with her and why he had said that she was never out of his sight. Nevertheless, against overwhelming evidence, she wondered if she wasn't making a mistake, if Don had been trying only to scare her from seeing other men and if Don's and the creep's going out at the same time wasn't just coincidence. And the fact that he knew her name virtually could be meaningless. After all, he must be interested in her, because of the intensity of his watching. He lived on the same floor as she, though in a different building. Figuring out her apartment number would not be tough, since each building had an identical layout as to apartment numbers. The directory downstairs would furnish her name in a second. Perhaps, she thought; but her final conclusion was hard. The two men were identical and any other rationale was simply fooling herself.

In the bedroom, the metal of the target pistol felt warm and humid to the touch. Carrying the weapon into the living room, she loaded it by candlelight and, going to the corner of the room, flanked by the draperies, she waited with gun pointing at the door.

"Marian, I'm going to kill you."

"Maybe you will," she whispered to herself. "We'll see."

With doors and windows shut and air conditioning off, the air in the room was getting sticky, and she felt a thin unladylike film spread across her, caused partially by rising temperature and humidity but mainly by the most terrifying experience of her existence.

Falling nearly horizontally, the rain beat a staccato pattern on the windows, and with water came wind howling with an eerie pitch around glass and concrete. Seven thousand people lived in the complex, she had heard, yet she could summon only a single person to help, a jilted suitor who for some warped reason imagined himself wronged, and one who had promised to kill her.

She was too far from the candle to see the gun held in her hand, though she suspected from the vicious grip on the butt that the hand would show white. Please come. Please come. So we can finish whatever it is you and I must finish.

In time he came. In uncounted hours to the waiting girl, in reality only the handful of minutes that it requires a strong man to run down 17 flights, cross a courtyard, climb 17 flights, he burst through the door, hitting it at a run at nearly shoulder height, entering the room in a shallow dive, unnaturally stiff as a creature drawn on wires.

The first shot she could identify individually, a sharp minor ping in the small room, but the rest ran together like a string of irritating firecrackers. The slightly plunging man never had the opportunity to straighten from his dive, for his trip was all one way—to the floor by the coffee table, face flush with the rug when the forward momentum had stopped.

Falling to the rug, the gun made a gentle anticlimactic thud, and the one large gulp of air she took was filled with smoke, so when she screamed, the sound came out hoarse and warbling, like the racket from a hurt animal.

"Shut up," Don Moretel said as he closed the door. In easy fashion, he swung a flashlight. "You'll wake the dead," he added, and laughed.

In the corner, Marian started to cry.

Jack Ritchie has appeared frequently in these anthologies with an admirable diversity of tales. You would do worse than track down a paperback collection of his tales, A New Leaf and Other Stories *(Dell, 1971). In the meantime, try this sneaky caper— which caught me entirely by surprise—as a worthy example of his art.*

JACK RITCHIE
The Magnum

Amos Weatherlee clutched a magnum of champagne in one hand and a hammer in the other.

He paused in the wide doorway of the hotel bar.

At this hour of the afternoon, the barroom was nearly empty except for three women in one booth with Pink Ladies and a middle-aged man alone in another.

Weatherlee approached him and extended the hammer. "Pardon me, but I would regard it as an extreme favor if you would smash my bottle."

Harry Sloan studied him warily. "Don't you think that would make quite a mess?"

Weatherlee's silver-gray hair was somewhat disheveled and he spoke with a slight slur. "I never thought of that. You don't suppose that the bartender has a basin or something like that we could use?"

Sloan sipped his whiskey and soda. "If you're really set on smashing that bottle, why don't you do it yourself?"

Weatherlee sighed. "I tried. I really tried. Captain O'Reilly did too. So did Carruthers and Larson and Cooper and I don't know how many more. It was quite a wild night."

"What was?"

"Our club meeting a year ago."

Sloan's attention was distracted by the procession of a dozen elderly men filing through the hotel entrance. At least half of them walked with canes. They moved slowly across the lobby toward the open doors of a private dining room.

Sloan showed some interest. "Who in the world are they?"

"Our club," Weatherlee said. "It's our annual reunion. The members just finished a sight-seeing bus tour of the city and now we're going to have dinner." He watched as the group entered the dining room. "We were all members of the same National Guard Company. We formed the club right after the war."

"World War I?"

"No," Weatherlee said. "The Spanish American War."

Sloan regarded him skeptically.

"That's Captain O'Reilly," Weatherlee said. "Wearing the broad-brimmed campaign hat." He sat down. "How old do you think I am?"

"I haven't the faintest idea."

"Ninety," Weatherlee said proudly. "I was eighteen when I enlisted."

"Sure," Sloan said. "And I suppose you were a member of Teddy Roosevelt's Rough Riders and charged up San Juan hill?"

"No. Actually our outfit never got beyond Tampa before the war ended. Our only casualties were to yellow fever."

"You look pretty spry for ninety."

"I am." Weatherlee said firmly. "I take a brisk half-hour walk every day and I'm still in full possession of all my faculties. In full possession."

"Sure," Sloan said. "Sure."

"Of course we weren't all the same age when we formed the club. Captain O'Reilly, for instance, our oldest man, was thirty-six. Twice as old as I at the time. He joined the club more in the spirit of good-fellowship, rather than really expecting to drink the bottle."

Sloan eyed the magnum of champagne. "Just what kind of a club was this?"

"A Last Man club. Perhaps you've heard of them? We founded ours in 1898. Right after the war ended and we were waiting to get shipped home. We wanted one hundred members, but actually we could get only ninety-eight to sign up."

"And those are the survivors? What's left?"

"Oh, no. Those are only the members who could make it. The others are in hospitals, old age homes, and the like."

Sloan did some mental arithmetic. "You said that Captain O'Reilly was thirty-six when the club formed in 1898?"

"Yes."

"Are you telling me that Captain O'Reilly is now one hundred and eight years old?"

"That's right. Our oldest man."

"And at ninety, you're the youngest?"

"Yes," Weatherlee said. "And I'm Custodian of the Bottle. According to our by-laws, the youngest surviving member is Custodian of the Bottle."

Sloan finished his drink. "Just how many club members are still alive?"

"Ninety-five."

Sloan stared at him for a few moments. "You mean to tell me that only three of you people have died since 1898?"

Weatherlee nodded. "There was Meyer. He died in a train accident back in 1909. Or was it 1910? And McMurty. He stayed in the Guard and worked himself up to full colonel before he was killed in the Argonne in 1918. And Iverson. He died of acute appendicitis in 1921."

Sloan considered his empty glass and then sighed. "Care for a drink?"

Weatherlee smiled affably. "I guess one more won't hurt. I'll take whatever you're having."

Sloan caught the bartender's eye and held up two fingers.

Weatherlee leaned forward and lowered his voice. "Actually this isn't the original champagne bottle. I broke that in 1924."

Sloan studied it again.

"It happened at our convention that year," Weatherlee said. "I was riding the elevator at the time. In those days they didn't operate as smoothly as they do now. There was this sudden jerk as the operator stopped at my floor. The suitcase I was carrying sprang open and the bottle dropped to the floor. Couldn't have fallen more than a foot, but there it lay, shattered on the floor."

Weatherlee shook his head at the memory. "I was absolutely panicstricken. I mean here I was the custodian of the club's bottle—a great responsibility—and there it lay, shattered on the elevator floor. Luckily I was the only passenger on the elevator at the time. No one but the operator knew what had happened."

"So you went out and bought another bottle?"

"No. I didn't see how I could duplicate it anywhere. The bottle was quite distinctive. Purchased in Tampa, twenty-six years before."

Sloan indicated the bottle. "Then what is that?"

"It was the elevator operator who saved me," Weatherlee said. "He went out and got an *exact* duplicate."

"How did he manage to do that?"

"I haven't the faintest idea. He seemed a little evasive, now that I remember, but I was too overjoyed to press him. He was really most apologetic about the accident. Most solicitous. Took care of the mess in the elevator and brought the new bottle to my room fifteen minutes later. Wouldn't even let me pay for it. Claimed that the entire incident was really his doing and wouldn't accept a cent."

Sloan took his eyes from the magnum. "You said something about Captain O'Reilly trying to break the bottle?"

"Yes. Last year at our meeting. I still don't know exactly why he tried it. But I do remember that he kept staring at the bottle all evening. That year I was the Treasurer and I'd just finished reading my report. We had $4,990 in the treasury. Our dues are actually almost nominal, but still after all those years and compounded interest, it reached that sum."

The bartender brought the drinks. Sloan paid him and took a swallow of his whiskey and soda. "So what about O'Reilly?"

Weatherlee watched the bartender leave. "Oh, yes. Well, just as I finished, he rose suddenly to his feet and began slashing at the bottle with his cane and shouting, 'That damn bottle! That damn bottle!' And then it seemed as though nearly everyone else went mad too. They shouted and cursed and smashed at the bottle, some even with chairs. I really don't know how it would all have ended if the waiters and other hotel people hadn't rushed in and restrained them."

"But they didn't break the bottle?"

"No. It was most remarkable. The blows were really resounding, and yet it didn't break. I thought about that all year. All this long year."

Weatherlee took a deep breath. "I arrived here early this morning. I am not a drinking man, but on impulse I bought a pint of whiskey and took it up to my room. I just sat there drinking and staring at that bottle. I even forgot all about the bus tour. And then I don't know what came over me, but I picked up an ashtray—one of those heavy glass things that are practically indestructible—and struck the bottle. Again and again, until finally the *ashtray* broke."

Weatherlee took the handkerchief from his breastcoat pocket. "I was in a perfect frenzy. I rushed out of my room with the bottle and down the hallway I found one of those maintainence closets with its door open. There was a hammer on one of the shelves. I put the magnum of champagne into the stationary tub in the cubicle and struck it again and again with the hammer."

"But the bottle still didn't break?"

Weatherlee dabbed lightly at his forehead with the handkerchief. "But what was most ghastly of all was that all the time I was trying to smash that bottle, I had the feeling that someone, somewhere, was *laughing* at me."

He glared at the magnum. "And then suddenly, the *conviction,* the *certainty,* came to me that neither I, nor *anybody* in the club could destroy that bottle. If it were done, it had to be done by someone on the outside."

Sloan frowned at his drink. "Just *why* do you want to destroy that bottle in the first place?"

Weatherlee sighed. "I don't know. I just know that I *do.*"

They were both silent for almost a minute and then Sloan said, "This elevator operator. What did he look like?"

"The elevator operator? Rather a distinguished sort of a person. I remember thinking at the time that he wasn't at all what one would expect of an elevator operator. Rather tall. Dark hair, dark eyes."

One of the doors of the dining room across the lobby opened and a waiter stepped out. He came into the bar. "Mr. Weatherlee, we're serving now."

Weatherlee nodded. "Yes. I'll be there in a moment."

Sloan waited until the waiter was out of hearing. "When did you say you broke the original bottle?"

"In 1924."

"And nobody's died since then?"

"Nobody's died since 1921. That was when Iverson got his acute appendicitis."

Sloan stared at the bottle again. "I'd like to join your club."

Weatherlee blinked. "But that's impossible."

"Why is it impossible?"

"Well . . . for one thing, you didn't belong to our National Guard company."

"Do your by-laws say anything about members having to belong to that particular company? Or any company at all?"

"Well, no. But it was *assumed.* . . ."

"And you did say that you never did fill your membership

quota? Only ninety-eight people signed up? That leaves a vacancy of two, doesn't it?"

"Yes, but you are so much younger than any of the rest of us. It would be unfair for us to have to compete with you for the bottle."

"Look," Sloan said. "I'm not a rich man, but I'll match what's in the treasury, dollar for dollar."

"That's very kind of you," Weatherlee said a bit stiffly, "but if you should outlive all of us, and that seems likely, you'd get it all back anyhow."

Sloan smiled patiently. "I'll sign an affidavit renouncing all claim to what's in the treasury."

Weatherlee rubbed his neck. "I don't know. I'm not the final authority on anything like this. I'm not even an officer this year, unless you want to count being Custodian of the Bottle. I really don't know what the procedure would be in a case like this. I suppose we'll have to take a vote or something."

He rose and put the magnum under his arm. "I suppose there's no harm in asking, but frankly I think they'll turn you down."

Sloan put his hand on the hammer. "Better leave this here with me."

Sloan came to Weatherlee's room at nine-thirty the next morning.

He took an envelope from his pocket and handed it to Weatherlee.

Weatherlee nodded acceptance. "To be quite honest, I was a bit surprised that the club decided to accept you. Not without exception, of course. Captain O'Reilly was quite against it."

Sloan moved to the bureau and picked up the magnum of champagne.

Weatherlee blinked. "What are you doing?"

"Taking the bottle with me. You told me yourself that according to the club's by-laws, the youngest member is Custodian of the Bottle."

"Yes, but. . . ."

Sloan opened the door to the corridor. He smiled broadly. "We wouldn't want you to go around asking strange people to break it, now would we?"

When Sloan was gone, Weatherlee locked the door.

He went to the bathroom and began removing the make-up from his face. As he worked, a half century disappeared.

Maybe he could have taken Sloan for more than five thousand, but you never know. Getting too greedy could have blown the whole deal.

He smiled.

Finding the sucker was the hardest part of it.

But once you did, and learned approximately how much he could part with without undue pain, you went about arranging the set-up. That included going to the nearest Old Soldiers' Home and offering to treat a dozen of their oldest veterans to a dinner.

And the old boys did so enjoy an afternoon out.

*Thomasina Weber, a newcomer to these anthologies, spins a grim
little web, with a sizeable aftershock in the final paragraph . . .*

THOMASINA WEBER
Loaded Quest

Tony Graybill stepped out of the bus, his joints stiff from the
long ride. It was eight thirty on a warm July evening, but the
Florida air was pleasingly fragrant after the air-conditoned
atmosphere of the bus. The cigar smoker who had been his
seatmate for the last two hundred miles had not helped matters.

Reclaiming his duffel bag from the luggage compartment,
Tony headed for the motel he had noticed a few blocks from the
depot. The night was young and, after cleaning up, he would
still have an hour or two to look for Millie.

The room he was given was clean, but far from luxurious.
Compared to where he had been, though, it was paradise. He
never wanted to see another jungle. He relished the hot shower,
letting gallons of water revitalize his weary body. He wondered if
he would ever feel rested again.

He still had not grown accustomed to the fact that he was his
own man, with no more orders and living with filth and death,
grateful every time a bullet whizzed past his ear to a less
fortunate target. Now he could do exactly as he pleased. At the

moment, he had one goal in mind, the goal that had kept him alive, day after hellish day.

Maybe that explained ghosts, he reflected, as he locked his motel room door behind him. They were probably dedicated persons who had died before achieving their goals. It seemed logical. Death would not be strong enough to quench *his* fire. He could readily picture himself as a dedicated ghost. A smile touched his lips and it felt strange, like something he had forgotten how to do.

The main street did not look familiar to him, but he had been away a long time, and towns change. People change too, he mused grimly. You can't blame a town; but a person, that's different. A faithful, worthwhile person does not change, not the way Millie did. So what did that make Millie?

Other wives waited, even though it wasn't easy. It wasn't easy for the men, either, but knowing they had someone to go home to made it bearable. Millie hadn't even given him that. He should have known something was wrong when her letters stopped coming. When he finally did get a letter, it was not from Millie but from her lawyer.

Before the ink was dry on the divorce papers, Millie had married again. That was all he knew. He did not know whom she had married, but he was willing to bet it was someone with money. When Tony and Millie had married, they had less than fifty dollars between them. At first Millie had thought it was a lark, sitting on a plank laid on concrete blocks and eating off lap trays. Rent and food, those were all his wages as a gas-pump jockey supplied.

The novelty soon wore off, for Millie was not the grin-and-bear-it type. Millie was strong, but in Millie's life, Millie came first. Her parents were well-to-do and she was used to an easy life. When Tony was drafted before their first anniversary, he had the feeling Millie was happier than she let on at the prospect of moving back into her parents' home. His only consolation was that even if he had not gone off to war, chances are their marriage still would not have survived.

So her new husband must have money. It followed, then, that they would live on the wealthy side of town. Every town had its Snob Hill, so he headed in that direction.

It was a waste of time, he discovered half an hour later. The houses were set well back from the streets and many of them were unlighted. The Party Set, of course. Those families that were at home had discreetly drawn their drapes. He would have to come back tomorrow, when it was daylight. Just as well; he was tired.

Next morning he had breakfast at The Diner and no one recognized him, but that was not surprising. He did not recognize them, either. It was probably under new management. Businesses were always changing hands, and waitresses never stay in one place very long. Besides, these waitresses looked as though they had still been in school when he went away.

He set out once again for Snob Hill. Refreshed by a good night's sleep and a satisfactory breakfast, Tony covered the neighborhood systematically. Another man might have been discouraged by the apparent futility of his quest, for very few people showed themselves, but Tony was determined to find Millie. He knew beyond a doubt that the intensity of his feeling would flush her out. It was his belief that by concentrating on what he sought, he emitted electromagnetic waves which attracted electromagnetic waves emitted by the object sought. This would bring them together.

Whether that was the case or not, Millie did emerge from a $100,000 house just as he was walking by. Thanks to the distance between the house and the sidewalk, she did not see him. Averting his face, he hurried on. He was not yet ready to confront her. He would know when the time was right.

He watched her for a week. He saw her in shorts, in slacks, in mini-skirts, in suits, in every sort of outfit money could buy; all expensive, nothing but the best. Millie had had a good figure, but it had never looked that good in the clothes she wore when she was married to Tony. He remembered with a pang how he used to run his fingers through the long red hair that was now bleached blonde and piled on top of her head so elegantly. His Millie—the same Millie—yet so different.

There were no children, he was glad to see. He didn't think he could have endured his Millie being mother to another man's children. It was bad enough that she was another man's wife. He wondered vaguely if her husband had done his part to defend his country. Probably not; money like that does not have to fight.

He wondered what she would say when she saw him. Would she cry? Back there, squinting through sweat and grime, he had thought he could not possibly wait another day to see her. Now that they were practically together, he could afford to wait. Everything had to be just right; he would not allow haste to spoil it. He would approach her when he was ready, and not a moment before. He had all the time in the world.

He watched her sunning in the yard and swimming in her pool. He followed her when she went shopping, even took a seat a row behind her in a movie one afternoon, watching her profile instead of the film. Her husband must have been out of town, for one evening a cab delivered a big, well-dressed man carrying an attaché case. She opened the door for him and he enfolded her in his arms. Tony watched the house all night; the man did not come out again.

The husband was about what Tony had expected—close to fifty, showing the effects of too much rich food, with a way of carrying himself that indicated years of commanding bellhops, porters and other lesser mortals. Money must have meant more to Millie than he realized.

It was toward the end of the second week that Tony knew the time had come. Apparently her husband had gone off on another business trip several days before. It was early evening, not quite dark, although the full moon was already visible. Millie came out of the house wearing a gold bikini. Concealed behind the hibiscus that ringed the pool, Tony followed her with his eyes as she seated herself on the edge of the pool, swinging her legs in the water. Hands flat beside her, she gazed downward into the green depths. Soundlessly, he came up behind her.

"Hello, Millie," he said as he grasped her shoulders and pushed. He had to go in with her for, fighting wildly, she started to scream. That would have spoiled everything, but she didn't scream long. He left her there, a shimmering stone on the bottom of the green pool.

Tony Graybill stepped out of the bus, his joints stiff from the long ride. It was nine o'clock on a hot August evening, but the Texas air was refreshing after the airconditioned atmosphere of the bus.

Reclaiming his duffel bag from the luggage compartment, Tony headed for the motel he had noticed on the way into town. The night was young and, after cleaning up, he would still have an hour or two to look for Millie.

This is a tale of impression and subtlety and suggestion, with many a nice turn of phrase. The beautiful opening line is almost a story in itself.

HENRY T. PARRY
Homage to John Keats

When Howard P. Ransom reached 55, he retired from his job, sold his house, murdered his wife, and settled down in Rome, thereby fulfilling four long-cherished ambitions. He loathed his house, detested his job, hated his wife and loved the prospect of taking up life, late but renewed, in a foreign capital of endless attraction.

His job, he felt, was far beneath one of his talent, but it paid so well that his love of money outweighed his distaste. His house was a constant burden, insatiable in its demands for repairs, rapacious in its tax requirements, an unstaunchable bleeding of the money and time that he would rather have spent on his boat. But it was his wife Hannah whom he regarded as the major obstacle to freedom and a new life.

As the years of their marriage passed, whatever of love and understanding there may have been had vanished, with Hannah exhibiting a half-hidden sufferance bordering on contempt, and he an impotent chafing and smoldering resentment. He found that the cute pussycat face of 22 became the snarling mask of a stalking tiger at 50.

Hannah had adamantly refused to agree to a divorce, primarily because Howard wanted it. For Howard to have simply walked out was repellent to his nature, which required order and planning and abhorred loose ends and unfinished business. This plus the fatal flaw in the mind of every killer—the conviction that his action was justified—led him to the murder of his wife.

The act itself was simple, well-planned, and swift. One of the few remaining things they did together was to take an occasional weekend cruise in the boat. Returning home just after dark one Sunday, they rounded the breakwater at the end of the Delaware-Chesapeake Canal and turned north against the ebbing tide where the river and bay met. Two miles upstream Howard put the engine on idle and came astern to where Hannah sat.

"I want you to put on this life jacket. The tide is ebbing quite strongly and there's all this debris floating about. If I have to make a quick turn and if you should be standing, you might go over the side."

"Oh, Howard, is that necessary? Such unusual precautions here on the river."

"This is practically the top end of Delaware Bay. And there's this heavy tanker traffic—"

"Oh, all right, all right. A lesson in geography. Always a lesson in something."

"Just this one last lesson then."

She stood and he helped her into the life jacket, steadying her as she staggered slightly, and swiftly tied the ribbons. He could smell the perfume she used, a smell that he had come to loathe as much as once it had attracted him.

"Howard," her voice rose in bewilderment, "what have you done to this jacket? It weighs a ton."

"Yes," he agreed, "it's packed with lead"—and he pushed her over the stern.

The greasy water was barely disturbed as she went under. He

switched on the spotlight and played it back and forth over the water. Crates, fruit baskets, odd pieces of lumber, all swam placidly by on the outward tide, but the surface betrayed no sign of what had happened.

For two hours he waited, to be sure that his plan had worked, and then headed for the nearest marina and a telephone to report his well-rehearsed story to the Coast Guard, with special care in placing the scene of the incident farther up the river than it had actually occurred.

It took Howard three months to make what he thought of as his getaway. Calls placed at lengthening intervals to the Coast Guard brought no news and elicited finally the opinion that there was no likelihood of the body being recovered.

The house was sold, removing forever the burden of wet basements, rising taxes, and ever more plentiful crops of crabgrass. Kindly neighbors offered sympathy and expressed understanding of his wish for a complete change of scene, expressions which Howard gravely accepted, inwardly relishing the contrast between his decently submissive outward manner and his inner satisfaction with the fruition of his plans.

Thoughtfully he arranged for a tombstone to be erected—a fact that was noted in the local paper—and had it incised with Hannah's name and the years of her birth and death, and, as indicative of his intentions, he had his own name added, followed by the year of his birth and a small uncarved rectangle in which at the proper time another year would be cut. With a touch of grim wholly uncharacteristic humor he thought that a suitable epitaph for Hannah might be "Lost at sea," but sensibly he restrained himself.

Late in the fall, after a dutiful and symbolic visit to the cemetery, Howard arrived in Rome. Through the columns of a newspaper aimed at the American tourist he rented a small furnished apartment in a converted palazzo on a street near the top of the Spanish Steps, a house reputed to have been owned by a cadet branch of the Medici.

After the spare trimness and openness of his suburban house he was struck by the stony, secretive exteriors of the Roman houses and the contrast with their ornate, pretentious interiors. His living room was furnished with heavy oaken furniture, elaborately carved; one chair with a faded damask cover on its tall back was supposed to have once been the property of the infamous Principe de Canisio who, it was said, had died in it, a messy affair of a jealous husband and a silken cord.

Dim acne-ed mirrors on the walls on each side of the door reflected windows with heavy velvet drapes looped back by tassled rope ties. It seemed that the same style of furniture that was suitable for the palazzo of a doge had been used in this small room, giving it a theatrical, shop-worn splendor. But Howard settled contentedly in these falsely elegant surroundings and gave himself over to the delights of leisurely explorations of the ancient city.

It was not until early summer that he saw Hannah. Or thought he saw Hannah.

He was returning from an afternoon of browsing among the many shops near the Piazza di Spagna and had begun to climb the magnificent stairway street of the Spanish Steps, the sweeping thoroughfare that leads majestically up to the Monte di Trinita. In the wall of the building to the right of the first landing was the shrine of millions of poetry-loving tourists, the window of the room where the poet Keats had died. He paused on the landing, looking up at the open window, and saw a woman looking down at him, a woman who resembled Hannah.

Shaken, he stared up at her, his mind rejecting the atavistic fear of the dead returned to life and telling himself to wait for a movement or gesture to dispel the likeness, for her aspect to shift from identity to mere similarity. The woman gazed down calmly, framed portraitlike in the window, an absent-minded half smile on her lips, and raised her hand; but whether or not the gesture was in greeting he could not determine. Then the woman slowly moved back from the frame of the window and was out of sight.

He stood and stared upward at the window not thirty feet away, his mind searching for the possibility of error in the execution of his plan, but at no point could he find a mistake. He was brought back to reality when he heard a passing American schoolteacher comment to her companion "Look. Another poetry lover paying homage to John Keats." As they passed him he smelled the faint fragrance of the same perfume Hannah had used and he wondered if he had smelled it unknowingly as he looked at the woman in the window and if it had not added a subliminal reinforcement to a chance likeness.

He concluded that the resemblance was accidental, but from that time forward, before he fell asleep at night, he saw again the face and form of Hannah framed in the window.

A week later he saw her again.

It was during the intermission before the last act of "Aida," which was performed outdoors at the Baths of Caracalla. He strolled among the crowds under the lights along the wide paths that skirted the towering walls with their shadowed arches recessing into darkness. She was standing under an arch, well back from the walk and partially obscured by the shadow of a tree as well as by the shadows of the arch.

He stopped, the crowd moving slowly past him, and stared at the figure that stood dwarfed by the tall arch, hugging itself as if chilled and idly watching the passing crowd. Her eyes swept over him with no sign of recognition and then swung back to look at him uncertainly as if she were not sure she knew him, and then she turned away toward the interior darkness of the arch, on her lips the same half smile that he had seen from the Steps.

He pushed his way through the crowd toward her but the overhead lights flicked off and on several times to signal the end of the intermission. By the time he made his way through the returning surge of the crowd she had vanished. He made his way to the entrance where the patrons were returning to their seats and although he observed each one until the first aria was well under way he did not see her again.

Similarly after the performance he watched the main exit but saw no one who remotely resembled his dead wife. But he found this occurrence less troubling than the previous one and although he thought about it constantly for days it did not cause the questioning and examination the first encounter had. A resemblance, close enough to be sure, but it was not Hannah. If it had been, he was certain she could not have resisted showing the new power which she would now have over him.

Three days later in the late afternoon he returned to his apartment, slipped his key into the handsome walnut door, swung the door inward, and froze. Delusions of sight and errors in identification were always possible but there is not auto-suggestion in the sense of smell. The living room smelled faintly of Hannah's perfume.

Terror spurted in him but he forced himself to stride into the room. Hannah sat in the Principe di Canisio's chair, her face as worn as the scarlet damask that covered the tall back of the chair, and in her hand was an ugly and unladylike .45 caliber automatic. She pointed it upward, directly at his face, so that he looked into its cruel, uncompromising muzzle that seemed small for such a deadly object.

For several seconds they stared at each other wordlessly, the woman who should have been dead and the man who should have been free. She waved the gun toward a slender gilt chair beside the door and he sat down facing her, the light from the window behind her chair making him feel, irrationally, that if only he could be in shadow he would be able to explain everything.

"How?" he managed to whisper.

"You thought of everything, Howard, everything but one small detail. I surfaced under an upturned fruit basket and stayed there while you were making certain with the spotlight that you had murdered me. My clothes made me buoyant for a time and the tide was carrying me downstream away from your light. When I was in sufficient darkness I grabbed a floating timber and paddled to shore just below a refinery. Murder and a polluted river, Howard! Some form of repayment is indicated, don't you agree?

"I floundered through the marshes until I came to a highway and walked along it until I found a filling station. It was closed but it was also a bus stop. After an hour's wait, during which most of the water dripped out of my clothes—but oh, the smell— a bus marked Ocean City came in and I got on. In the two-hour ride down the coast to Ocean City I planned what I would do.

"First of all, I couldn't let you, or anyone else, know I had survived. You would surely try again. I decided that this was no matter for the law and, besides, what could I prove? I had $48 in my purse. The next day I got a job as a summer waitress at a restaurant and worked there all summer under an assumed name. I even got a new Social Security number. I worked hard and they liked hard-working steady help who showed up seven days a week and didn't irritate the customers. I also subscribed to our hometown paper so that I would have some way of finding out about you. That tombstone now, that was touching.

"After the summer was over they offered me a job in their Florida place and I worked there until two weeks ago when I had enough money saved for this trip. The paper had reported your departure to live in Rome 'for an indefinite period,' it said, and how wrong that is now. My one fear was that my money would run out before I located you. I didn't realize how easy it is to find an American in Rome. Just watch the tourist attractions long enough and you'll find them.

"I saw you first at the Colosseum one day and followed you to this address. I thought at the time what a fitting place the Colosseum would be to do what I had come to do if it weren't so public. Too bad we didn't meet there by moonlight."

"May I get up and stand by the window?" he asked. "I can't breathe."

"Do," she answered, "but don't get too close. It's too late for accidents."

He walked to the window in the wall behind her chair and

stood looking down into the street. Shielded from her direct view by the tall back of the chair she was sitting in, he slowly slid one hand under the window drapery and unhooked the ropelike tie that looped the drape back.

"How did you get out of the life jacket?" he asked, not turning toward her chair.

"Oh, it almost worked. But you made one mistake—one small detail. When you tied the ribbons of the life jacket your reflexes took over. You tied the same knot that you, and nearly everybody else, ties every day of their lives—a simple bow knot. Under water I gave one pull at the ends of the ribbons and the knots came apart and I slipped out of the jacket. It was simple compared to untying and taking off my sneakers under water as we used to do when I was a girl in camp. If you had tied a good hard square knot, Howard, things would have been different for me. And for you.

"If you're wondering about the gun, I borrowed it—stole it really—from the Florida restaurant. They always kept one near the cash register."

He whirled from the window and leaped toward the back of her chair, the drapery tie outstretched between his hands. Her first shot, fired in frightened reflex at his reflection, shattered the mirror on the wall opposite her chair. Hanging over the chair back, he fumbled desperately to twist the rope tie around her neck. She slid from the chair to the floor and fired backward and upward in the blind instinct of selfpreservation.

Howard staggered backward from the impact of the shot, one hand jerking upward and holding the moth-eaten drapery tie as though in some baroque scalp dance, the other clutching the window drape which he pulled to the floor with him as he fell, his body becoming partly hidden in its pretentious folds. She pulled herself to her feet and stood over the body, sickened at the reality of what her plans had brought to pass, and dreading the possibility of having to fire again. But the thing that lay there was still and dead, the rope tie grasped in one hand.

She replaced the gun in her bag, inspected the room carefully to be sure she left no trail, and left the apartment without looking back. She made her way through the streets to the top of the Spanish Steps, rejecting the waiting taxis in case the drivers would be questioned later. Going down the long cascade of the Spanish Steps, she stopped at the landing one flight from the street below and looked up at the figures that drifted aimlessly past the open window of the room where Keats had died.

She wondered what historic shrine this house might be but knew that now she would never find out, any more than she would learn whether operas were performed in ruined bathhouses, as advertised. She had already placed a foot on the next descending step when her body contracted with rigid terror. Looking down at her from the open window of Keats's room was Howard, or a man who at this distance resembled Howard in startling detail.

He stood in full view immediately in front of the window, looking patient and expectant. She stared up at him in a paralysis of fear; he gazed down at her with serene assurance.

Then the figure slowly disappeared backward into the room, smiling as if in anticipation and passing confidently, amost negligently, through one hand and then the other a faded rope tie.

Ed McBain (Evan Hunter) is the foremost American practitioner of that most important and popular modern variant of crime fiction, the police procedural. McBain has recently shown the versatility of the form by using it imaginatively as political satire (Hail to the Chief), but meanwhile here is one of his infrequent novelet-length studies of the procedural (also expanded to novel length and published under the same title). It's McBain's justly famed 87th Precinct, with Detective Steve Carella interviewing the unmourning husband of the victim of a particularly messy murder . . .

ED MCBAIN
Sadie When She Died

"I'm very glad she's dead," the man said.

He wore a homburg, muffler, overcoat and gloves. He stood near the night table, a tall man with a narrow face, and a well-groomed gray moustache that matched the graying hair at his temples. His eyes were clear and blue and distinctly free of pain or grief.

Detective Steve Carella wasn't sure he had heard the man correctly. "Sir," Carella said, "I'm sure I don't have to tell you——"

"That's right," the man said, "you don't have to tell me. It happens I'm a criminal lawyer and am well aware of my rights. My wife was no good, and I'm delighted someone killed her."

Carella opened his pad. This was not what a bereaved husband was supposed to say when his wife lay disemboweled on the bedroom floor in a pool of her own blood.

"Your name is Gerald Fletcher."

"That's correct."

"Your wife's name, Mr. Fletcher,"

"Sarah. Sarah Fletcher."

"Want to tell me what happened?"

"I got home about fifteen minutes ago. I called to my wife from the front door, and got no answer. I came into the bedroom and found her dead on the floor. I immediately called the police."

"Was the room in this condition when you came in?"

"It was."

"Touch anything?"

"Nothing. I haven't moved from this spot since I placed the call."

"Anybody in here when you came in?"

"Not a soul. Except my wife, of course."

"Is that your suitcase in the entrance hallway?"

"It is. I was on the Coast for three days. An associate of mine needed advice on a brief he was preparing. What's your name?"

"Carella. Detective Steve Carella."

"I'll remember that."

While the police photographer was doing his macabre little jig around the body to make sure the lady looked good in the rushes, or as good as any lady *can* look in her condition, a laboratory assistant named Marshall Davies was in the kitchen of the apartment, waiting for the medical examiner to pronounce the lady dead, at which time Davies would go into the bedroom and with delicate care remove the knife protruding from the blood and slime of the lady, in an attempt to salvage some good latent prints from the handle of the murder weapon.

Davies was a new technician, but an observant one, and he noticed that the kitchen window was wide open, not exactly usual on a December night when the temperature outside hovered at twelve degrees. Leaning over the sink, he further noticed that the window opened onto a fire escape on the rear of the building. He could not resist speculating that perhaps some-one had climbed up the fire escape and then into the kitchen.

Since there was a big muddy footprint in the kitchen sink, another one on the floor near the sink, and several others fading as they traveled across the waxed kitchen floor to the living room, Davies surmised that he was onto something hot. Wasn't it pos-sible that an intruder *had* climbed over the windowsill, into the sink and walked across the room, bearing the switchblade knife that had later been pulled viciously across the lady's abdomen from left to right? If the M.E. ever got through with the damn body, the boys of the 87th would be halfway home, thanks to Marshall Davies. He felt pretty good.

The three points of the triangle were Detective-Lieutenant Byrnes, and Detectives Meyer Meyer and Steve Carella. Fletcher sat in a chair, still wearing homburg, muffler, overcoat and gloves as if he expected to be called outdoors at any moment. The interrogation was being conducted in a windowless cubicle labeled Interrogation Room.

The cops standing in their loose triangle around Gerald Fletcher were amazed but not too terribly amused by his brutal frankness.

"I hated her guts," he said.

"Mr. Fletcher," Lieutenant Byrnes said, "I *still* feel I must warn you that a woman has been murdered—"

"Yes. My dear, wonderful wife," Fletcher said sarcastically.

". . . which is a serious crime. . . ." Byrnes felt tongue-tied in Fletcher's presence. Bullet-headed, hair turning from iron-gray to ice-white, blue-eyed, built like a compact linebacker, Byrnes looked to his colleagues for support. Both Meyer and Carella were watching their shoelaces.

"You have warned me repeatedly," Fletcher said. "I can't imagine why. My wife is dead—someone killed her—but it was not I."

"Well, it's nice to have your assurance of that, Mr. Fletcher, but this alone doesn't necessarily still our doubts," Carella said, hearing the words and wondering where the hell they were coming from. He was, he realized, trying to impress Fletcher. He continued, "How do we know it *wasn't* you who stabbed her?"

"To begin with," Fletcher said, "there were signs of forcible entry in the kitchen and hasty departure in the bedroom, witness the wideopen window in the aforementioned room and the shattered window in the latter. The drawers in the dining-room sideboard were open——"

"You're very observant," Meyer said suddenly. "Did you notice all this in the four minutes it took you to enter the apartment and call the police?"

"It's my *job* to be observant," Fletcher said. "But to answer your question, no. I noticed all this *after* I had spoken to Detective Carella here."

Wearily, Byrnes dismissed Fletcher, who then left the room.

"What do you think?" Byrnes said.

"I think he did it," Carella said.

"Even with all those signs of a burglary?"

"*Especially* with those signs. He could have come home, found his wife stabbed—but not fatally—and finished her off by yanking the knife across her belly. Fletcher had four minutes, when all he needed was maybe four seconds."

"It's possible," Meyer said.

"Or maybe I just don't like the guy," Carella said.

"Let's see what the lab comes up with," Byrnes said.

The laboratory came up with good fingerprints on the kitchen window sash and on the silver drawer of the dining-room sideboard. There were good prints on some of the pieces of silver scattered on the floor near the smashed bedroom window. Most important, there were good prints on the handle of the switchblade knife. The prints matched; they had all been left by the same person.

Gerald Fletcher graciously allowed the police to take *his* fingerprints, which were then compared with those Marshall Davies had sent over from the police laboratory. The fingerprints on the window sash, the drawer, the silverware and the knife did not match Gerald Fletcher's.

Which didn't mean a damn thing if he had been wearing his gloves when he'd finished her off.

On Monday morning, in the second-floor rear apartment of 721 Silvermine Oval, a chalked outline on the bedroom floor was the only evidence that a woman had lain there in death the night before. Carella sidestepped the outline and looked out the shattered window at the narrow alleyway below. There was a distance of perhaps twelve feet between this building and the one across from it.

Conceivably, the intruder could have leaped across the shaftway, but this would have required premeditation and calculation. The more probable likelihood was that the intruder had fallen to the pavement below.

"That's quite a long drop," Detective Bert Kling said, peering over Carella's shoulder.

"How far do you figure?" Carella asked.

"Thirty feet. At least."

"Got to break a leg taking a fall like that. You think he went through the window headfirst?"

"How else?"

"He might have broken the glass out first, then gone through," Carella suggested.

"If he was about to go to all that trouble, why didn't he just *open* the damn thing?"

"Well, let's take a look," Carella said.

They examined the latch and the sash. Kling grabbed both handles on the window frame and pulled up on them. "Stuck."

"Probably painted shut," Carella said.

"Maybe he *did* try to open it. Maybe he smashed it only when he realized it was stuck."

"Yeah," Carella said. "And in a big hurry, too. Fletcher was opening the front door, maybe already in the apartment by then."

"The guy probably had a bag or something with him, to put the loot in. He must have taken a wild swing with the bag when he realized the window was stuck, and maybe some of the stuff fell out, which would explain the silverware on the floor. Then he probably climbed through the hole and dropped down feet first. In fact, what he could've done, Steve, was drop the bag down first, and *then* climbed out and hung from the sill before he jumped, to make it a shorter distance."

"I don't know if he had all that much time, Bert. He must have heard that front door opening, and Fletcher coming in and calling to his wife. Otherwise, he'd have taken his good, sweet time and gone out the kitchen window and down the fire escape, the way he'd come in."

Kling nodded reflectively.

"Let's take a look at that alley," Carella said.

In the alleyway outside, Carella and Kling studied the concrete pavement, and then looked up at the shattered second-floor window of the Fletcher apartment.

"Where do you suppose he'd have landed?" Kling said.

"Right about where we're standing." Carella looked at the ground. "I don't know, Bert. A guy drops twenty feet to a concrete pavement, doesn't break anything, gets up, dusts himself off, and runs the fifty-yard dash, right?" Carella shook his head. "My guess is he stayed right where he was to catch his breath, giving Fletcher time to look out the window, which would be the natural thing to do, but which Fletcher didn't."

"He was anxious to call the police."

"I still think he did it."

"Steve, be reasonable. If a guy's fingerprints are on the handle of a knife, and the knife is still in the victim——"

"*And* if the victim's husband realizes what a sweet setup he's stumbled into, wife lying on the floor with a knife in her, place broken into and burglarized, why *not* finish the job and hope the burglar will be blamed?"

"Sure," Kling said. "Prove it."

"I can't," Carella said. "Not until we catch the burglar."

While Carella and Kling went through the tedious routine of retracing the burglar's footsteps, Marshall Davies called the 87th Precinct and got Detective Meyer.

"I think I've got some fairly interesting information about the suspect," Davies said. "He left latent fingerprints all over the apartment and footprints in the kitchen. A very good one in the sink, when he climbed in through the window, and some middling-fair ones tracking across the kitchen floor to the dining room. I got some excellent pictures and some good blowups of the heel."

"Good," Meyer said.

"But more important," Davies went on, "I got a good walking picture from the footprints on the floor. If a man is walking slowly, the distance between his footprints is usually about twenty-seven inches. Forty for running, thirty-five for fast walking. These were thirty-two inches. So we have a man's usual gait, moving quickly, but not in a desperate hurry, with the walking line normal and not broken."

"What does that mean?"

"Well, a walking line should normally run along the inner edge of a man's heelprints. Incidentally, the size and type of shoe and angle of the foot clearly indicate that this *was* a man."

"OK, fine," Meyer said. He did not thus far consider Davies' information valuable nor even terribly important.

"Anyway, none of this is valuable nor even terribly important," Davies said, "until we consider the rest of the data. The bedroom window was smashed, and the Homicide men were speculating that the suspect had jumped through the window into the alley below. I went down to get some meaningful pictures, and got some pictures of where he must have landed— on both feet, incidentally—and I got another walking picture and direction line. He moved toward the basement door and into the basement. But the important thing is that our man is injured, and I think badly."

"How do you know?" Meyer asked.

"The walking picture downstairs is entirely different from the one in the kitchen. When he got downstairs he was leaning heavily on the left leg and dragging the right. I would suggest that whoever's handling the case put out a physicians' bulletin. If this guy hasn't got a broken leg, I'll eat the pictures I took."

A girl in a green coat was waiting in the apartment lobby when Carella and Kling came back in, still retracing footsteps, or trying to. The girl said, "Excuse me, are you the detectives?"

"Yes," Carella said.

"The super told me you were in the building," the girl said. "You're investigating the Fletcher murder, aren't you?" She was quite softspoken.

"How can we help you, miss?" Carella asked.

"I saw somebody in the basement last night, with blood on his clothes."

Carella glanced at Kling and immediately said, "What time was this?"

"About a quarter to eleven," the girl said.

"What were you doing in the basement?"

The girl sounded surprised. "That's where the washing machines are. I'm sorry, my name is Selma Bernstein. I live here in the building."

"Tell us what happened, will you?" Carella said.

"I was sitting by the machine, watching the clothes tumble, which is simply *fascinating*, you know, when the door leading to the back yard opened—the door to the alley. This man came down the stairs, and I don't even think he saw me. He went straight for the stairs at the other end, the ones that go up into the street. I never saw him before last night."

"Can you describe him?" Carella asked.

"Sure. He was about twenty-one or twenty-two, your height and weight, well, maybe a little bit shorter, five ten or eleven, brown hair."

Kling was already writing. The man was white, wore dark trousers, high-topped sneakers, and a poplin jacket with blood on the right sleeve and on the front. He carried a small red bag, "like one of those bags the airlines give you."

Selma didn't know if he had any scars. "He went by in pretty much of a hurry, considering he was dragging his right leg. I think he was hurt pretty badly."

What they had in mind, of course, was identification from a mug shot, but the I.S. reported that none of the fingerprints in their file matched the ones found in the apartment. So the detectives figured it was going to be a tough one, and they sent out a bulletin to all of the city's doctors just to prove it.

Just to prove that cops can be as wrong as anyone else, it turned out to be a nice easy one after all.

The call came from a physician in Riverhead at 4:37 that afternoon, just as Carella was ready to go home.

"This is Dr. Mendelsohn," he said. "I have your bulletin here, and I want to report treating a man early this morning who fits your description—a Ralph Corwin of 894 Woodside in Riverhead. He had a bad ankle sprain."

"Thank you, Dr. Mendelsohn," Carella said.

Carella pulled the Riverhead directory from the top drawer of his desk and quickly flipped to the C's. He did not expect to find a listing for Ralph Corwin. A man would have to be a rank amateur to burglarize an apartment without wearing gloves, then stab a woman to death, and then give his name when seeking treatment for an injury sustained in escaping from the murder apartment.

Ralph Corwin was apparently a rank amateur. His name was in the phone book, and he'd given the doctor his correct address.

Carella and Kling kicked in the door without warning, fanning into the room, guns drawn. The man on the bed was wearing only undershorts. His right ankle was taped.

"Are you Ralph Corwin?" Carella asked.

"Yes," the man said. His face was drawn, the eyes in pain.

"Get dressed, Corwin. We want to ask you some questions."

"There's nothing to ask," he said and turned his head into the pillow. "I killed her."

Ralph Corwin made his confession in the presence of two detectives of the 87th, a police stenographer, an assistant district attorney, and a lawyer appointed by the Legal Aid Society.

Corwin was the burglar. He'd entered 721 Silvermine Oval on Sunday night, December 12, down the steps from the street where the garbage cans were. He went through the basement, up the steps at the other end, into the back yard, and climbed the fire escape, all at about ten o'clock in the evening. Corwin entered the Fletcher apartment because it was the first one he saw without lights. He figured there was nobody home. The kitchen window was open a tiny crack; Corwin squeezed his fingers under the bottom and opened it all the way. He was pretty desperate at the time because he was a junkie in need of cash. He swore that he'd never done anything like this before.

The man from the D.A.'s office was conducting the Q. and A. and asked Corwin if he hadn't been afraid of fingerprints, not wearing gloves. Corwin figured that was done only in the movies, and anyway, he said, he didn't own gloves.

Corwin used a tiny flashlight to guide him as he stepped into the sink and down to the floor. He made his way to the dining room, emptied the drawer of silverware into his airline bag. Then he looked for the bedroom, scouting for watches and rings, whatever he could take in the way of jewelry. "I'm not a pro," he said. "I was just hung up real bad and needed some bread to tide me over."

Now came the important part. The D.A.'s assistant asked Corwin what happened in the bedroom.

A. There was a lady in bed. This was only like close to ten-thirty, you don't expect nobody to be asleep so early.

Q. But there was a woman in bed.

A. Yeah. She turned on the light the minute I stepped in the room.

Q. What did you do?

A. I had a knife in my pocket. I pulled it out to scare her. It was almost comical. She looks at me and says, "What are you doing here?"

Q. Did you say anything to her?

A. I told her to keep quiet, that I wasn't going to hurt her. But she got out of bed and I saw she was reaching for the phone. That's got to be crazy, right? A guy is standing there in your bedroom with a knife in his hand, so she reaches for the phone.

Q. What did you do?

A. I grabbed her hand before she could get it. I pulled her off the bed, away from the phone, you know? And I told her again that nobody was going to hurt her, that I was getting out of there right away, to just please calm down.

Q. What happened next?

A. She started to scream. I told her to stop. I was beginning to panic. I mean she was really yelling.

Q. Did she stop?

A. No.

Q. What did you do?

A. I stabbed her.

Q. Where did you stab her?

A. I don't know. It was a reflex. She was yelling, I was afraid the whole building would come down. I just . . . I just stuck the knife in her. I was very scared. I stabbed her in the belly. Someplace in the belly.

Q. How many times did you stab her?

A. Once. She . . . She backed away from me. I'll never forget the look on her face. And she . . . she fell on the floor.

Q. Would you look at this photograph, please?

A. Oh, no. . . .

Q. Is that the woman you stabbed?

A. Oh, no . . . I didn't think . . . Oh, no!

A moment after he stabbed Sarah Fletcher, Corwin heard the door opening and someone coming in. The man yelled, "Sarah, it's me, I'm home." Corwin ran past Sarah's body on the floor, and tried to open the window, but it was stuck. He smashed it with his airline bag, threw the bag out first to save the swag because, no matter what, he knew he'd need another fix, and he climbed through the broken window, cutting his hand on a piece of glass. He hung from the sill, and finally let go, dropping to the ground. He tried to get up, and fell down again. His ankle was killing him, his hand bleeding. He stayed in the alley nearly fifteen minutes, then finally escaped via the route Selma Bernstein had described to Carella and Kling. He took the subway to Riverhead and got to Dr. Mendelsohn at about nine in the morning. He read of Sarah Fletcher's murder in the newspaper on the way back from the doctor.

On Tuesday, December 14, which was the first of Carella's two days off that week, he received a call at home from Gerald Fletcher. Fletcher told the puzzled Carella that he'd gotten his number from a friend in the D.A.'s office, complimented Carella and the boys of the 87th on their snappy detective work, and invited Carella to lunch at the Golden Lion at one o'clock. Carella wasn't happy about interrupting his Christmas shopping, but this was an unusual opportunity, and he accepted.

Most policemen in the city for which Carella worked did not eat very often in restaurants like the Golden Lion. Carella had never been inside. A look at the menu posted on the window outside would have frightened him out of six months' pay. The place was a faithful replica of the dining room of an English coach house, circa 1627: huge oaken beams, immaculate white cloths, heavy silver.

Gerald Fletcher's table was in a secluded corner of the restaurant. He rose as Carella approached, extending his hand, and said, "Glad you could make it. Sit down, won't you?"

Carella shook Fletcher's hand, and then sat. He felt extremely uncomfortable, but he couldn't tell whether his discomfort was caused by the room or by the man with whom he was dining.

"Would you care for a drink?" Fletcher asked.

"Well, are you having one?" Carella asked.

"Yes, I am."

"I'll have a Scotch and soda," Carella said. He was not used to drinking at lunch.

Fletcher signaled for the waiter and ordered the drinks, making his another whiskey sour. When the drinks came, Fletcher raised his glass. "Here's to a conviction," he said.

Carella lifted his own glass. "I don't expect there'll be any trouble," he said. "It looks airtight to me."

Both men drank. Fletcher dabbed his lips with a napkin and said, "You never can tell these days. I hope you're right, though." He sipped at the drink. "I must admit I feel a certain amount of sympathy for him."

"Do you?"

"Yes. If he's an addict, he's automatically entitled to pity. And when one considers that the woman he murdered was nothing but a——"

"Mr. Fletcher. . . ."

"Gerry, please. And I know: it isn't very kind of me to malign the dead. I'm afraid you didn't know my wife, though, Mr. Carella. May I call you Steve?"

"Sure."

"My enmity might be a bit more understandable if you had. Still, I shall take your advice. She's dead, and no longer capable of hurting me, so why be bitter. Shall we order, Steve?"

Fletcher suggested that Carella try either the trout *au meunière* or the beef and kidney pie, both of which were excellent. Carella ordered prime ribs, medium rare, and a mug of beer.

As the men ate and talked, something began happening, or at least Carella *thought* something was happening; he might never be quite sure. The conversation with Fletcher seemed on the surface to be routine chatter, but rushing through this inane, polite discussion was an undercurrent that caused excitement, fear, and apprehension. As they spoke, Carella knew with renewed certainty that Gerald Fletcher had killed his wife. Without ever being told so, he knew it. *This* was why Fletcher had called this morning; *this* was why Fletcher had invited him to lunch; *this* was why he prattled on endlessly while every contradictory move of his body signaled on an almost extrasensory level that he *knew* Carella suspected him of murder, and was here to *tell* Carella (*without* telling him) that, "Yes, you stupid cop, I killed my wife. However much the evidence may point to another man, however many confessions you get, I killed her and I'm glad I killed her. And there isn't a damn thing you can do about it."

Ralph Corwin was being held before trial in the city's oldest prison, known to law enforcers and lawbreakers alike as Calcutta. Neither Corwin's lawyer nor the district attorney's office felt that allowing Carella to talk to the prisoner would be harmful to the case.

Corwin was expecting him. "What did you want to see me about?"

"I wanted to ask you some questions."

"My lawyer says I'm not supposed to add anything to what I already said. I don't even *like* that guy."

"Why don't you ask for another lawyer? Ask one of the officers here to call the Legal Aid Society. Or simply tell him. I'm sure he'd have no objection to dropping out."

Corwin shrugged. "I don't want to hurt his feelings. He's a little cockroach, but what the hell."

"You've got a lot at stake here, Corwin."

"But I killed her, so what does it matter *who* the lawyer is? You got it all in black and white."

"You feel like answering some questions?" Carella said.

"I feel like dropping dead, is what I feel like. Cold turkey's never good, and it's worse when you can't yell."

"If you'd rather I came back another time. . . ."

"No, no, go ahead. What do you want to know?"

"I want to know exactly how you stabbed Sarah Fletcher."

"How do you *think* you stab somebody? You stick a knife in her, that's how."

"Where?"

"In the belly."

"Left-hand side of the body?"

"Yeah. I guess so."

"Where was the knife when she fell?"

"I don't know what you mean."

"Was the knife on the *right*-hand side of her body or the *left?*"

"I don't know. That was when I heard the front door opening and all I could think of was getting out of there."

"When you stabbed her, did she *twist* away from you?"

"No, she backed away, straight back, as if she couldn't believe what I done, and . . . and just wanted to get *away* from me."

"And then she fell?"

"Yes. She . . . her knees sort of gave way and she grabbed for her belly, and her hands sort of—it was terrible—they just . . . they were grabbing *air,* you know? And she fell."

"In what position?"

"On her side."

"*Which* side?"

"I could still see the knife, so it must've been the opposite side. The side opposite from where I stabbed her."

"One last question, Ralph. Was she dead when you went through that window?"

"I don't know. She was bleeding and . . . she was very quiet. I . . . guess she was dead. I don't know. I guess so."

Among Sarah Fletcher's personal effects that were considered of interest to the police before they arrested Ralph Corwin, was an address book found in the dead woman's handbag on the bedroom dresser. In the Thursday afternoon stillness of the squad room, Carella examined the book.

There was nothing terribly fascinating about the alphabetical listings. Sarah Fletcher had possessed a good handwriting, and most of the listings were obviously married couples (Chuck and Nancy Benton, Harold and Marie Spander, and so on), some were girlfriends, local merchants, hairdresser, dentist, doctors, restaurants in town or across the river. A thoroughly uninspiring address book—until Carella came to a page at the end of the book, with the printed word MEMORANDA at its top.

Under the word, there were five names, addresses and telephone numbers written in Sarah's meticulous hand. They were all men's names, obviously entered at different times because some were in pencil and others in ink. The parenthetical initials following each entry were all noted in felt marking pens of various colors:

Andrew Hart, 1120 Hall Avenue, 622-8400 (PB&G) (TG)
Michael Thornton, 371 South Lindner, 881-9371 (TS)
Lou Kantor, 434 North 16 Street, FR 7-2346 (TPC) (TG)
Sal Decotto, 831 Grover Avenue, FR 5-3287 (F) (TG)
Richard Fenner, 110 Henderson, 593-6648 (QR) (TG)

If there was one thing Carella loved, it was a code. He loved a code almost as much as he loved German measles. He flipped through the phone book and the address for Andrew Hart matched the one in Sarah's handwriting. He found an address for Michael Thornton. It, too, was identical to the one in her book.

He kept turning pages in the directory, checking names and addresses. He verified all five.

At a little past eight the next morning, Carella got going on them. He called Andrew Hart at the number listed in Sarah's address book. Hart answered, and was not happy. "I'm in the middle of shaving," he said. "I've got to leave for the office in a little while. What's this about?"

"We're investigating a homicide, Mr. Hart."

"A *what*? A homicide? Who's been killed?"

"A woman named Sarah Fletcher."

"I don't know anyone named Sarah Fletcher," he said.

"She seems to have known you, Mr. Hart."

"Sarah *who*? Fletcher, did you say?" Hart's annoyance increased.

"That's right."

"I don't know anybody by that name. Who says she knew me? I never heard of her in my life."

"Your name's in her address book."

"*My* name? That's impossible."

Nevertheless, Hart agreed to see Carella and Meyer Meyer at the offices of Hart and Widderman, 480 Reed Street, sixth floor, at ten o'clock that morning.

At ten, Meyer and Carella parked the car and went into the building at 480 Reed, and up the elevator to the sixth floor. Hart and Widderman manufactured watchbands. A huge advertising display near the receptionist's desk in the lobby proudly proclaimed "H&W Beats the Band!" and then backed the slogan with more discreet copy that explained how Hart and Widderman had solved the difficult engineering problems of the expansion watch bracelet.

"Mr. Hart, please," Carella said.

"Who's calling?" the receptionist asked. She sounded as if she were chewing gum, even though she was not.

"Detectives Carella and Meyer."

"Just a minute, please," she said, and lifted her phone, pushing a button in the base. "Mr. Hart," she said, "there are some cops here to see you." She listened for a moment and then said, "Yes, sir." She replaced the receiver on its cradle, gestured toward the inside corridor with a nod of her golden tresses, said, "Go right in, please. Door at the end of the hall," and then went back to her magazine.

The gray skies had apparently infected Andrew Hart. "You didn't have to broadcast to the world that the police department was here," he said immediately.

"We merely announced ourselves," Carella said.

"Well, okay, now you're here," Hart said, "let's get it over with." He was a big man in his middle fifties, with iron-gray hair and black-rimmed eyeglasses. "I told you I don't know Sarah Fletcher and I don't."

"Here's her book, Mr. Hart," Carella said. "That's your name, isn't it?"

"Yeah," Hart said, and shook his head. "But how it got there is beyond me."

"Is it possible she's someone you met at a party, someone you exchanged numbers with?"

"No."

"Are you married, Mr. Hart?"

"No."

"We've got a picture of Mrs. Fletcher. I wonder——"

"Don't go showing me any pictures of a corpse," Hart said.

"This was taken when she was still very much alive, Mr. Hart."

Meyer handed Carella a manila envelope. He opened the flap and removed from the envelope a framed picture of Sarah Fletcher which he handed to Hart. Hart looked at the photograph, and then immediately looked up at Carella.

"What is this?" he said. He looked at the photograph again, shook his head, and said, "Somebody killed her, huh?"

"Yes, somebody did," Carella answered. "Did you know her?"

"I knew her."

"I thought you said you didn't."

"I didn't know Sarah Fletcher, if that's who you think she was. But I knew *this* broad, all right."

"Who'd *you* think she was?" Meyer asked.

"Just who she told me she was. Sadie Collins. She introduced herself as Sadie Collins, and that's who I knew her as. Sadie Collins."

"Where was this, Mr. Hart? Where'd you meet her?"

"A singles' bar. The city's full of them."

"Would you remember when?"

"At least a year ago."

"Ever go out with her?"

"I used to see her once or twice a week."

"When did you stop seeing her?"

"Last summer."

"Did you know she was married?"

"Who, Sadie? You're kidding."

"She never told you she was married?"

"Never."

Meyer asked, "When you were going out, where'd you pick her up? At her apartment?"

"No. She used to come to my place."

"Where'd you call her when you wanted to reach her?"

"I didn't. She used to call me."

"Where'd you go, Mr. Hart? When you went out?"

"We didn't go out too much."

"What *did* you do?"

"She used to come to my place. The truth is, we never went out. She didn't want to go out much."

"Didn't you think that was strange?"

"No," Hart shrugged. "I figured she liked to stay home."

"Why'd you stop seeing her, Mr. Hart?"

"I met somebody else. A nice girl. I'm very serious about her."

"Was there something wrong with Sadie?"

"No, no. She was a beautiful woman, beautiful."

"Then why would you be ashamed——"

"Ashamed? Who said anything about being ashamed?"

"I gathered you wouldn't want your girlfriend——"

"Listen, what *is* this? I stopped seeing Sadie six months ago. I wouldn't even talk to her on the phone after that. If the crazy babe got herself killed——"

"Crazy?"

Hart suddenly wiped his hand over his face, wet his lips, and walked behind his desk. "I don't think I have anything more to say to you gentlemen."

"What did you mean by crazy?" Carella asked.

"Good day, gentlemen," Hart said.

Carella went to see Lieutenant Byrnes. In the lieutenant's corner office, Byrnes and Carella sat down over coffee. Byrnes frowned at Carella's request.

"Oh, come on, Pete!" Carella said. "If Fletcher *did* it——"

"That's only *your* allegation. Suppose he *didn't* do it, and suppose *you* do something to screw up the D.A.'s case?"

"Like what?"

"I don't know like what. The way things are going these days, if you spit on the sidewalk, that's enough to get a case thrown out of court."

"Fletcher hated his wife," Carella said calmly.

"Lots of men hate their wives. Half the men in this city hate their wives."

"But her little fling gives Fletcher a good reason for . . . Look, Pete, he had a motive; he had the opportunity, a golden one, in fact; and he had the means—another man's knife sticking in Sarah's belly. What more do you want?"

"Proof. There's a funny little system we've got here—it requires proof before we can arrest a man and charge him with murder."

"Right. And all I'm asking is the opportunity to *try* for it."

"Sure, by putting a tail on Fletcher. Suppose he sues the city?"

"Yes or no, Pete? I want permission to conduct a round-the-clock surveillance of Gerald Fletcher, starting Sunday morning. Yes or no?"

"I must be out of my mind," Byrnes said, and sighed.

Michael Thornton lived in an apartment building several blocks from the Quarter, close enough to absorb some of its artistic flavor, distant enough to escape its high rents. A blond man in his apartment, Paul Wendling, told Kling and Meyer that Mike was in his jewelry shop.

In the shop, Thornton was wearing a blue work smock, but the contours of the garment did nothing to hide his powerful build. His eyes were blue, his hair black. A small scar showed white in the thick eyebrow over his left eye.

"We understand you're working," Meyer said. "Sorry to break in on you this way."

"That's okay," Thornton said. "What's up?"

"You know a woman named Sarah Fletcher?"

"No," Thornton said.

"You know a woman named Sadie Collins?"

Thornton hesitated. "Yes," he said.

"What was your relationship with her?" Kling asked.

Thornton shrugged. "Why? Is she in trouble?"

"When's the last time you saw her?"

"You didn't answer my question," Thornton said.

"Well, you didn't answer ours either," Meyer said, and smiled. "What was your relationship with her, and when did you see her last?"

"I met her in July, in a joint called The Saloon, right around the corner. It's a bar, but they also serve sandwiches and soup. It gets a big crowd on weekends, singles, a couple of odd ones for spice—but not a gay bar. I saw her last in August, a brief, hot thing, and then good-bye."

"Did you realize she was married?" Kling said.

"No. Is she?"

"Yes," Meyer said. Neither of the detectives had yet informed

Thornton that the lady in question was now unfortunately deceased. They were saving that for last, like dessert.

"Gee, I didn't know she was married." Thornton seemed truly surprised. "Otherwise, nothing would've happened."

"What *did* happen?"

"I bought her a few drinks and then I took her home with me. Later, I put her in a cab."

"When did you see her next?"

"The following day. It was goofy. She called me in the morning, said she was on her way downtown. I was still in bed. I said, 'So come on down, baby.' And she did. *Believe* me, she did."

"Did you see her again after that?" Kling asked.

"Two or three times a week."

"Where'd you go?"

"To my pad on South Lindner."

"Never went anyplace but there?"

"Never."

"Why'd you quit seeing her?"

"I went out of town for awhile. When I got back, I just didn't hear from her again. She never gave me her number, and she wasn't in the directory, so I couldn't reach her."

"What do you make of this?" Kling asked, handing Thornton the address book.

Thornton studied it and said, "Yeah, what about it? She wrote this down the night we met—we were in bed, and she asked my address."

"Did she write those initials at the same time, the ones in parentheses under your phone number?"

"I didn't actually see the page itself, I only saw her writing in the book."

"Got any idea what the initials mean?"

"None at all." Suddenly he looked thoughtful. "She *was* kind of special, I have to admit it." He grinned. "She'll call again, I'm sure of it."

"I wouldn't count on it." Meyer said. "She's dead."

His face did not crumble or express grief or shock. The only thing it expressed was sudden anger. "The stupid. . . ." Thornton said. "That's all she ever was, a stupid, crazy. . . ."

On Sunday morning, Carella was ready to become a surveillant, but Gerald Fletcher was nowhere in sight. A call to his apartment from a nearby phone booth revealed that he was not in his digs. He parked in front of Fletcher's apartment building until 5:00 P.M. when he was relieved by Detective Arthur Brown. Carella went home to read his son's latest note to Santa Claus, had dinner with his family, and was settling down in the living-room with a novel he had bought a week ago and not yet cracked, when the telephone rang.

"Hello?" Carella said into the mouthpiece.

"Hello, Steve? This is Gerry. Gerry Fletcher."

Carella almost dropped the receiver. "How are you?"

"Fine, thanks. I was away for the weekend, just got back a little while ago, in fact. Frankly I find this apartment depressing as hell. I was wondering if you'd like to join me for a drink."

"Well," Carella said. "It's Sunday night, and it's late. . . ."

"Nonsense, it's only eight o'clock. We'll do a little old-fashioned pub crawling."

It suddenly occurred to Carella that Gerald Fletcher had already had a few drinks before placing his call. It further occurred to him that if he played this *too* cozily, Fletcher might rescind his generous offer.

"Okay. I'll see you at eight-thirty, provided I can square it with my wife."

"Good," Fletcher said. "See you."

Paddy's Bar & Grill was on the Stem, adjacent to the city's theater district. Carella and Fletcher got there at about nine o'clock while the place was still relatively quiet. The action began a little later, Fletcher explained.

Fletcher lifted his glass in a silent toast. "What kind of person would you say comes to a place like this?"

"I would say we've got a nice lower-middle-class clientele bent on making contact with members of the opposite sex."

"What would you say if I told you the blonde in the clinging jersey is a working prostitute?"

Carella looked at the woman. "I don't think I'd believe you. She's a bit old for the young competition, and she's not *selling* anything. She's waiting for one of those two or three older guys to make their move. Hookers don't wait, Gerry. *Is* she a working prostitute?"

"I haven't the faintest idea," Fletcher said. "I was merely trying to indicate that appearances can sometimes be misleading. Drink up, there are a few more places I'd like to show you."

He knew Fletcher well enough by now to realize that the man was trying to tell him something. At lunch last Tuesday, Fletcher had transmitted a message and a challenge: *I killed my wife, what can you do about it?* Tonight, in a similar manner, he was attempting to indicate something else, but Carella could not fathom exactly what.

Fanny's was only twenty blocks away from Paddy's Bar and Grill, but as far removed from it as the moon. Whereas the first bar seemed to cater to a quiet crowd peacefully pursuing its romantic inclinations, Fanny's was noisy and raucous, jammed to the rafters with men and women of all ages, wearing plastic hippie gear purchased in head shops up and down Jackson Avenue.

Fletcher lifted his glass. "I hope you don't mind if I drink myself into a stupor," he said. "Merely pour me into the car at the end of the night." Fletcher drank. "I don't usually consume this much alcohol, but I'm very troubled about that boy."

"What boy?" Carella asked.

"Ralph Corwin," Fletcher said. "I understand he's having some difficulty with his lawyer and, well, I'd like to help him somehow."

"Help him?"

"Yes. Do you think the D.A.'s office would consider it strange if I suggested a good defense lawyer for the boy?"

"I think they might consider it passing strange, yes."

"Do I detect a note of sarcasm in your voice?"

"Not at all."

Fletcher squired Carella from Fanny's to, in geographical order, The Purple Chairs and Quigley's Rest. Each place was rougher, in its way, than the last. The Purple Chairs catered to a brazenly gay crowd, and Quigley's Rest was a dive, where Fletcher's liquor caught up with him, and the evening ended suddenly in a brawl. Carella was shaken by the experience, and still couldn't piece out Fletcher's reasons.

Carella received a further shock when he continued to pursue Sarah Fletcher's address book. Lou Kantor was simply the third name in a now wearying list of Sarah's bedmates, until she turned out to be a tough and striking woman. She confirmed Carella's suspicions immediately.

"I only knew her a short while," she said. "I met her in September, I believe. Saw her three or four times after that."

"Where'd you meet her?"

"In a bar called The Purple Chairs. That's right," she added quickly. "That's what I am."

"Nobody asked," Carella said. "What about Sadie Collins?"

"Spell it out, Officer, I'm not going to help you. I don't like being hassled."

"Nobody's hassling you, Miss Kantor. You practice your religion and I'll practice mine. We're here to talk about a dead woman."

"Then talk about her, spit it out. What do you want to know? Was she straight? Everybody's straight until they're *not* straight anymore, isn't that right? She was willing to learn. I taught her."

"Did you know she was married?"

"She told me. So what? Broke down in tears one night, and spent the rest of the night crying. I knew she was married."

"What'd you say about her husband?"

"Nothing that surprised me. She said he had another woman.

Said he ran off to see her every weekend, told little Sadie he had out-of-town business. *Every* weekend, can you imagine that?"

"What do you make of this?" Carella said, and handed her Sarah's address book, opened to the MEMORANDA page.

"I don't know any of these people," Lou said.

"The initials under your name," Carella said. "TPC and then TG. Got any ideas?"

"Well, the TPC is obvious, isn't it? I met her at The Purple Chairs. What else could it mean?"

Carella suddenly felt very stupid. "Of course. What else could it mean?" He took back the book. "I'm finished," he said. "Thank you very much."

"I miss her," Lou said suddenly. "She was a wild one."

Cracking a code is like learning to roller-skate; once you know how to do it, it's easy. With a little help from Gerald Fletcher, who had provided a guided tour the night before, and a lot of help from Lou Kantor, who had generously provided the key, Carella was able to crack the code wide open—well, almost. Last night, he'd gone with Fletcher to Paddy's Bar and Grill, or PB&G under Andrew Hart's name; Fanny's, F under Sal Decotto; The Purple Chairs, Lou Kantor's TPC; and Quigley's Rest, QR for Richard Fenner on the list. Probably because of the fight, he hadn't taken Carello to The Saloon, TS under Michael Thornton's name—the place where Thornton had admitted first meeting Sarah.

Except, what the hell did TG mean, under all the names but Thornton's?

By Carella's own modest estimate, he had been in more bars in the past twenty-four hours than he had in the past twenty-four years. He decided, nevertheless, to hit The Saloon that night.

The Saloon was just that. A cigarette-scarred bar behind which ran a mottled, flaking mirror; wooden booths with patched, fake leather seat cushions; bowls of pretzels and potato chips; jukebox gurgling; steamy bodies.

"They come in here," the bartender said, "at all hours of the night. Take yourself. You're here to meet a girl, am I right?"

"There *was* someone I was hoping to see. A girl named Sadie Collins. Do you know her?"

"Yeah. She used to come in a lot, but I ain't seen her in months. What do you want to fool around with her for?"

"Why? What's the matter with her?"

"You want to know something?" the bartender said: "I thought she was a hooker at first. Aggressive. You know what that word means? Aggressive? She used to come dressed down to here and up to there, ready for action, selling everything she had, you understand? She'd come in here, pick out a guy she wanted, and go after him like the world was gonna end at midnight. And always the same type. Big guys. You wouldn't stand a chance with her, not that you ain't big, don't misunderstand me. But Sadie liked them gigantic, and mean. You know something?"

"What?"

"I'm glad she don't come in here anymore. There was something about her—like she was compulsive. You know what that word means, compulsive?"

Tuesday afternoon, Arthur Brown handed in his surveillance report on Gerald Fletcher. Much of it was not at all illuminating. From 4:55 P.M. to 8:45 P.M. Fletcher had driven home, and then to 812 North Crane and parked. The report *did* become somewhat illuminating when, at 8:46 P.M., Fletcher emerged from the building with a redheaded woman wearing a black fur coat over a green dress. They went to Rudolph's restaurant, ate, and drove back to 812 Crane, arrived at 10:35 P.M. and went inside. Arthur Brown had checked the lobby mailboxes, which showed eight apartments on the eleventh floor, which was where the elevator indicator had stopped. Brown went outside to wait again, and Fletcher emerged alone at 11:40 P.M. and drove home. Detective O'Brien relieved Detective Brown at 12:15 A.M.

Byrnes said, "This woman could be important."

"That's just what I think," Brown answered.

Carella had not yet spoken to either Sal Decotto or Richard Fenner, the two remaining people listed in Sarah's book, but saw no reason to pursue that trail any further. If the place listings in her book had been chronological, she'd gone from bad to worse in her search for partners.

Why? To give it back to her husband in spades? Carella tossed Sarah's little black book into the manila folder bearing the various reports on the case, and turned his attention to the information Artie Brown had brought in last night. The redheaded woman's presence might be important, but Carella was still puzzling over Fletcher's behavior. Sarah's blatant infidelity provided Fletcher with a strong motive, so why take Carella to his wife's unhappy haunts, why *show* Carella that he had good and sufficient reason to kill her? Furthermore, why the offer to get a good defense attorney for the boy who had already been indicted for the slaying?

Sometimes Carella wondered who was doing what to whom.

At five o'clock that evening, Carella relieved Detective Hal Willis outside Fletcher's office building downtown, and then followed Fletcher to a department store in midtown Isola. Carella was wearing a false moustache stuck to his upper lip, a wig with longer hair than his own and of a different color, and a pair of sunglasses.

In the department store, he tracked Fletcher to the Intimate Apparel department. Carella walked into the next aisle, pausing to look at women's robes and kimonos, keeping one eye on Fletcher who was in conversation with the lingerie salesgirl.

"May I help you, sir?" a voice said, and Carella turned to find a stocky woman at his elbow, with gray hair, black-rimmed spectacles, wearing Army shoes and a black dress. Her suspicious smile accused him of being a junkie shoplifter or worse.

"Thank you, no," Carella said. "I'm just looking."

Fletcher made his selections from the gossamer undergarments which the salesgirl had spread out on the counter, pointing first to one garment, then to another. The salesgirl wrote up the order and Fletcher reached into his wallet to give her either cash or a credit card; it was difficult to tell from an aisle away. He chatted with the girl a moment longer, and then walked off toward the elevator bank.

"Are you *sure* I can't assist you?" the woman in the Army shoes said, and Carella answered, "I'm positive," and moved swiftly toward the lingerie counter. Fletcher had left the counter without a package in his arms, which meant he was *sending* his purchases. The salesgirl was gathering up Fletcher's selections and looked up when Carella reached the counter.

"Yes, sir," she said. "May I help you?"

Carella opened his wallet and produced his shield. "Police officer," he said. "I'm interested in the order you just wrote up."

The girl was perhaps nineteen years old, a college girl working in the store during the Christmas rush. Speechlessly, she studied the shield, eyes bugging.

"Are these items being sent?" Carella asked.

"Yes, *sir*," the girl said. Her eyes were still wide. She wet her lips and stood up a little straighter, prepared to be a perfect witness.

"Can you tell me where?" Carella asked.

"Yes, *sir*," she said, and turned the sales slip toward him. "He wanted them wrapped separately, but they're all going to the same address. Miss Arlene Orton, 812 North Crane Street, right here in the city, and I'd guess it's a swell—"

"Thank you very much," Carella said.

It felt like Christmas day already.

The man who picked the lock on Arlene Orton's front door, ten minutes after she left her apartment on Wednesday morning, was better at it than any burglar in the city, and he happened to work for the Police Department. It took the technician longer to set up his equipment, but the telephone was the easiest of his jobs. The tap would become operative when the telephone company supplied the police with a list of so-called bridging points that located the pairs and cables for Arlene Orton's phone. The monitoring equipment would be hooked into these and whenever a call went out of or came into the apartment, a recorder would automatically tape both ends of the conversation. In addition, whenever a call was made from the apartment, a dial indicator would ink out a series of dots that signified the number being called.

The technician placed his bug in the bookcase on the opposite side of the room. The bug was a small FM transmitter with a battery-powered mike that needed to be changed every twenty-four hours. The technician would have preferred running his own wires, but he dared not ask the building superintendent for an empty closet or workroom in which to hide his listener. A blabbermouth superintendent can kill an investigation more quickly than a squad of gangland goons.

In the rear of a panel truck parked at the curb some twelve feet south of the entrance to 812 Crane, Steve Carella sat behind the recording equipment that was locked into the frequency of the bug. He sat hopefully, with a tuna sandwich and a bottle of beer, prepared to hear and record any sounds that emanated from Arlene's apartment.

At the bridging point seven blocks away and thirty minutes later, Arthur Brown sat behind equipment that was hooked into the telephone mike, and waited for Arlene Orton's phone to ring. He was in radio contact with Carella.

The first call came at 12:17 P.M. The equipment tripped in automatically and the spools of tape began recording the conversation, while Brown simultaneously monitored it through his headphone.

"Hello?"

"Hello, Arlene?"

"Yes, who's this?"

"Nan."

"Nan? You sound so different. Do you have a cold or something?"

"Every year at this time. Just before the holidays. Arlene, I'm terribly rushed, I'll make this short. Do you know Beth's dress size?"

The conversation went on in that vein, and Arlene Orton spoke to three more girlfriends in succession. She then called the local supermarket to order the week's groceries. She had a fine voice, deep and forceful, punctuated every so often (when she was talking to her girlfriends) with a delightful giggle.

At 4:00 P.M., the telephone in Arlene's apartment rang again.

"Hello?"

"Arlene, this is Gerry."

"Hello, darling."

"I'm leaving here a little early. I thought I'd come right over."

"Good."

"I'll be there in, oh, half an hour, forty minutes."

"Hurry."

Brown radioed Carella at once. Carella thanked him, and sat back to wait.

On Thursday morning, two days before Christmas, Carella sat at his desk in the squad room and looked over the transcripts of the five reels from the night before. The reel that interested him most was the second one. The conversation on that reel had at one point changed abruptly in tone and content. Carella thought he knew why, but he wanted to confirm his suspicion:

FLETCHER: I meant after the *holidays,* not the trial.

MISS ORTON: I may be able to get away, I'm not sure. I'll have to check with my shrink.

FLETCHER: What's he got to do with it?

MISS ORTON: Well, I have to pay whether I'm there or not, you know.

FLETCHER: Is he taking a vacation?

Miss Orton: I'll ask him.

Fletcher: Yes, ask him. Because I'd really like to get away.

Miss Orton: Ummm. When do you think the case (inaudible).

Fletcher: In March sometime. No sooner than that. He's got a new lawyer, you know.

Miss Orton: What does that mean, a new lawyer?

Fletcher: Nothing. He'll be convicted anyway.

Miss Orton: (Inaudible).

Fletcher: Because the trial's going to take a lot out of me.

Miss Orton: How soon after the trial. . . .

Fletcher: I don't know.

Miss Orton: She's dead, Gerry, I don't see. . . .

Fletcher: Yes, but. . . .

Miss Orton: I don't see why we have to wait, do you?

Fletcher: Have you read this?

Miss Orton: No, not yet. Gerry, I think we ought to set a date now. A provisional date, depending on when the trial is. Gerry?

Fletcher: Mmmm?

Miss Orton: Do you think it'll be a terribly long, drawn-out trial?

Fletcher: What?

Miss Orton: Gerry?

Fletcher: Yes?

Miss Orton: Where are you?

Fletcher: I was just looking over some of these books.

Miss Orton: Do you think you can tear yourself away?

Fletcher: Forgive me, darling.

Miss Orton: If the trial starts in March, and we planned on April for it. . . .

Fletcher: Unless they come up with something unexpected, of course.

Miss Orton: Like what?

Fletcher: Oh, I don't know. They've got some pretty sharp people investigating this case.

MISS ORTON: What's there to investigate?

FLETCHER: There's always the possibility he didn't do it.

MISS ORTON: (Inaudible) a signed confession?

FLETCHER: One of the cops thinks I killed her.

MISS ORTON: You're not serious. Who?

FLETCHER: A detective named Carella. He probably knows about us by now. He's a very thorough cop. I have a great deal of admiration for him. I wonder if he realizes that.

MISS ORTON: Where'd he even get such an idea?

FLETCHER: Well, I told him I hated her.

MISS ORTON: What? Gerry, why the hell did you do that?

FLETCHER: He'd have found out anyway. He probably knows by now that Sarah was sleeping around with half the men in this city. And he probably knows I knew it, too.

MISS ORTON: Who cares what he found out? Corwin's already confessed.

FLETCHER: I can understand his reasoning. I'm just not sure he can understand mine.

MISS ORTON: Some reasoning. If you were going to kill her, you'd have done it ages ago, when she refused to sign the separation papers. So let him investigate, who cares? Wishing your wife dead isn't the same thing as killing her. Tell that to Detective Copolla.

FLETCHER: Carella. (Laughs).

MISS ORTON: What's so funny?

FLETCHER: I'll tell him, darling.

According to the technician who had wired the Orton apartment, the living room bug was in the bookcase on the wall opposite the bar. Carella was interested in the tape from the time Fletcher had asked Arlene about a book—"Have you read this?— and then seemed preoccupied. It was Carella's guess that Fletcher had discovered the bookcase bug. What interested Carella more, however, was what Fletcher had said *after* he knew the place was wired. Certain of an audience now, Fletcher had:

(1) Suggested the possibility that Corwin was not guilty.

(2) Flatly stated that a cop named Carella suspected him.

(3) Expressed admiration for Carella, while wondering if Carella was aware of it.

(4) Speculated that Carella had already doped out the purpose of the bar-crawling last Sunday night, was cognizant of Sarah's promiscuity, and knew Fletcher was aware of it.

(5) Made a little joke about "telling" Carella.

Carella felt as eerie as he had when lunching with Fletcher and later when drinking with him. Now he'd spoken, through the bug, directly to Carella. But what was he trying to say? And why?

Carella wanted very much to hear what Fletcher would say when he *didn't* know he was being overheard. He asked Lieutenant Byrnes for permission to request a court order to put a bug in Fletcher's automobile. Byrnes granted permission, and the court issued the order.

Fletcher made a date with Arlene Orton to go to The Chandeliers across the river, and the bug was installed in Fletcher's 1972 car. If Fletcher left the city, the effective range of the transmitter on the open road would be about a quarter of a mile. The listener-pursuer had his work cut out for him.

By ten minutes to ten that night, Carella was drowsy and discouraged. On the way out to The Chandeliers, Fletcher and Arlene had not once mentioned Sarah or the plans for their impending marriage. Carella was anxious to put them both to bed and get home to his family. When they finally came out of the restaurant and began walking toward Fletcher's automobile, Carella actually uttered an audible, "At *last,*" and started his car.

They proceeded east on Route 701, heading for the bridge, and said nothing. Carella thought at first that something was wrong with the equipment, then finally Arlene spoke and Carella knew just what had happened. The pair had argued in the restaurant, and Arlene had been smoldering until this moment when she could no longer contain her anger.

"Maybe you don't want to marry me at all," she shouted.

"That's ridiculous," Fletcher said.

"Then why won't you set a date?"

"I have set a date."

"You haven't set a date. All you've done is say after the trial. *When,* after the trial? Maybe this whole damn thing has been a stall. Maybe you *never* planned to marry me."

"You know that isn't true, Arlene."

"How do I know there really *were* separation papers?"

"There were. I told you there were."

"Then why wouldn't she sign them?"

"Because she loved me."

"If she loved you, then why did she do those horrible things?"

"To make me pay, I think."

"Is that why she showed you her little black book?"

"Yes, to make me pay."

"No. Because she was a slut."

"I guess. I guess that's what she became."

"Putting a little TG in her book every time she told you about a new one. *Told Gerry,* and marked a little TG in her book."

"Yes, to make me pay."

"A slut. You should have gone after her with detectives. Gotten pictures, threatened her, forced her to sign——"

"No, I couldn't have done that. It would have ruined me, Arl."

"Your precious career."

"Yes, my precious career."

They both fell silent again. They were approaching the bridge now. Carella tried to stay close behind them, but on occasion the distance between the two cars lengthened and he lost some words in the conversation.

"She wouldn't sign the papers and I (   ) adultery because (   ) have come out."

"And I thought (   )."

"I did everything I possibly could."

"Yes, Gerry, but now she's dead. So what's your excuse now?"

"I'm suspected of having *killed* her, damn it!"

Fletcher was making a left turn, off the highway. Carella stepped on the accelerator, not wanting to lose voice contact now.

"What difference does that make?" Arlene asked.

"None at all, I'm sure," Fletcher said. "I'm sure you wouldn't mind at all being married to a convicted murderer."

"What are you talking about?"

"I'm talking about the possibility . . . Never mind."

"Let me hear it."

"All right, Arlene. I'm talking about the possibility of someone accusing me of the murder. And of my having to stand trial for it."

"That's the most paranoid——"

"It's not paranoid."

"Then what is it? They've caught the murderer, they——"

"I'm only saying suppose. How could we get married if I killed her, if someone says I killed her?"

"No one has said that, Gerry."

"Well, *if* someone should."

Silence. Carella was dangerously close to Fletcher's car now, and risking discovery. Carella held his breath and stayed glued to the car ahead.

"Gerry, I don't understand this," Arlene said, her voice low.

"Someone could make a good case for it."

"Why would anyone do that? They know that Corwin——"

"They could say I came into the apartment and . . . They could say she was still alive when I came into the apartment. They could say the knife was still in her and I . . . I came in and found her that way and . . . finished her off."

"Why would you do that?"

"To end it."

"You wouldn't kill anyone, Gerry."

"No."

"Then why are you even suggesting such a terrible thing?"

"If she wanted it . . . If someone accused me . . . If someone said I'd done it . . . that I'd finished the job, pulled the knife across her belly, they could claim she *asked* me to do it."

"What are you saying, Gerry?"

"I'm trying to explain that Sarah might have——"

"Gerry. I don't think I want to know."

"I'm only trying to tell you——"

"No, I don't want to know. Please. Gerry, you're frightening me."

"Listen to me, damn it! I'm trying to explain what *might* have happened. Is that so hard to accept? That she might have *asked* me to kill her?"

"Gerry, please, I——"

"I *wanted* to call the hospital, I was *ready* to call the hospital, don't you think I could *see* she wasn't fatally stabbed?"

"Gerry, please."

"She begged me to kill her, Arlene, she begged me to end it for her, she . . . Damn it, can't *either* of you understand that? I tried to show him, I took him to all the places, I thought he was a man who'd understand. Is it that difficult?"

"Oh, my God, *did* you kill her? *Did* you kill Sarah?"

"No. Not Sarah. Only the woman she'd become, the slut I'd forced her to become. She was Sadie, you see, when I killed her—when she died."

"Oh, my God," Arlene said, and Carella nodded in weary acceptance.

Carella felt neither elated nor triumphant. As he followed Fletcher's car into the curb in front of Arlene's building, he experienced only a familiar nagging sense of repetition and despair. Fletcher was coming out of his car now, walking around to the curb side, opening the door for Arlene, who took his hand and stepped onto the sidewalk, weeping. Carella intercepted them before they reached the front door of the building. Quietly, he charged Fletcher with the murder of his wife, and made the arrest without resistance.

Fletcher did not seem at all surprised.

So it was finished, or at least Carella thought it was.

In the silence of his living room, the telephone rang at a quarter past one. He caught the phone on the third ring.

"Hello?"

"Steve," Lieutenant Byrnes said. "I just got a call from Calcutta. Ralph Corwin hanged himself in his cell, just after midnight. Must have done it while we were still taking Fletcher's confession in the squad room."

Carella was silent.

"Steve?" Byrnes said.

"Yeah, Pete."

"Nothing," Byrnes said, and hung up.

Carella stood with the dead phone in his hands for several seconds and then replaced it on the hook. He looked into the living room, where the lights of the tree glowed warmly, and thought of a despairing junkie in a prison cell, who had taken his own life without ever having known he had not taken the life of another.

It was Christmas day.

Sometimes, none of it made any sense at all.

This story might be regarded as having an unlikely theme for a maiden literary venture—that of the hired killer. Molloy was syndicate hit man for years. Now weary of murder he longed for quiet retirement; the mob said okay (these being more civilized times), but first one final assignment, a fast and easy one . . .

MARIE DIGIOIA
The Last Contract

The warm desert air engulfed him as he leaned toward the open window and focused his binoculars on the white clapboard building on the opposite side of the street. In one of the screen-covered windows was a sign: *Dr. Horace Hanley, M.D.* A man in cowboy duds came out, carrying a little girl with tear-stained eyes. Then she appeared. She wore her blonde hair in a casual shoulder-length style and had deep-set, sad-looking eyes and a slender figure that made her seem curiously fragile—so that for a fleeting moment Malloy wished he hadn't been given the contract.

She stood in the doorway, glancing warily about her. Then she walked quickly down the street to a nearby coffee shop and vanished inside. Malloy tossed the binoculars into the duffel bag, then reached inside his suitcase to finger the .38 revolver lying under his clothing. He locked the suitcase and put it and the duffel bag into the closet. Finally he slipped a piece of cardboard under the door and closed it behind him.

There wasn't anyone else out on the street. It was as if the whole town of Reamore, Arizona, populated 1,573, had curled up within itself like a snail until the anonymity of evening made it safe for the residents to come out of their shell. The blazing sun beat down on him and he quickened his step as he drew near the service station.

A heavy-set man in grease-stained coveralls sat inside the garage, sipping a soft drink.

"You must be Rick Malloy. Jim Turner here." The big man offered his hand. "Pete Hanson tells me you can pinch hit while my regular grease monkey's laid up. For a one-horse town you'd be surprised at all the traffic passing through here."

"Yeah, it's a regular Times Square." Malloy moved toward the exit. "I'll see you on Wednesday morning, okay?"

He walked back in the direction of the boardinghouse. The car he had bought at the used-car lot in Phoenix was parked on a side street and he got in, cursing as his body touched the burning seat. Then he drove away from the town.

He made his call from a telephone booth facing Highway 9.

"I'm here," Malloy announced after Hanson's gravel voice came over the wire, "and I've made contact with my cover."

"And how does the customer look to you?"

"Like a lame deer I once bagged in the Canadian woods. It got tired of running, too."

"So you've got yourself an easy mark. What could be better, your last time around?"

"Maybe a blind guy with a seeing-eye dog."

"Relax." Hanson laughed nervously. "Soon it'll be all over and you'll be back on the farm. Keep thinking about that."

"It's all I think about."

The cardboard was still under the door when he returned to his room. Stripping to the waist, he stretched out on the iron bed. Drifting off into semiconsciousness, he saw himself walking through the tall cornfields on the farm in Pennsylvania. It was May, and the crisp morning air filled his lungs.

Malloy got up abruptly and walked over to the bureau. He stared at the reflection of himself in the mirror, noting the deep lines under his eyes, the gray accenting his dark hair. The years of hard living had left their mark. He suddenly felt tired—an indefinable weariness he'd felt ever since he decided to leave the organization.

It hadn't been easy. As the old man had told him, competent gunmen were hard to find in these days of discontented, turned-on youth. For weeks the old man had exerted all the pressure of the organization to try to dissuade Malloy, but he had managed to stand firm. Finally the summons to visit the old man's home in San Francisco came, bringing about the confrontation Malloy had looked forward to and yet feared.

The living room was almost the same as he remembered it when he had first entered it more than twenty years before as an eager young hood. It was as if time and the old man had stood still. They stared across the room at one another before moving forward and clasping hands.

"I'll miss you, Rick." The old man's eyes were moist. "You've been like a son to me."

Malloy's shoulders relaxed. "Then my resignation has been accepted?"

"It's not like the old days." The old man shrugged. "When a loyal man wants to retire from active duty now, we don't stop him."

"But it wasn't necessary to invite me all the way out here to tell me so." Malloy met the old man's gaze. "There's something else."

"One last favor, Rick—one last hit." The old man's voice took on a note of urgency. "We've found Jesse Delano's girl."

Delano had headed up the mob's narcotics operations on the eastern coast until an anonymous phone call two years before to the F.B.I. had resulted in a raid which caught him red-handed with $2,000,000 worth of heroin. The organization failed to uncover the leak in its top ranks until the girl suddenly disappeared after Delano's trial, and it was learned she'd been planted by a rival mob conducting a personal vendetta against the old man and his chiefs. A contract was put out on her, but apparently she had vanished from the face of the earth—until now.

"How did you nail her?"

"She used to be a registered nurse. We kept checking out all the hospitals and doctors."

You dumb broad, Malloy thought; the first rule of survival is to cut all old ties. Aloud he said, "All right, I'll take the contract."

The old man nodded a silent thanks, walked over to a rolltop desk, and took out a large manila envelope. "Here's all the information you'll need. There's one thing, Rick." The old man's eyes darkened. "Hit her as fast as you can. The Feds haven't stopped looking for her either. If they get to her first, it could be the end of the ball game for a lot of us."

For the next few days Malloy observed the girl's movements, noting that she arrived punctually at the doctor's office in the morning at 10:00 A.M., took a half-hour lunch break at noontime, returned to the office, and left for the day around 6:00 P.M. The name she used was Anne Winslow and she had rooms over the nearby drug store. A tour of the town's bars and the single movie house confirmed what Malloy already suspected—that she kept to herself after working hours.

He also made a check on the local police. The sheriff was an aging ex-state trooper named Bill McGregor who was assisted by Tom Grayson, an arrogant young deputy with longish hair whom Malloy took an instant dislike to. Finally Malloy drove away from the isolated town and into the desert. He got out of the car with pick and shovel and walked between the balls of cactus, stopped before a cluster of heat-baked rocks, and prodded the surrounding earth. Returning to the car, he stared out into the vast emptiness, thinking how easy it would be for a person to lose his way.

It was the third morning after Malloy started working at the service station that the "accident" occurred. The jack he was turning to prop up an auto slipped out of his hands and he suffered a deep gash on the calf of his left leg. Jim Turner hurried over to assist him up.

"Doc Hanley will fix you up. Hang on while I get the Jeep."

She wore a crisp white uniform over her tall slim figure, assisting adeptly as Dr. Hanley, a man in his early sixties who spoke in short hurried sentences, gave Malloy an antibiotic shot and started treating the injury. Malloy glanced over at her during the procedure and once she looked up and met his gaze, then quickly lowered her eyes.

Later the girl led Malloy into the small reception room to ask him some questions, efficiently writing down his answers on a file card. When he got up to leave and she lingered beside the door he knew she'd been hooked by the bait he'd fed her.

"I'm sorry, Mr. Malloy—about your wife leaving you and taking your son." Her eyes were dark with sympathy.

"You can't blame a woman for wanting security for herself and her child." He looked past her. "I've been running away from myself for twenty-five years now."

The late morning heat mingled with the air-conditioned coolness of the reception room. "You're wondering why I've come to Reamore, aren't you?" he asked, and he saw her body stiffen. "You know nobody comes to this hot hole-in-the-ground if they have a choice. Tell me, Miss Winslow, what are you running away from?"

The girl stood rigid, her face flushed with color as if he had just struck her. Then she retreated inside, closing the door quickly behind her.

He was seated at the counter in the coffee shop when she walked in later that afternoon. She hesitated when she spied him, then recovered herself and moved toward a booth in the farthest corner. Malloy waited until the proprietor, a husky ex-cowpoke called Jake, had served her, before picking up his beer and walking over to her table.

"I must apologize for my behavior this morning." He flashed a friendly grin. "My scars were showing."

"You hit on a sensitive nerve, that's all. We all bear scars in one form or another."

"Care to tell me about it?" He sat down opposite her.

"It's a long story. And this is neither the time nor the place."

"Okay, then, are you free tonight?"

She looked amused. "Do you usually come on like a bulldozer when you meet a girl?"

"Not always." He returned her smile. "What time shall I pick you up?"

She told him and he got up and left, aware as he paid Jake at the cash register and walked outside that her eyes would be following him.

Her apartment was a three-roomer with contemporary-styled furniture, accessible by a flight of stairs to the right of the drug-store entrance. Malloy quickly scanned it while she gathered her belongings, noting there were no photographs or mementoes to tie the girl in with anyone else. It was the kind of home he was familiar with—the impersonal domain of one who always had to be ready to move on to another town, another country if neces-sary. He had stayed in similar places himself during the passing years.

They drove out to a roadside bar just south of the town and elbowed their way past the circle of denim-trousered cowboys standing at the bar, to the accompaniment of a rock tune being played on the jukebox. He guided the girl to a table at the rear and ordered drinks.

She sat silently sipping a martini, her eyes quickly darting to the entrance whenever a newcomer appeared.

"You were supposed to tell me your long story. Remember?"

"Would you be annoyed if I told you this still isn't the right time?"

"It's your story, baby." He stared down at her in the dimly lit room, studying the expression on her face. It was almost vulnerable, certainly sad. "But I can guess this much. Whatever it is, you're knee-deep in trouble. The unsolvable kind."

She gazed at him with eyes darkened by fear. "You have a vivid imagination, Mr. Malloy. But even if that were true——" She broke off suddenly. "Please, let's leave."

The girl stared straight ahead as they jostled their way out. Malloy waited until they'd reached the exit before casually glancing back. His eyes met those of the deputy, Grayson, who stood lounging against the wall at the rear of the bar.

She remained silent and uptight during the long drive down the highway and back into town.

"Anne——" He put out a restraining hand as she reached for the car door. "I won't pry any more. But if you do decide to confide in me I'm ready to listen. And to help, if I can."

She looked up at him as if she were memorizing the lines on his face, then she quickly got out of the car.

The next morning after a restless sleep during which he dreamed he was driving back to the farm and lost his way, Malloy called Hanson.

"Tom Grayson, the local deputy—what have you got on him?" he demanded.

"Has he been eyeing you? He's clean, like we told you."

"Yeah, pure as a skunk. It's not me he's eyeing, it's the girl. She's scared of him for some reason—and I want to know why."

Malloy and the girl had dinner that evening at a posh steak house in town. She seemed more relaxed.

"You're not really the penniless drifter you claim to be," she teased, "if you can afford these prices."

"All right, I confess. I've recently acquired a great deal of money. An inheritance, in fact." He adopted her light tone.

"You're looking at the proud owner of eighteen acres of Pennsylvania cornfields."

"That explains the far-away look in your eyes. The farm's for real, isn't it?"

Malloy nodded. "You might say I've come full circle. I was born there, hated it as a boy and ran away when I was fifteen. Many things have happened since—service in the Navy, marriage, divorce, trouble with the law. Now that it's mine it's become the most important thing in the world to me. I want to go back to where it all started. Ironic, isn't it?"

"Maybe, but I envy you. You can go home again." Her eyes were suddenly downcast. "How much longer are you planning to stay in Reamore?"

"A week, maybe two at the most." He lit a cigarette, watching her through the haze of smoke.

"I'll be sorry to see you go."

"Then why stay here? What is it about this damned desert town that makes it so attractive to you?"

"You're coming on strong again, Rick." A pleading look came into her eyes. "Please, let me think this over."

They left the restaurant later arm in arm. When her fingers suddenly entwined tighter around his, he looked up. Parked across the street was the police station wagon with Grayson seated behind the wheel watching them.

Malloy spent another uneasy night, phoning Hanson around 5:30 in the morning.

"What's the matter, couldn't you wait for the birds to get up?" Hanson growled. "We've checked out the fuzz again—there's not a scratch on him."

"Yeah, so you say. Last night he was eyeing the girl again."

"That's her problem." Hanson yawned loudly. "There's nothing to get uptight about. Say, you're not softening up towards that broad, are you?"

Malloy hung up the receiver without answering.

He saw the girl on the following three evenings and on the

third night they made love. Afterward, when he left in the early morning hours, she clung to him like a frightened child afraid of the dark and he pushed her roughly away from him. Back in his room he lay back against the pillows of the bed, downing bourbon steadily until drowsiness overcame him and he fell into a heavy slumber which blotted out all images.

The next afternoon he went to see Dr. Hanley again. He felt her touch his elbow as she was ushering him out.

"We'll have dinner at my place tonight, Rick." She looked anxiously up at him. "That long story you wanted to hear—I'm ready to tell it now."

She did tell him later that evening as they sat in the living room of her apartment, only it was a modified version of the facts as Malloy knew them. It seemed that at one time, between nursing jobs, she had worked in New York as a confidential secretary to a man who turned out to be an underworld figure and who was later arrested and sent to prison. During her employment she had seen some papers she wasn't supposed to see and had fled the city, fearing for her life.

"Why are you so sure they're looking for you?"

"I lived for a while in Chicago, thinking it would be easy to get lost in another big city. But I was wrong. One evening as I entered my apartment a man came towards me from the hallway and I panicked, running down the stairs." She paused, sighing. "I left that same night by bus, winding up here eventually. That was a year and a half ago."

"You could have gone to the police."

"I didn't want to become another police file number, and the last thing I wanted was publicity." In the softly lit room she looked more helpless than ever. "I just wanted to forget the whole thing—if only they'd let me."

"It could be they've given you up for lost by now," Malloy persisted.

"I only wish I could believe that." Her eyes suddenly filled with tears. "I don't want you to leave me, Rick."

"I've stopped running, Anne. So why can't you? Besides,

there's an alternative." Malloy grasped her by the shoulders. "You can get swallowed up by the Pennsylvania countryside with me."

He left her shortly afterward, a frail figure on the sofa, sobbing.

On his way to the coffee shop at noon the next day he saw Grayson approach the girl at the entrance. She brushed him angrily aside and when Malloy entered she was already seated, her face pale and without expression.

"Tell me why the fuzz is bugging you, Anne," he said, "so I'll have a legitimate reason for punching him in the jaw."

"It's not your problem, Rick." She stared at the marble-topped table.

"Really? After last night I thought there'd be no more secrets between us."

"He has this thing about me." She relaxed then, her anger spent. "I've tried to discourage him, but he just doesn't get the message."

"Has he ever made a pass at you?"

She shook her head. "He just follows me around, staring at me, sometimes making ambiguous remarks—like now."

"I suggest you have a talk with the sheriff about his erring boy, angel. Or I will."

She promised to speak to McGregor that same afternoon, and for the next few days Grayson was nowhere in sight whenever Malloy and the girl were together.

During this time he dreamed that he reached down to pick up the stalks of corn on the farm and found his arms covered with blood. He woke up in a sweat, rubbing his arms frantically.

It was with relief that he heard from Turner that the regular mechanic was returning to work the following Monday. He called up Anne and told her to meet him at Jake's coffee shop at noon. When he went outside he saw the police station wagon pulled up beside one of the gas pumps. Grayson was leaning against the rear door, his thin lips forming an unpleasant grin as Malloy walked by.

Anne was waiting for him in the corner booth, apprehension clouding her face.

"Well, it's happened. I'm out of a job. But more important, I've received title to the farm," he told her. "I'm leaving Sunday afternoon. Are you coming with me?"

She stared back at him, trembling.

"Yes," she said finally in a shy voice. "Yes, I'm coming with you."

He reached for her hand. "You won't let me down, will you, Anne?"

Her only answer was the pressure of her hand.

On Sunday morning he took the car to the service station to have it gassed and oiled.

"You don't let moss grow under your shoes, do you?" Turner grinned.

"Not if I can help it. But I do remember faces." Malloy kept his tone casual. "Like that long-haired deputy of yours. I'd swear I've met him somewhere before."

"Could be. Tom Grayson's only been in Reamore about eighteen months."

Back at the boardinghouse Malloy carefully rubbed all traces of his fingerprints from the furniture in the room. After bringing his suitcase and duffel bag out to the car, he drove around to the girl's apartment. Her luggage was in the hallway and he quickly locked it in the trunk compartment.

He drove to the edge of town, parked in a deserted back street leading to Highway 9, waited a half hour before she appeared. She was breathing heavily as she got into the car, as if she'd been running instead of riding on a bus.

"Have some of this." He took a flask from the glove compartment.

He glanced over at her before starting the engine and a queasy feeling attacked him in the pit of his stomach. What the devil was the matter with him? He couldn't cop out now. Think about the farm, man. Hell, all he wanted was to get away from this infernal heat and from this girl who stirred uncomfortable longings inside of him. But he had to keep a cool head. So for the first few miles he kept his eyes on the road, calculating how long it would take to reach the spot he had selected for the hit.

When she finally spoke her voice was barely audible. "For almost two years I've avoided any real contact with people because of this fear I've lived with. Then you come along and ask me to go away with you—and here I am."

"How does it feel—to be out in the open?"

"Not so frightening—with you here." Her fingertips stroked his arm and again the nervous feeling swelled inside him.

"Don't," he said sharply.

She settled back against the seat, respecting his mood. After what seemed an eternity to Malloy the sun sank in the distance and a charcoal darkness enveloped the highway. He glanced in the rear-view mirror to make sure there were no cars behind them.

He spotted the side road about a half a mile farther down and stepped on the accelerator, the car jerking over the rock-laden, cactus-filled dirt, throwing the girl roughly against the door. Malloy brought the car to a screeching halt and pulled the girl to an upright position, holding the .38 close against her ribs.

"Sorry, baby," he said. "This is where we split."

She was shivering again, wide-eyed with fear. "Oh, no—not you. Please, I'll do anything—only *please*."

He looked down at her for a moment, almost with contempt. She was like all the rest, after all. "Get out of the car—real slow. We're going for a little walk."

The girl moved out in clumsy motions like a doll manipulated by strings. He forced her to walk in front of him, listening for any sounds that might disturb the tranquility he now felt. She was murmuring incoherent words, but he made no effort to understand them. His mind and eyes were focused ahead to where a cluster of rocks loomed like shadowy ghosts. Once or twice she collapsed, and he pulled her to her feet.

"This is where we stop." She turned halfway around, but he halted her. "No, stay just the way you are."

"What's the matter, Rick?" she said. "Don't you like to look at your victims when you hit them?"

"I'm not enjoying this either, baby. I could have gone ape for you if things were different."

"Then give me a chance, Rick! Say I ran away, that you couldn't find me——"

"Save your breath, angel. I don't make the rules in this game, I only enforce them. And you committed one of the cardinal sins." He stepped back, putting more distance between them.

He backed into the cold barrel of a revolver and froze.

"Drop it, Malloy. Nice and easy."

Malloy's fingers slowly released their grip on the .38. The thumping sound the gun made as it hit the ground matched the pounding of his heart. "How did you figure it out, fuzz?"

"I pegged you for one of the old man's guns the day you drove into town, Malloy." Grayson's sneer sent shivers down Malloy's spine. "And I'm not the fuzz. It was a cover to watch out for Little Orphan Annie here. You see, my organization looks out for its own, too."

"You certainly took your time getting here," the girl snapped at Grayson.

"You're still breathing, aren't you? Get his gun."

This time the chill spread throughout Malloy's body, numbing him. He watched in a daze as the girl moved in closer and picked up his gun. Her eyes were dry and hard as they met his.

"I should have realized. You both arrived in Reamore at about the same time," Malloy said to no one in particular.

"Right on, Malloy. And we'll be leaving together, too—before another one of the old man's boys shows up. But you don't have to worry about it any longer." Grayson's lanky figure moved directly in front of Malloy. "Thanks for setting up everything so neatly for us. I couldn't have done a better job myself."

A muted sound filled the night air as Malloy fell to his knees, a bright kaleidoscope of the farm appearing in his mind's eye before he collapsed face down and tasted the cool dry sand in his mouth. Then everything was darkness.

Lawrence Treat has been given credit for creating the modern police procedural story, which is one of the most important developments in crime fiction since World War II. The following tale might be taken as evidence that others than police may take advantage of their procedure . . .

LAWRENCE TREAT and CHARLES M. PLOTZ

The Good Lord Will Provide

April 3

Dear Judy,

It's been a whole year now a whole long year without you. But I been a real good prisoner staying out of trouble like a cat stays away from water. They all say I'll get my parole next April, plenty of time to put in a crop. So hang on, you and Uncle Ike. The only thing bothering me is I ain't heard from you in so long. Why? What's happening?

Judy, it's not like I done anything wrong. All I did was drive that car. I didn't know they had guns and itchy fingers, I didn't even know them good. They was just a couple of city fellas hanging around a bar and I got chinning with them and happened to let drop I was the champeen stock car racer of Hadley County. I done a little bragging maybe. I musta told them I could just about drive a car up the side of a wall and down the other side and if they wanted to see how good I was, why come on out and look. Which they did.

Maybe I was a little stupid but when they allowed they'd pay me right then and there to take them to the bank next day and then on out to the back hills where there was no roads, which they said they wanted to do just for the hell of it—well all I did was ask how much. And when they told me I plumb near keeled over. Because it was almost as much as we needed for that mortgage payment. I figured money was money and if they was taking a lot of it out of the bank, why wouldn't they be generous? What I didn't know was they didn't have no account there.

So I reckon I was real stupid. But stupid or not I sure was lucky because if I'd stayed with that pair much longer I'da got killed too. But they paid me to get them out of town and up into the hills and after I done that I took off and come straight back to you.

When Ike heard the news on the radio he knowed right off it was me at the wheel of the car. Nobody else could have outdrove and outsmarted the cops and I bet I could have got clear off to Mexico or maybe China if I'da wanted to. And if the airplanes hadn't spotted me like they did that pair. But I done what I was paid for, so I come back where I belonged. And if they took fifty thousand like the papers said or a million I wouldn't know. I was waiting out in the car and all the money I ever seen was what I give you. And like I said, I got it the day before and it wasn't stolen from the bank. Not that bank anyhow.

The sheriff kept asking me where the stolen money was. After all the two bank robbers was dead with no trace of the money and all the sheriff had was me. Just a poor dumb farmer with a knack for handling a car.

But I don't want to worry you with all this. I'm real lonesome for you like I said. So when are you coming up here to visit me? And how are you and how's Ike and the farm?

Your loving husband
Walt

R.F.D. 2, Hadley

April 10

Dear Walt,

I got your letter and the reason I ain't come to see you is that I just don't have the money for the trip. Besides I got to do all the chores now. Uncle Ike's down with the rhumatiz again and Doc Saunders says he won't be up and around until the warm spring weather sets in and that's not liable to happen until May. And when Ike's feeling puny he wants me around all the time and all he does is complain and tell me everybody's out to take the skin off me. He even tried to chase George off the place when George come around in his new car to ask me out for a ride. And I sure needed to get away from the farm for awhile.

George was real nice to me too. He wanted to know how I was getting along without you and if I missed you much. Well I said it was kind of lonesome, there was things a girl needed sometimes and who was around except Ike? Seems George got my meaning wrong but I straightened him out real good. Afterwards I told him right out that we was liable to lose the farm unless we got that mortgage installment paid and how could I pay it until I got a crop in? And I said that what with George getting promoted to be vice president of the bank he could maybe do something. He said he'd see what he could manage and that was about as far as we got. Anyhow it was nice getting away from Ike for awhile, specially when George took me to dinner at that new place in town.

Walt, I wish you was a banker too.

Your loving wife
Judy

STATE PENITENTIARY

April 15

Dear Judy,

I know it's hard on you with Ike to take care of it's even worse. He's tetchy enough when he feels good but when he's got the aches he's enough to try the patience of a saint. But the good Lord will provide, Judy, and I know what I'm saying.

About George and the bank holding off—you want to get it writ down. So next time you see him you want to ask him about Ruthie Watkins which I found out about from a guy up here named Ernie Taylor. Ernie, his business is selling letters. And like he says, if I got a cow or a bushel of wheat I can sell them, can't I? So why can't he sell letters?

Ernie and me get along fine because the both of us we're innocent men and we shouldn't ought to be here. But as long as we are we talk about things and Ernie happened to mention some letters he got hold of which George writ to this Ruthie Watkins. So maybe you better mention them to George next time you see him.

Your loving husband
Walt

R.F.D. 2, Hadley

April 22

Dear Walt,

George took me out to dinner again and we talked about a lot of things. And like you told me to I just happened to mention Ruthie Watkins and then I said about the mortgage and how it ought to be writ down. And the very next day I got a letter from the bank promising to hold off until autumn but I don't know what good it's going to do. Because next time I was out with George, Ike got hold of some of that white mule stuff and after that he got the idea he ought to go riding in the tractor. Which he did, as far as that big ditch on the west side. Ike didn't get hurt bad, just a bruise or two that he's relaxing from, but you ought to see what's left of that tractor. So how do I make that mortgage payment in the fall with no crop coming in? And if I don't pay up we got no farm.

I'm tired, Walt. I'm plumb tired and just about at the end of my tether. You said the good Lord will provide—but how? How?

Your loving wife
Judy

STATE PENITENTIARY

April 28

Dear Judy,

You got to be patient like I said and if you're real patient the Lord *will* provide. Because He come to me in a dream and He said that there was something buried in the south field that would take care of us. So you tell Ike to get over that rhumatiz of his. Tell him I only got a year to go and then I'm going to dig up that something in the south field and after that everything's going to be all right.

Your loving husband
Walt

R.F.D. 2, Hadley

May 4

Dear Walt,

I don't know just how to tell you this but I guess I'll just set it down the way it happened.

You know how Ike hates the law ever since they come around and took you away. So when the sheriff and six deputies showed up the day before yesterday Ike tried to chase them away. He got up out of bed and ran all over the place looking for his shotgun, only I had it hid. Then he yelled at them and called them all kinds of names and they finally grabbed him and tied him up for a spell, so he never did see what they done. He's spry again, all that running after the deputies loosened him up and now he's as good as ever. But I don't rightly know what the sheriff come for and you'll never tumble to what those deputies of his done.

Walt, they went down to that south field and the six of them spent the whole day digging and then they come back the next day and kept on until they dug up just about every inch of that field. And I never did see any six men look so tired and they sure was mad. I asked them lots of questions and one of them—I think he come all the way down from the prison—he allowed as how all your mail gets read. Walter, what did he say that for?

Your loving wife
Judy

STATE PENITENTIARY

May 7

Dear Judy
  Now plant.

Your loving husband
Walt

Joe Gores does not ordinarily write in a humorous vein; in fact, I wouldn't have seriously resisted the assertion that he hadn't one in his literary corpus. More fool, I; this MWA scroll winner is a wholly delightful, whacky car-tracing caper that bubbles from bumper to bumper (Memo to Hollywood: my mind keeps running this story as a motion picture . . .)

JOE GORES
The O'Bannon Blarney File

"March seventeenth!" Dan Kearny fell back weakly in his chair, cold gray eyes fixed in disbelief on his desk calendar. "My God, Giselle, it's——"

"—St. Paddy's Day," she said hollowly. Giselle Marc was a tall, slender, wickedly curved blonde who was much too intelligent to be so attractive. "To O'B, it's Christmas and New Year's and the Fourth of July and Happy Hanukkah and his Saint's Day all rolled into one."

"And *you* send him off to Sacramento! Out of town, on St. Paddy's Day, with one of the new men. . . ."

"Larry Ballard isn't exactly *new*, Dan. He's been a field investigator with DKA going on two years."

They were in Kearny's soundproofed cubbyhole in the basement of the old narrow Victorian ex-bawdy house which served as head offices for Daniel Kearny Associates. Kearny scowled, hunched ex-prizefighter shoulders, stuck out his ice-breaker jaw. He was a stocky, thick-chested, compact man with thinning curly hair.

"Too new to ride with O'B on St. Paddy's Day. Remember last year? O'Bannon came off the freeway, loaded, at seventy miles an hour and broadsided a new Pelara with a cop standing on the corner——"

"He talked the cop out of the ticket, Dan," said Giselle meekly.

"An *Irish* cop. And by some miracle the other guy was driving on a suspended license." He shook his heavy graying head bitterly. "How could you *do* this to me, Giselle?"

It must be admitted: O'Bannon Had Been Drinking. But, as he pointed out to Larry Ballard, Kearny was to blame. Expecting O'B to work on St. Paddy's Day! And worse, in *Sacramento* instead of San Francisco! As well Dismal Seepage, Arkansas.

"It isn't *Dan's* fault that our Sacramento man let that guy slam a car hood on his back," Ballard pointed out.

"I'm not so sure," said O'B darkly, leading the younger man into yet another bar's cool shadowy interior. It seemed to Ballard that they had spent the day playing liar's dice for drinks in a succession of undistinguished bistros; yet they had somehow closed out a disconcerting number of open cases.

"Sacrilege!" exclaimed O'Bannon.

Ballard, who admitted to no ethnic affiliations, stared about in bewilderment. "What do you mean?"

The Rathskeller, as its name implied, was a German-style *Bierhaus* of darkly vanished woodwork, a back bar lined with heavy steins, and imported beer on tap. Now, however, the place was wildly decorated with giant shamrocks, cardboard LJepre-cauns, and twisted streamers of green crepe paper. Behind the stick was an apparently Teutonic gentleman with thick hairy forearms and the pale butch-cut hair of a Hitler Youth. He was just raising a mug to his lips; festive green food coloring had been added to the beer therein.

"Sacrilege," repeated O'Bannon brokenly.

The bartender lowered his tankard, did a slow take around his establishment, then took in the Irishman's shamrock green tie, flaming red hair, and lean freckled drinker's face. Finally he nodded.

"I'll lay you a double shot of Bushmill's that I'm more Irish than you are, Red."

An unholy light came into O'Bannon's eyes; he began shamelessly gargling his r's. "Holy Mither presairve us." He rubbed his hands briskly together, then laid his driver's license on the bar beside the three doubles the bartender was pouring. "Faith, and 'tis Patrick Michael O'Bannon I be, begorra—as confirmed by the Department of Motor Vehicles of this gr-r-reat state."

"Man, you're a Mick, all right. But. . . ."

The bartender almost regretfully produced his own license and laid it next to O'Bannon's. Their heads drew close over it. After a long moment, O'B heaved a bitter shuddering sigh, and very slowly laid a ten-dollar bill on the stick next to the three double Bushmill's.

The publican's name was Seamus Sean Irish.

"We should have phoned in *hours* ago," Ballard said weakly.

O'B, in the outdoor phone booth next to The Rathskeller, was having a little trouble finding the slot with his dime. He paused to pontificate. "The trouble with you, Ballard me lad, is that you're too cautious. *Strike.* . . ." his gesture would have carried him outside the booth if the metal flex from the receiver hadn't stopped him. His dime popped from between his fingers and catapulted into the slot. ". . . while the iron is hot. Observe people, Ballard me lad. Study them. Every man has his weakness. . . ."

"What's my weaknesh . . . ah, weakness, O'B?"

"Sad-eyed women who either kill themselves or put something

in your coffee." He paused to give the long-distance operator the collect call. "Mine is never taking *a* drink. Dan Kearny's is a deplorable lack of faith in my ability to . . . what? Hello?"

Ballard could hear Giselle, clearly speaking with her mouth pressed close to the phone. "The Great White Father is on the warpath, O'B! He wants——"

"O'BANNON, WHY IN HELL HAVEN'T YOU PHONED IN? WHERE ARE YOU?"

O'B held the blaring phone from his ear, wincing, then answered in a tour-guide's singsong. "Sacramento, the historic capital of California, is center of the 'forty-nine gold rush——"

"DON'T GET CUTE WITH ME, O'BANNON! I sent you up there to work cases, not get Ballard drunk in some cheap gin mill. What about that Drake Plymouth? We've been chasing that guy for three months——"

"Plymouth's in the barn, Dan. It was laying on the residence address with two flat tires and cobwebs on the steering wheel." He tipped a wink at Ballard; they actually had spent two hours digging the guy out of the woodwork by convincing a relief mail carrier that they were telephone repairmen.

"Oh." Kearny sounded almost crestfallen. "The client thinks the MacDonald woman who embezzled those negotiable bonds skipped——"

"Her new address is 6316 North Rosebury, St. Louis, Missouri."

"I . . . see." Then Kearny's voice became triumphant. "What about the Wellman Toronado, huh? The client's really *screaming*——"

"Toronado's on the tow-bar, Dan. I'm looking at it right now."

Ten minutes later, slouched in the rider's side of O'Bannon's Chev Caprice with a headache, Larry Ballard wondered why O'B was the only person he'd ever met who could leave Dan Kearny speechless. Hell, here was Ballard, twenty-five years old, half an inch under six feet and weighing 184 pounds; but when Kearny cut loose, he just hung on grimly, like a barnacle on a rock. There was O'B, forty-two years old, just touching five-eight, 155 pounds, whose only admitted sports were bar whiskey at night and steam baths in the morning. But *he* calmly ignored Kearny's outbursts as an umpire ignores heckling from the stands.

Was it because O'B had heard all of the world's sad tales at least twice, and had never believed any of them? While Ballard believed almost all of them?

"I thought you were going to tell me what files we have to work on the way home," said O'Bannon from behind the wheel.

Ballard studied the cases as the linked Caprice and Toronado sped southwest through the Sacramento River flatlands. There were two of them. First was a 1972 Cougar registered to a Dorothy Soderberg, last known address of 458 West D Street, Dixon. Client was Fairfield First National Bank.

"Where the hell is Dixon, O'B?"

"Little burg twenty miles down the road."

Orders were REPOSSESS ON SIGHT, which meant they didn't have to talk to anyone, just grab. If, of course, they could spot the car. Fairfield, home of their client bank on the Cougar, was a somewhat larger town another twenty miles beyond Dixon. Fairfield was also where the second case was located.

But first, *la* Soderberg and her 1972 Cougar; one case at a time was all his aching head could encompass. Then he realized that O'B, who had taken the Dixon overpass, was pulling off on the shoulder.

"What's the matter?"

"Let's drop the Toronado off the tow-bar here by the overpass. We can pick it up again on our way back out after we work the Cougar."

Dixon reminded Ballard of his own home town. The same grid of north-south streets intersecting similar east-west streets; the same drive-in where the teen-agers would congregate; the movie house, volunteer fire department, drugstore, bars, churches, supermarket; trees arching over frame-housed residential streets.

The address on West D was the O-Kay Kleaners. Closed.

"Let's try the volunteer firemen," said Ballard.

On duty was a teen-age boy watching television. "That'd be the Soderbergs," he said. "Two blocks past the stop sign, right-hand side on the street. They just seeded the front lawn. . . ."

They drove past the Soderberg house, circled the block, went down the alley. No Cougar. Dusk had fallen, lights were winking on; through the front window they could see a middle-aged man watching TV. He wore old-fashioned arm garters. A fresh-faced girl of high school age opened the door.

"Dorothy Soderberg?" Ballard asked.

The girl's dark eyes slid away. "I . . . she isn't. . . ." She turned toward the front-room TV-watcher. "Pops. . . ."

The man asked them in as a gray-haired stocky woman came from the kitchen to appraise them with shrewd faded eyes.

"Dorothy owe you, too?" she demanded harshly.

Ballard hesitated, but O'Bannon said immediately, "That she does, ma'am, that she does. For the Cougar."

"She's our daughter-in-law," said Soderberg. "She's a *good* girl, but our son was killed in Vietnam, and Dot . . . well, she . . ."

Sorrow and scorn had been battling in the woman's face; sorrow lost. "Six weeks, and already she's dating other boys!"

"Now, Mother, these men aren't interested in——"

"Well, I don't care. She got that government insurance money, and she just went crazy spending. Big fancy car, running up to Tahoe weekends to ski . . ." Her shrewd eyes pried at the investigators. "If we tell where she is, do you intend to take that car away from her?"

Again Ballard hesitated; again O'Bannon spoke immediately. "Yes, ma'am, that's what we're here for."

She looked defiantly at her sad-eyed husband.

"She's moved back in with her pa out west of town—three miles beyond the freeway overpass. Tudor, his name is. Can't probably read the mailboxes in the dark, but being it's a chicken ranch. . . ."

It was dark out. As they drove back out past their parked Toronado, Ballard opened his window. Through it came clean fresh country air, the scent of new grass, the rich smell of damp earth, the . . .

"Whew!" exclaimed O'B. "That's *got* to be our chicken ranch."

From the road they could see lights; O'B played his spotlight across the barnyard, the coops, the open-ended machinery shed. No Cougar. They stumbled across a rutted yard; faint light through the screen door showed that a long and skinny man wearing bib overalls was sitting on the top step in the dark.

"Mr. Tudor?" asked O'Bannon.

"Yep." He uncoiled his length until he was an easy six-and-a-half feet tall, slat-thin. He thrust a thumb through his overalls bib. "Pointa fac', *Royal* Tudor. *De*scended of the Tudors of England. Lookin' fer Dot, ain'tcher? Men come, nights, it's gen'ally fer her. T'other one's too little yit—least, hope she is. Dot's in town. . . ."

The screen door creaked open, then slammed three diminishing times. A girl about fourteen paused where the light from inside would clearly outline her shape through her thin cotton dress.

"Bet she's drivin' 'round after a *boy*." She turned to silhouette her precocious bustlin. "Taldy *Ben*son. *He* works at the garage, an' *he's* got a new Corvette Stingray auto*mo*bile."

They returned to the scattered lights of Dixon, where O'B parked across from the drive-in and changed places with Ballard. "I've just got a feeling this is going to call for a finesse from the Old Maestro." He chuckled. "How did you like the little sister? Tobacco Rhoda. Makes you feel that old lady Soderberg probably had a point about Dot. She must wear those widow's weeds pretty lightly."

Ballard stiffened. "There she is."

A new Corvette had passed, tail-gated by a screaming red Cougar with a laughing blonde behind the wheel. She had good facial bones and wide-set reckless eyes. Beside her was a round-faced brunette.

"Next time around, join the parade."

Within a few minutes, Taldy Benson had pulled into the drive-in. As O'B had expected, Dorothy kept going.

"The Old Maestro is about to strike. Pull alongside."

Ballard gunned up even with the red car. The girl looked over, then slammed on her brakes and called through her open window.

"Why are you following us? We'll tell the police!"

"*Do*rothy *ba*by!" yipped O'Bannon.

"Who . . . are you?" But her wide, go-to-hell mouth was already quirking at O'B's lean, freckled, equally go-to-hell features.

"This is *Red!* Don't you remember? Tahoe. . . ."

"Were . . . you the man who helped us with the tire chains. . . ."

"That's right!" cried O'B. He muttered, "follow us," to Ballard, and slid from the Chev. He opened Dorothy's door, in a moment was behind the wheel with the girls emitting shrill squeals of laughter beside him. Ballard heard, "Your Old Man said . . . in town . . . my car conked out . . . the overpass. . . ."

But it wasn't until the tail lights of the red Cougar, a quarter-mile ahead, brightened just behind the parked black Toronado that Ballard understood. He cut his lights, drifted closer in the dark. They were clearly visible by the glare of the Cougar's headlights. It was pulled up close behind the parked Toronado, and the brunette was out on the shoulder to check the match of the bumpers. That left Dot . . .

Ballard went slowly by, tires crunching gravel. O'B was gesturing. "Dot . . . check on this side, will you?"

Ballard pounded his steering wheel gleefully. The Old Maestro indeed! She had slid obediently out, was standing in the road to watch the bumpers come gently together.

"Don't scratch . . . car. . . ."

She was out of earshot by then, but Ballard could see in the rear-view mirror that the cars were nose-to-tail. Then the red Cougar moved. It shot *backwards,* away from the car that the open-mouthed girls had thought O'B was going to push. He paused momentarily before whipping a U-ie to speed safely away.

"Lady," he declared solemnly, "you've just been repossessed!"

"Gailani Funeral Home." Ballard was reading aloud from the file. He stifled a satisfied belch; his headache was gone. "Client is California-Citizens Bank, San Mateo Branch. Hmmm . . . Short $76.85 on the January payment, down $193.75 each for February and March. . . ."

"And we're after a 1969 Oldsmobile hearse," mused O'B.

They had rendezvoused at a pizza joint in Fairfield. Ballard had driven the Caprice, with the recovered Toronado dragging behind on the tow-bar. In the unencumbered Soderberg Cougar, O'B had been half a pizza and a whole pitcher of beer ahead when Ballard finally had arrived.

"What are the instructions?"

"Contact subject, collect all delinquent funds or store unit. No exceptions. O'B, why in hell wouldn't a funeral home pay for its hearse?"

O'Bannon shrugged. "Maybe the guy's got expensive tastes. Let's hit the residence address first; he's probably home this time of night."

It was just after midnight when they pulled up across from the rambling ranch-style house. Ballard parked his linked vehicles behind the Cougar, joined O'B on the walk. A dog thundered inside. O'B punched the bell, to be rewarded with a female voice asking who it was.

"Sorry to bother you so late, Mrs. Gailani, but it's important that we speak with your husband."

The dog growled softly. The woman said, through the closed door, "He's down at the shop, finishing up some work."

"The *shop?*" muttered O'B as they returned to the cars.

Gailani's Funeral Home was a fine new box of aluminum, glass, and Permastone, set off Massachusetts Street between a hospital and a branch bank. It looked like a liquor store with pretensions. Ballard made a loop through the hospital drive to end up behind the red Cougar. He grinned as he noted the name of the bank next door. Fairfield First National. Talk about coincidences! In the mortuary's blacktop lot gleamed a row of three hearses. O'B jerked a thumb at them.

"I'll check if it's one of those—you go talk to the man like the instructions say. Remember, cash only."

"Hell, O'B, he won't have cash tonight."

O'B winked. "I've always wanted to repo a hearse."

The night bell brought forth a fortyish man in white shirt, no tie, and black trousers. His shoes and his eyes gleamed blackly, his hair was too black to be convincing. Ballard was assailed by the rolling chords of an organ and warm air cloyed with too many flowers.

"Mr. Gailani?"

"Yes." His voice was a well-oiled baritone.

"I represent the San Mateo Branch of California-Citizens Bank." The subject maintained his oily beam, so Ballard said in a harder tone, "About the Oldsmobile hearse."

A frown marred Gailani's hitherto tranquil brow. "Ah. Of course. Come in."

A coffin was laid out in the same chapel as the organ; flowers and ornate candlesticks bearing dull orange tapers flanked it. The upper half was open to display a stern waxy profile, but it was the organ which made Ballard's hackles rise.

No one was playing it.

"Runs off a tape," beamed Gailani. "I've just been . . . ah . . . clearing up a few odds and ends. . . ."

Which one was the corpse, Ballard wondered. An odd or an end?

"Ah . . . there was something?"

"There was—is—$464.35 in cash, Mr. Gailani, plus my charges. Or I'll be forced to store the vehicle.

"The Olds hearse? Oh dear. You didn't receive word I'd paid?"

"Do you have proof of payment, Mr. Gailani?"

"I spoke with Mr. Verdugo on the phone at four-thirty today."
Ballard surreptitiously checked the case sheet; Verdugo was
indeed the bank zone man who had assigned it. "I asked if my
check for the payment had arrived, and he said it had." Gailani
frowned. "He said investigators from a . . . Kenny Associates?
Kearny? That was it, Daniel Kearny Associates, were on the case,
but that he would call them and tell them to close their file."

Ballard sighed inwardly. O'Bannon had called in *before* 4:30,
so they had not gotten the cancellation. No hearse-repossession
for O'B that night. Gailani was shoving an open check book
under his nose.

"See? There's the check stub, dated yesterday, made out——"

"I believe you, I believe you," said Ballard.

"I'm *most* relieved. You've no idea how I feel about my
hearses." His mouth pursed erotically. "That Olds is a . . .
mighty . . . fine . . . *piece* . . . OF . . . *IRON!* And business
has been so *brisk* that I need it! Tomorrow the departed in the
next room makes his final journey; there's a delivery to San
Francisco early in the morning. . . ."

Ballard paused outside to breathe air not cloyed with death's
cosmetics. After 1 A.M., fifty miles to the city towing that damned
Toronado. He pulled open the door of the red Cougar.

"O'B, the guy already paid—"

He stopped. O'Bannon was not within. Ballard swiveled to
look at the three hearses in the parking lot, feeling distinctly
unwell as he did.

Only two hearses were left. The Old Maestro had struck again.

O'B would wait for him—but where? Fairfield was too small;
the subject might see his repossessed hearse parked outside a bar
and just take it back again. A bar it would be, of course. But
. . . Yeah. A bar in the next big town south toward San Francisco. Near the freeway.

Ballard drove at the even 50 m.p.h. the law allowed vehicles
with a tow, took Vallejo's Magazine Street off-ramp, pulled into a

slanting blacktop lot beside a bar, from which he could swing the linked autos easily back onto the freeway. His hunch had been right. Behind the building, out of sight, was the hearse.

Inside, on a stool, was O'Bannon. "You have the makings of a detective after all, Ballard me boy." He clapped a dice box on the bar. "I'll fight you for last call."

Ballard sat down, shook his dice box idly until the bartender had departed for their beers. He said: "O'B, the guy paid."

O'Bannon's freckled face paled. Repossessing a vehicle on which the payments were current could lead to lawsuits; lawsuits led banks to quit using the investigation firm which got them sued.

"What proof did he have? Certified check carbon? Stamped payment book? Canceled check?"

"Just a check stub. But. . . ." Ballard outlined the facts, concluding, ". . . and he obviously *had* talked with Dick Verdugo at San Mateo. Do we try to sneaky-pete the hearse back to his lot——"

"No way. I reported the repo to the Fairfield police; they'll have an official record of it." He brightened. "After all, Larry, check stubs aren't *proof* of payment. If we take it back to DKA, in the morning get to Verdugo before the subject does——"

"That isn't all, O'B." Ballard stared glumly into the mirror. "I moved the Soderberg Cougar to the mortuary lot, but——"

"So? Hell, one of us can pick it up tomorrow. . . ."

"The bank? Next door? That's our client on that car."

Watching O'B take the news was like watching one of the Roadrunner TV ads, where the coyote ran into a wall and then cracked apart and fell into several separate pieces. Finally O'Bannon sighed deeply.

"So if our client happens to look out the window tomorrow and recognizes that red Cougar—which isn't exactly inconspicuous—he'll wonder why it isn't safely in the DKA storage garage in San Francisco where it's supposed to be, and. . . ."

Ballard nodded. "Scratch one client."

"So I've blown both of them. And on St. Paddy's Day, yet." Then O'B shrugged and stood up. "Well, let's get the hearse down to the city. We can make out the condition report right here—there's plenty of light in the lot."

They circled the hearse, noting dents, scratches, general mechanical condition, the amount of usable tread left on the tires. They checked mileage; extras such as power steering, brakes, seats, windows; the condition of the interior upholstery. That left the itemization of all personal property found in the vehicle.

"I'll check the back end," grunted O'B.

But when he drew aside the curtains behind the seat, there was one of the long pauses of the sort Victorian novels delighted in characterizing as pregnant.

A casket reposed in the curtained hearse.

Ballard began, in a hushed voice, "You don't suppose. . . ."

O'Bannon lifted the display half of the coffin's top. He shone his flashlight within. They craned forward, then pivoted to look at each other. O'B lowered the lid reverently.

"Now *that's* what I call personal property," he breathed. Then he snapped his fingers, began rummaging through the glove box. "Just a second, I thought . . . yeah." He read aloud. *"George: consign to Eternal Rest."* He looked up at Ballard. "Gailani said they had one to deliver to San Francisco, didn't he? There's an SF directory in the Caprice. . . ."

Larry Ballard returned riffling the Yellow Pages. "Here it is! Eternal Rest Funeral Home, Geary Boulevard at Twelfth Avenue. But we can't just——"

"We sure as hell can't store it in the personal property lockers at the office." O'Bannon rummaged again, came up with a chauffeur's cap. He touched the visor with a diffident finger. "Call me George."

Eternal Rest was to be found in a narrow rose-colored building flanked by a florist's shop and a bank parking lot. An alley slanted up between the florist and the mortuary to a small concrete loading platform with double doors. Ballard was beside O'Bannon in the hearse; the Chev and Toronado were parked a block away. At 3:30 A.M. the boulevard was deserted and dark.

"Now, as the Great White Father says, we shall play it by ear."

O'Bannon backed the hearse's long shining shape up the alley. Cap in place, he mounted to the double doors and tapped on the glass with his ring. Finally the single caged light bulb over the platform went on, a bolt snicked, handles clanked, and the doors opened outward. A short dumpy man appeared, egg-bald and wearing a rumpled morning face armored with bad breath.

"You guys are early enough." He shivered, clicked porcelain teeth together. "Which one's this?"

"From Fairfield," said O'Bannon with a picturesque yawn.

"That'd be Anna Osborne—died all over the cake at her daughter's wedding reception. Chapel B. Lemme get my shoes on, this cement's cold."

When he returned, Ballard and O'B had the rear doors open and the casket slid out on its oiled telescope runners. The three men wrestled it on to a wheeled dolly. Then the two detectives stole quickly away.

"Like falling off a log," chortled O'B as they drove away. He sobered. "After we dump this and the Toronado at the storage lot let's find an all-night Turkish bath. We have to be on Verdugo's phone when he comes into the office at eight-thirty."

Four hours later, at 8:20, they arrived at the DKA basement rumpled but refreshed. Along the left wall were the field agent cubicles; along the right, banks of screened personal property lockers into which Anna Osborne would not possibly have fit. As they entered, the sliding glass door of Kearny's office at the far end of the basement opened to let his massive jaw emerge. It was followed by Kearny. Kearny was beaming, like a spitting cobra about to spit.

"You lads are up bright and early," he said toothily.

"You know us, Dan. Company Time is Company Money."

"I'll bet you fellows repossessed a Cougar from a little girl named Dorothy Soderberg up in Dixon last night, didn't you?"

O'B and Ballard exchanged glances. O'B cleared his throat. Dan Kearny beamed invincibly.

"And you know what? Fairfield First National Bank has been on the horn. Our clients. Miss Soderberg came into their Auto Contracts at eight o'clock—beat on the doors until they opened them up. And she *paid off that car!* In cash. And *now*—she wants her car. *Right now* she wants it. AND I SUPPOSE YOU HAVE THE CAR DOWN HERE——"

It was O'Bannon at his finest. He cut in airily, "Tell them to look out the window."

"DOWN HERE AND . . . What?"

"Tell our client to look out of his side window and he'll see the Cougar parked in the lot that's . . . ah . . . next to the bank."

"But . . . how did you. . . ."

O'B spread deprecatory hands. "I *knew* she'd pay it off this morning, so I left it there. We had a long chat with her before the repo—right, Larry?"

Ballard had trouble with some obstruction in his throat, but finally nodded. "Right," he got out.

Kearny looked from one to the other, rapidly, like a tennis spectator. Dammit, O'Bannon had done *some* unorthodox thing that . . .

The intercom buzzed. He snatched up the closest phone, listened to Giselle from the clerical offices above. He nodded, eying O'B and Ballard malevolently. When he spoke, there was honey in his voice.

"Tell Mr. Verdugo that we have the field agents on that Gailani repossession right here. Yes. Assure him that any charge-backs will come right from their salaries. . . ." He said crisply to O'Bannon, "Take extension three."

O'B picked up the phone as if it were booby-trapped, but his voice bubbled with carefree *bonhomie*. "Dicky Verdugo! How's tricks, reverend?"

He listened, nodded, then finally spoke with virtuous horror. "A *corpse?* In the hearse *we* repossessed? Dicky, I can *personally* assure you that there's no corpse in that vehicle. And. . . ."

Kearny jerked his own phone back to his ear. Dammit, O'Bannon *couldn't* be getting away with it after all! If . . . He heard Verdugo speaking.

". . . real *relief*, O'B. A stray stiff would make some real *waves*." Admiration filled his voice. "What I can't figure out is how the hell you *knew* that guy's check was rubber, and repossessed the hearse anyway. I mean, he conned me *plenty* on the phone yesterday. It was only when our Vallejo branch called this morning that I found out he's been sailing kites all over Solano County. . . ."

Kearny had no stomach for further listening. He tossed the receiver in the general direction of the phone and stalked majestically back into his cubbyhole, slamming the door behind him hard enough to rattle it on its padded runners. Once safely alone, he plucked a cigarette from his pack with outraged fingers, then flopped in the chair behind his big blondewood desk.

By God, how in *hell* did O'Bannon do it? Pull all sorts of cute crap, ignore proper procedure, give a younger man like Ballard every sort of bad example—and come out rosewater. St. Paddy's Day, that had to be it. What had Giselle called it? O'Bannon's Saint's Day?

He puffed furiously at his cigarette, stubbed it out, lit another. And there would be more to come, he knew. The redheaded Irishman would try to ram an eye-popping expense account from the Sacramento foray down his throat. And expect him, Dan Kearny, to swallow it.

Yes, and even *that* wasn't the worst of it. Hell no.

The *worst* of it was that Dan Kearny would.

An intriguing gambit in crime fiction explores the terrors of the man who, arising with a stupifying hangover from a mind-obliterating drunk, discovers by slow revelation what horrors have been wrought in the blackness of his night. But in this story the awakening news seems good . . .

GEORGE ANTONICH
Late, Late Call

The telephone screamed. I came out of my nightmare muttering obscenities. I peered at the bedside clock. Two minutes past midnight. I wondered vaguely why the lamp was still on. The bedroom reeked of stale bourbon. My mouth tasted like the bottom of an alligator pit. On the phone a voice I hadn't heard for a long, painful time said: "Mike? Is that you? This is Cindy. Cindy Tasman."

Her words splashed over me like a pail of chilling ice water. At the first syllable from that low-pitched, heavily sensual voice, my entire body throbbed instantly awake as if touched by an electric prod.

"Mike? Don't you remember me?"

Remember? Could I ever forget the woman I'd killed two years before?

"Mike?"

I heard my own thinly drawn breath. I asked, "Cindy——" as if my throat had suddenly rusted.

"It's really me, Mike. Are you all right? You sound so strange."

The once-familiar voice stirred up a boiling cauldron of memories I'd fought for two bourbon-soaked years to forget. In the past six months, with Debra's tender loving help, I'd almost succeeded in moving Cindy to the back burner of my mind. Until now. Until the raucous ringing of the telephone told me the flame had not gone out.

My fingers ached on the receiver.

"I'm all right," I said. "You woke me out of a bad dream." With my free hand I reached for the open bottle on the nightstand. I took a long swallow and wondered why I'd mentioned the nightmare. Trying, I couldn't remember what I'd been dreaming. My head felt spun with cobwebs.

On the phone, Cindy sighed wearily. "Mike, would you rather I just hung up? You needn't talk to me if you don't want to."

"No!" It came out as a sharply cried plea. "Don't hang up. I do want to talk to you. How—how are you, Cindy?"

"I'm fine, Mike, Just fine." She paused briefly. "Look, I don't want to bother you. If you'd rather not talk to me, I'll understand."

I took another deep gulp from the bottle. She was apologizing to me! It didn't make sense.

Quickly, I said, "Don't hang up on me, Cindy. Just give me a moment or two to collect my wits."

I put down the receiver and fumbled for a cigarette. Thumbing the lighter, my right hand ached. I looked at it. The middle knuckle was slightly split. Around it, purplish blotches were beginning to form. I moaned, wondering what I'd stumbled into this time. After each wobble-kneed bender the cost of repairs to my bachelor apartment grew. I shook my head. There would be plenty of time to think about that later. Right now I must concentrate on Cindy.

The image of her was bright and burning through my mind. The old consuming desire almost blotted out what I'd done to her—or what I thought I'd done to her. Was it only two years before? Slightly more. I'd met her that summer I was twenty-four and working in a picturesque North Beach bar. She had come to San Francisco to visit a relative. At the end of a week I was so out-of-my-head in love with her I was actually pricing wedding bands. Over the bar, I'd made an elaborate ceremony of tearing up my little black book to prove my sincerity.

Cindy! A tall girl with extra-bright copper-colored hair that was long and stimulating to the touch. Everything about her was extra-special. She had almond shaped green eyes and a wide, soft mouth with lips that were a deep rose red without makeup. She'd dressed in thigh-high miniskirts and turquoise turtlenecks that hot summer. And when I held her in my arms it was as if I'd died and gone to a very special heaven all my own.

And then, abruptly, it had all come to a screeching halt. We'd planned a weekend together, a drive down the coast to Santa Barbara. It had been the most perfect thing in my life. Until Sunday night. Sunday night Cindy told me she was leaving me.

I couldn't believe my ears. "What did I do wrong?"

She'd taken a deep breath and reached out for my hand. "You did everything right, darling. But this is the end of the line. When I met you I was already engaged to be married. I should have told you about Terry, but I didn't want to lose you. I thought I'd have this one last fling before settling down. But it got out of hand, darling. I'm getting much too serious about you."

"Forget Terry," I pleaded. "I love you. I want to marry you."

"I know," she said. "But I just can't see a life of scrimping, trying to make it on your bartender's salary. With Terry I'll have everything I've ever wanted."

"You can't do this to me," I moaned. "I can't live without you."

"You can," she said. "You will. Time will help. In a few weeks you'll have trouble trying to remember what I look like. Your male ego is bruised, Mike. You're not a very good loser."

"I should be." I laughed thinly. "I've been a loser all my life.

But you're right, I've never learned to accept rejection grace-
fully." I forgot everything then, my pride, my independence, my
manhood. I groveled and begged her not to leave.

Then Cindy drew away from me. "This is disgusting, Mike.
You're acting like a sulky little boy who can't have his own
way."

I hit her then. Just one blow. A short right cross to her lovely
chin. She crumpled like a rag doll. Without a sound. I paced the
hotel room, bottle in hand for comfort, waiting for her to revive.
But she didn't. I panicked then. I didn't rant or rave or fall
apart. Instead, very methodically, as if I'd rehearsed it, I went
into the bathroom. I filled the tub. Then I carried Cindy's limp
body into the tiled room and lowered her into the water.

I fell on my knees beside the tub. Crazily, I hoped the cold
water might bring her around. The gurgling, pleading sounds
that came up from my throat brought no response. Cindy's eyes
remained closed. Her body began to sag. It slid slowly, slowly,
down in the tub. Before her head went under, I ran.

I'd been running for two years. After a time I stopped searching the out of town papers for some account of her death. After a
time I stopped flinching whenever someone laid a hand on my
shoulder. After a time, with Debra's help, I'd almost succeeded in
forgetting—until the ringing telephone brought it all back into
mind-boggling focus.

Grimly now, I ground out the cigarette butt and picked up the
receiver. I said, "Cindy—are you still there?"

"Yes, darling, I'm here."

"About that night in Santa Barbara," I began. "I'm sorry,
Cindy. I'm so very sorry."

"Stop putting all the blame on yourself," she said. "I certainly
can't fault you for leaving me there alone. I had it coming, Mike.
I did treat you very badly."

"It's all so fuzzy in my mind," I said. "I—I can't seem to put it
all together."

Cindy laughed. "No wonder, darling. We were both very

drunk. I remember telling you about Terry, then the lights went out for me. That must have been when you left. Apparently I tried to sober up with a cold bath. I must have slipped. At any rate, I came to in the tub, with a sore jaw and half drowned. But that's all in the past, darling. Don't you want to know why I called you?"

Relief flooded over me like a sudden spring rain. I made some weird, mewing sounds into the receiver.

"Terry is dead," Cindy told me. "His private plane crashed on our Palm Springs ranch. Mike, darling, I'm a rich widow!"

Stunned, all I could say was, "Oh?"

"Not just rich, darling—not even merely wealthy, but stinking, filthy rich! Everything Terry owned is mine now—and yours." Her voice broke off. "That is, unless you're one of those foolish men who object to marrying money."

Giddy with relief, I said, "That foolish I am not! All my life I've dreamed of finding a wealthy, sexy widow with a liquor store."

Cindy said with childlike glee, "I qualify on all counts. But it's not just one liquor store, darling. It's six. Six liquor stores, three bars in Palm Springs, an apartment house and two motels. How does that grab you?"

I let out a hissing *whoosh* of appreciation. "That sounds just great," I said. Then a sudden, haunting vision of Debra flashed through my mind. After what she'd done for me, how could I let her down? Into the phone, I said, "There's something you should know, Cindy. I—I've become pretty involved with someone. A wonderful girl."

Cindy said, "Debra Parson?"

I nodded dumbly. "After that night in Santa Barbara I went on a monumental bender. I didn't draw a sober breath for a year and a half. It's all pretty fuzzy, but I remember meeting her when I was broke and sick. She took me in hand and tried to straighten me out."

"I know," Cindy said. "Debra Parson. Age, twenty-three.

Occupation, part-time social worker and habitual do-gooder. She bailed you out of the drunk tank and made you her pet project for salvation. As I understand it, she even tried a bit of extra curricular loving care to keep you on the straight and narrow."

My mouth dropped open. "How could you possibly know all that?"

"It's simple, Mike. I've had you followed and watched for over three months, since Terry died."

"You had me followed? But why?"

Cindy laughed. "People do change in two years. Before I could bring myself to share all that lovely community property with you, I had to know what sort of a person you'd become."

"I'm afraid I haven't changed much," I said, then sighed. "I'm still a loser, Cindy."

"I don't understand."

"I mean, now, with you back, with everything I've ever wanted within my grasp, I'm in no position to accept."

"Because of Debra?"

"She's been wonderful to me, Cindy. I could never let her down. Don't you see? Of all people, I know just how devastating rejection can be."

"Mike, you are a fool!"

I took a slow, deliberate breath.

"Maybe so," I said. "But for the first time in two years I feel a small measure of peace. My bouts with the bottle are becoming fewer and farther between. I've got a part time job, and a woman who knows the meaning of love and selflessness for a man."

"Then you don't know?" Cindy asked, her voice rising. "Obviously, she hasn't told you yet?"

"Told me what? What are you talking about?"

"I'm talking about Royce Cargill, the man she's going to marry."

It was my turn to laugh. Crazily, the sound that came from my lips was more of a strangled gasp. "You're out of your mind." I said. "Debra is completely devoted to me. We had dinner earlier and she never mentioned another man." Even as I spoke the words, a slight glimmer of recognition teased the corners of my mind. *Where had I heard that name?*

"Royce Cargill," Cindy cut in, as if reading my thoughts, "is a young law student, about to graduate from Stanford. He and Debra have been sweethearts since childhood. At two o'clock this afternoon they took out a marriage license. In three days they'll be man and wife. And where does that leave you?"

Where did it leave me? It took a long moment for the full impact to hit me. "Do you know what this means?" I cried. "It means I'm free of her! What I thought was love was only my blind dependence on her—she was my crutch. Now I don't have to worry about letting her down. It means that you and I can do everything we've ever dreamed of."

"Are you sure, Mike? Have you matured enough to take a jolt like this?"

"I have," I assured her. "I know I have. Where are you now, Cindy? I want to see you. I must see you. We have so many plans to make."

"I'm at the Fairmont, darling. I can be at your place in ten minutes."

"Make it fifteen," I said. "Give me time to clean up, to put my head on straight."

I cradled the receiver and stretched out on the bed for a full minute, savoring the pure, unadulterated joy of it. Cindy and I together again, for the rest of our lives. It was too much! I reached out for the bottle on the nightstand. Then I changed my mind. I wouldn't be needing that again. As I replaced the bottle I noticed the middle knuckle of my right hand. The wound had opened. I tried to remember if there were bandages in the medicine cabinet. I got out of bed, my knees wobbling shakily.

I looked around the room. It was a cluttered mess. My dresser was at a drunken angle, as if I'd stumbled into it—again. The portable TV lay on the floor beside an overturned table. I groaned. I'd have to hurry to get everything put right before

Cindy arrived. But first things first. Right now I needed a bandage for my hand.

I went into the bathroom.

And wished I hadn't. A sharp cry of shock and revulsion tore out of my throat. Debra's limp body lay in the water-filled tub. Her sightless eyes were fixed accusingly on me.

Abruptly, I remembered where and when I had heard the name, Royce Cargill. And I knew, too, that the late, late telephone call had not brought me out of a bad dream.

My nightmare had only now begun.

Frederick Forsyth's runaway bestseller The Day of the Jackal
*(1971) was an easy Edgar winner as best mystery of the year and
a choice with which I, as chairman of the MWA committee,
enthusiastically concurred. Though promoted as a straight novel,
Jackal was from beginning to end a detective story—and a
superb one.*

*There's no detection in the tale that follows, but I think you'll
enjoy Forsyth in a mood not entirely dissimilar to that of* Jackal.

FREDERICK FORSYTH
No Comebacks

Sitting in the bright July sunshine, two men ordered a drink one
day at a café in the Rue Miollin. The Englishman's name was
not Barrie—that was borrowed from a dimly remembered writer
—and the Corsican's name was not Calvi—that was a village in
Corsica where he had been born, but these were the names they
used for the moment. A voice on the telephone, belonging to a
man they had never seen, had arranged the precise time and
place of this meeting. It was to last no more than 20 minutes.

After their drinks had been brought, the Englishman laid two
snapshots on the table. The first one was in black and white, a
photo of the dust jacket of a book. From the print peered a
middleaged man with weedy hair, a clipped mustache and a

chin in despondent retreat. Beneath the face, a caption read: "Major Archibald Summers has again added to our knowledge of and delight in our avian friends with his new volume on the birds of the Western Mediterranean lands. I read it with much pleasure.—Lady Clara Whitehope-Smith." The Corsican turned the picture over. A caption on the back read: "Villa San Crispin, Playa Caldera, Ondara, Alicante, Spain."

The other photo was in color. It showed a small villa with white walls and lemon-yellow shutters. Next to it was a rose garden with a number of bird feeders among the bushes.

"He's always at home between three and four in the afternoon. There are no servants and he should be alone." Barrie said.

"Five thousand pounds," Calvi said. "Border crossings are treacherous and the Spanish police are like wolves."

"Half now," said the Englishman and he laid a flat pasteboard box on the table. It was labeled as a box of photographic film. "Here is a London number where you can ring me between seven-thirty and eight any morning. Just say, 'Your picture is ready.' Written next to the number is the name of a café near the Invalides. I'll give you another box of film at two P.M. the day of your call."

"D'accord," said the Corsican. He put the box and the photos into his jacket pocket.

"Most important of all—no witnesses. He must be quite alone when it happens. Don't let yourself be seen by anyone who could identify you in connection with the villa."

The Corsican sighed and spread his huge hands. "Thus far, we had managed to proceed without platitudes, monsieur. I can only reply that I have a very vivid notion of life inside Tolédo Penal. Would you warn a noted surgeon that he must sterilize his instruments before an operation?"

After Barrie had gone, the Corsican rose and walked slowly in the direction of the Place Vendôme. In his mind, he was trying to get two things across a border in a perfectly normal, inconspicuous way. One was a package and the other was himself—but every time they attempted to cross together, his mind came to an impasse. At Orly nowadays, what with all the hijackings, every parcel was minutely checked. The Paris—Barcelona train entailed a customs check. The obvious problem was how A and B could enter separately and successfully and become AB again on the other side.

Now he noticed that, without being aware of her, he had been following a pretty girl. She was probably an American tourist— she was carrying a large, illustrated guidebook with a title in English. Excellent! he thought suddenly. What is more boring than a book? When he came to a bookshop near the Place Vendôme, he entered and began to browse.

About a half hour later, now carrying a bulky package under his arm, he paid a visit to the Spanish tourist office. His next stop was at the Iberia Air Lines office; from there, he took a taxi to his flat in Neuilly.

That evening, he rang the Astoria Palace, the best hotel in Valencia, and introduced himself as Monsieur Calvi, who desired two rooms for one night only, a fortnight hence. One was for himself and one was booked for another gentleman—and the name he gave was the name he used on his own passport. He told the registration clerk that he would write a letter of confirmation at once.

In fact, he had already written the letter. It reiterated his directions and added, as a postscript, that he'd ordered a book from a Paris bookstore. It should be held for his arrival. At the bottom of the letter, he wrote Calvi's signature with his left hand.

Then he rolled up his sleeves, unwrapped his purchase of the afternoon, weighed it and set to work to create a solander. The book for the purpose was a history of Spain in French, a thick quarto volume on heavy paper, bound in tan buckram. He bent the two covers and the first ten pages back and fastened them with a stout band. Then he took two carpenter's clamps and secured the remaining 400 pages at the edge of his kitchen table.

He produced a pair of flat steel L bars and a surgeon's scalpel. Leaving a margin of an inch and a half all around, he began to slice a neat rectangular cavity in the body of the book. After about an hour, 2973 years of Spanish history had been excised and reduced to ashes in the fireplace. He now had a box with a hollow measuring 6½″ × 9½″. He now applied bookbinder's glue in a thin coat to what remained of the pages and to the inner edges. He smoked three cigarettes as he waited for it to dry. As soon as it had hardened, his solander was ready for special fitting.

In the hollow, he carefully glued a cushion of foam rubber, cut to size for each surface. Then, from a concealed drawer in his desk, he produced a ninemillimeter "Le Français" model automatic he'd never employed before. The front sight had been ground off and a half inch of the Browning's barrel had been threaded to take a silencer—he had done this job some months before with his own lathe. He was a man with a number of specialized skills, of which he was rather proud.

A silencer on an automatic is never truly quiet, despite the delusion of scriptwriters and sound-effects men in television thrillers. An automatic makes a very respectable bang—because, as the bullet leaves the barrel, the jacket is forced back to expel the spent cartridge and to inject a fresh one. In this split second, half the noise of the explosion comes out through the open breech, making the silencer only 50 percent effective. Thus, Calvi would have preferred a revolver, but he needed a flat weapon for this particular purpose.

The silencers seen on television—usually about the size of a champagne cork—are about as useful for secrecy as a home fire extinguisher would be against Vesuvius in eruption. His was a heavy cylinder about six and a half inches long. He thrust the loaded magazine into the automatic's handle to save space.

Then, with a felt-nib pen, he marked out a place on the foam rubber for each component of the disassembled Browning. With a new scalpel, he cut neat beds for each part. By midnight, all the pieces lay snugly in their foam nests, the long silencer vertical along the book's spine, the barrel, frame and slide in a neat pattern. It made a deadly book, but one could hardly call it boring.

He covered the aperture with a small slab of foam rubber that protruded just slightly above the edges of the cavity. Over this he fastened a precisely cut sheet of firm plastic and secured it with six long, slender, brass screws. The last loose page was pasted over the plastic. Now the cover and the first pages could be opened—as a casual inspector might glance at them—but the rest of the book was a solid block that would require a knife to penetrate.

He weighed the solander; it was now just a half ounce heavier than the original. Next, he slipped it into a polyethylene case of the kind publishers use to protect expensive books from wear and scratching. The open end of this case he bonded together with a soldering iron heated over the flame of his gas stove. If a mildly curious official opened the outer wrapping, he would see a history volume and would let it go at that. If a somewhat more inquisitive type actually opened the plastic covering, he would find a book whose cover and first pages turned easily. The odds were a million to one that the Spanish postal system embraced a scholar so interested in the history of Spain in French that he would pursue the matter as far as page ten.

Calvi now brought out a page of Letraset letters in 12-point Caslon and a small instrument, like a pen, with a tiny brass knob at one end. He carefully placed the sheet over a shipping label and began to transfer, by pressure, the letters to the surface of the label. When he had finished, the legend read: "GALIGNANI. *Livres.* 224 Rue de Rivoli, Paris," and its look was indistinguishable from real printing. He typed the address—M. Alfred Calvi, Hotel Astoria Palace, Calle de Rodrigo Botet, Valencia, Espagne. With a rubber-stamp printing set, he made up the words LIBROS —IMPRESOS—LIVRES and stamped that on the outside wrapping.

The following morning, he mailed the letter by airmail and the package by surface post, which meant shipment by train and a ten-day delay.

Mark Sanderson was nervous as he let himself into the small London flat he had rented under the name of Barrie. Dark shabbiness made him uncomfortable and the flat was his momentary prison. Its only function was to enclose the telephone that stood on a rickety little table. And the telephone's only function was to receive one ten-second call. Sanderson loved telephones —in his Regent's Park penthouse, his Elizabethan manor in Worcestershire, his château on the Loire and his villa at Cap d'Antibes, there were telephones everywhere. His Riviera servants even had a joke about the apocryphal telephone under the surface in his swimming pool. But the fact was that he'd closed many deals worth millions of pounds, dollars or francs on the telephone; he was waiting for the greatest, the most golden deal of all.

The rather bizarre fact was that Mark Sanderson was in love. He'd been in love many times, of course, but never before with a woman. There'd been a passionate affair with South African gold-mining stock, an infatuation with his own jet plane, a romance with a huge resort-property investment in the West Indies and many others. There was also a continuing love for travel, fine food and wines, an art collection and flattering newspaper publicity. Most of these loves had been ornamented by one or another expensive beauty in female form—an actress, a model, a society girl. But their attentions and their well-acted gasps of arousal in bed had never been any more to him than a passing compliment paid to wealth and power. Then he had met Angela Summers.

The season had been Maytime, the place a fashionable house in Belgravia, the occasion a cocktail party in aid of some charity—and his hostess was saying in a casual way, "I don't believe you've met Mrs. Summers." He had looked at Mrs. Summers and suddenly had become 16 years old, a gawky lover, all the self-assurance of wealth and command suddenly vanished. Had he actually said, "An Angel of summer!" to her? And had he actually blushed? That was the way he recollected it later.

She was startlingly out of vogue for the thin lines and the high-fashion affectations of the Seventies. She had a deep bosom, slender waist, rounded hips. Her shining chestnut hair was drawn back and coiled. She wore a simple white dress that set off her medium-gold suntan and she had just a hint of make-up around her eyes. A Renoir in a room full of Helmut Newton photos.

He blundered into conversation on the subject of suntan. Was it from a skiing vacation that had been prolonged into spring? Or a Caribbean cruise?

Wrong on both counts, she replied with charming honesty—she simply didn't have that sort of money. She'd managed it mostly while working in the garden. That and her daily swim every afternoon from three to four while her husband worked on his book. They lived in a little house on the Costa Blanca.

"An author?" Sanderson asked. "Should I know his books?"

Not really, she explained, Archie was a retired Signals major who wrote books about birds. "Rather good books of their kind," she said bravely and defensively. They lived on his retirement pay and the small earnings she got from teaching English. Not a terribly glamorous life, she supposed, but they did like their privacy, the climate and the small house. "And Archie is mad about the Costa Blanca birds—he says they're rather special," she added with a slightly forlorn note coming into her voice.

Sanderson immediately asked her to go out to dinner with him that evening. "Oh, yes!" she whispered, almost as if she had been waiting for that. There was a minute of silence between them. Then she said in a cool and normal voice, "I must make some excuses to the friends who brought me. And we shouldn't leave together. Where shall we meet?"

The week that followed was the strangest in Sanderson's life. It was a little like a Georgian romance, rescued from time, illicit but not sinful. His other girls, modern girls, had been impressed by the chauffeured Rolls-Royce, the elegant dinner at the Mirabelle, his spacious penthouse—but for them these things all made up a dotted line that led directly to an episode in his bed. Not Angela. It seemed to occur to her not at all.

She noticed and she admired, but she was not overwhelmed. She would return his kiss warmly, but when he tried to put his hand inside her dress, she stopped him firmly. She was affectionate, but there was an old-fashioned boundary in her mind beyond which she would not go. Sanderson was dazed with love and rejection.

The evening before she was to fly back to Spain, as they were sitting over brandy in his flat, he suddenly asked her to divorce her husband and to marry him.

She smiled her usual, candid smile. "It would be nice, wouldn't it?" she said, "but I'm afraid not."

"Oh, don't be so bloody cool and English," he said. "I love you in a perfectly honest, simple-minded way. I admit that I've been trying to seduce you by all the old gambits—but being rich enough to have everybody do what I want has made me stupid. I don't even know enough to convince you that all of that was a sham. But there is one true thing: I love you. And I think that you love me."

She shook her head gently. "Now I'll say something perfectly simple-minded. I'm married to Archie. I can't destroy him. Have you ever seen a child whose puppy has been run over by a motorcar? That comparison sounds a bit grotesque, but it's close to what I mean."

"He has his birds, after all," said Sanderson.

She smiled and was silent. After a while, she said, "Would it help any if I went to bed with you just once and then never saw you again?"

"No," he said. "It wouldn't."

"Very well, now I believe what you've been saying," Angela answered, "and just in order to give our little story a firm ending, I'll say yes twice. Yes, I've fallen in love with you. And yes, I am going back to Archie in spite of it."

At the airport the next day, she was more heartbreakingly beautiful than ever. Before she kissed him goodbye, she said, "Mark, you can stop thinking and go back to being rich. In

Spain, I'll have a lot of lonely time to think and remember." She
was crying as she went to the plane.

The Iberia Caravelle drifted into the airport at Valencia and
touched down as the sun was setting. It was still furiously hot
and the 30 passengers, mostly villa owners from Paris arriving for
six weeks' vacation, grumbled at the usual baggage delays in the
customs shed.

Calvi carried one medium-sized suitcase as hand baggage. It
was opened and inspected carefully, then he was out of the airport building and into the taxi rank. First he wandered over to
the airport car park and was glad to see that a large area of it was
screened by trees from the airport buildings. The cars stood in
rows beneath the trees waiting for their owners. He decided to
return the next morning and take his transport from there. Then
he took a taxi into town.

The clerk at the hotel was more than helpful. As soon as the
Corsican presented himself and his passport, the desk clerk recalled the booking and the letter of confirmation written by
Monsieur Calvi and dived into the back office to emerge with the
package containing the book. The Corsican explained that,
unfortunately, his friend Calvi would not be joining him but
that he would settle both room bills when he left the following
morning. He produced a letter from the absent Calvi authorizing
him to take receipt of the book awaiting collection. The clerk
glanced at the letter, thanked the Corsican for offering to settle
both room bills and handed over the package.

In his room, Calvi checked the padded envelope. It had been
opened: The metal staples had been bent together to pass
through the sealing aperture and then bent back again. The blob
of glue he had placed on one of the metal lugs was missing. But
inside, the book was still in its polyethylene wrapper untouched,
for it would have been impossible to open it without tearing or
distorting it.

He opened it, forced the book covers apart with the blade of his penknife and extracted the parts of his gun. These he assembled back together, then he screwed on the silencer and checked the bullets in the magazine. They were all there—his special cartridges, with half the load removed to cut down the noise to a low crack. Even with half the usual load behind it, a nine-millimeter slug still goes straight into a human head at ten-foot range, and Calvi never fired at more than ten feet on a job.

He locked the gun into the bottom of the wardrobe, pocketed the key and smoked a cigarette on the balcony, gazing out at the bull ring in front of the hotel and thinking of the day ahead. From the hotel clerk he learned there was a plane to Madrid at eight in the morning and he had himself called at six.

The next morning he checked out at seven and took a taxi to the airport. Standing at the gate, he watched a dozen cars arrive, noting the make and number of the car and the appearance of the driver. Seven cars were driven by men without passengers, in what looked like business suits. From the observation terrace of the airport building, he watched the passengers stream out to the plane for Madrid, and four of the drivers were among them. He looked at the notes on the back of an envelope in his hand and found he had a choice of a Simca, a Mercedes, a Jaguar and an old Spanish SEAT, the local version of the Fiat 600.

After the plane had taken off, he went to the men's room and changed from his gray suit into jeans, pale-blue sport shirt and blue zip-front nylon windbreaker. The gun he wrapped in a towel and stowed in the soft airline bag he took from his suitcase. He checked the case, confirmed his evening booking for the Paris flight and walked back to the car park.

He tried the Mercedes and the Simca and found them both locked. Luckily, the third car, a well-worn SEAT, was not. He preferred a SEAT, in any case, because it is the most common car on Spanish streets. He opened the engine compartment and clipped two wires to the voltage regulator. One of these he attached to the engine coil, the other to the engine solenoid. He climbed into the car quickly. There was no hitch—the engine turned over at once and he bowled out of the car park onto the road to Valencia and the new seaboard highway N. 332 south to Alicante.

It is 92 kilometers or 57 miles from Valencia to Ondara, through the orange-growing centers of Gandia and Oliva, and he took it easy, making the trip in two hours. The whole coast was blistering in the morning sun, a long ribbon of golden sand dotted with brown bodies and splashing swimmers. The heat was oppressive, without a breath of wind, and along the sea horizon lay a faint and misty haze.

In Ondara's town center, he had no trouble asking the way to Playa Caldera, which, he was told by helpful townspeople, lay four miles out of town. He drove into the residential sprawl of villas just before noon and began to cruise, looking for the Villa San Crispin. To ask directions to the beach was one thing, to ask them to the villa might stick in someone's memory.

He found the yellow shutters and the white-painted terra-cotta walls just before one o'clock, checked the name painted on a tile set into the pillar by the front gate and parked the car 200 yards farther on. Walking idly, his bag slung over one shoulder like a tourist heading for the beach, he cased the back entrance. It was easy. From farther up the earth road on which the villa stood, a small footpath led away into a plantation of orange trees behind the row of houses. From the cover of the trees he could see that only a low fence separated the red earth of the orange orchard from the unshaded patio at the back of the villa with the yellow shutters, and he could see his man pottering about the garden with a watering can. There were French windows leading from the back garden into the main ground-floor room, wide open to allow a draft to blow through, if there should be a breath of wind. He checked his watch—time for lunch—and drove back to Ondara.

He sat till three in the Bar Valencia on Calle Doctor Fleming and had a large plate of enormous grilled prawns and two glasses of the local light white wine. Then he paid and left.

As he drove back to the *playa,* the rain clouds finally moved in off the sea and there was a dull rumble of thunder across the oil-smooth water, very unusual for the Costa Blanca in mid-July. He parked the car close to the path into the orange grove, tucked the silenced Browning into his belt, zipped the windbreaker up to the neck and headed into the trees. It was very quiet when he came back out of the grove and stepped across the low wall into the garden of the villa. The locals were all taking siestas in the heat, and the rain began to patter onto the leaves of the orange trees; large drops hit his shoulders as he crossed the flagstones, and when he reached the French windows, the shower broke at last, drumming into the pink tiles of the roof. He was glad, no one would hear a thing.

From a room to the left of the sitting room he heard a typewriter clack several times. He eased the gun out, standing immobile in the center of the lounge. Then he walked across the rush matting to the open study door.

Major Summers probably never knew what happened or why. He must have seen a man standing in the doorway of his study, and he half rose to ask what he wanted. Then he could see what was in the stranger's hand. There were two soft plops, hardly louder than the sound of the rain outside, and the major took two bullets in his chest. The third was fired vertically downward into his temple, but it was unlikely that he felt that one at all. The Corsican knelt and put a forefinger on the major's wrist. Then, rising to a crouch, he swiveled around toward the sitting-room door.

Sanderson arrived at the Café Grognard just a few minutes late. As soon as he had hung up the telephone in the shabby flat, he had taken a taxi to the airport, but there had been several delays. Calvi, in a pair of dark sunglasses, was sitting inside the café. All the other customers had chosen the sidewalk tables and the sun.

Sanderson sat down and, with a briskness he didn't feel, asked, "Done?"

Calvi nodded slowly.

Sanderson waited for a moment to hear if Calvi would add anything. Finally, he asked, "Any problems? The kind we spoke of?"

Calvi nodded ponderously again. "One. But I solved it."

"Explain!" said Sanderson sharply.

"A small mishap—simply that a woman came into the room just after I'd done the job. But there is no need for alarm, monsieur. As you ordered, no witnesses. I finished her off and concealed them both."

Sanderson seized the Corsican by his upper arms; his face was suddenly distorted and red; his jaw was working strangely. Finally, he was able to say. "What woman? Who? Tell me!"

Calvi stared at him and was afraid. All at once, it struck him that he had been hired by a madman. This English gentleman who had seemed so selfpossessed was actually a maniac. Even though Calvi had powerful biceps, the pressure on them was crushing. "A woman. Just a woman," he said in confusion.

"Tall, beautiful, chestnut-colored hair?" asked Sanderson wildly. Calvi, who knew a great deal about such things, saw death in the other man's eyes. He knew that he was going to be killed by this madman. Here at this table in the Café Grognard. Then, in a flash, something came back to him about the photograph of the book jacket with the major's picture.

"I have no notion of what you mean," he said. "As I say, a woman came into the room. It was a bright, sunny day and there were many birds in the garden. She had a pair of binoculars around her neck. She was quite short, had white hair and a bony face. She said something in English."

Sanderson's grip relaxed, but it was several minutes before he could calm himself enough to extract the firm box from his pocket, rise and walk out of the café.

Calvi watched him go. It was a near miss, that one, he told himself. Thinking it over, he sincerely regretted that it hadn't been a little, white-haired woman with binoculars who had come into the room. The other had been truly beautiful. Beautiful enough to do murder for.

*Florence V. Mayberry is surely one of the strongest women con-
tributors to current short crime fiction. Here the events and the
crime that results are secondary to her expert probing of character and emotion and weakness: those, first, of Milly, the wife who
places love of her husband above pride; and of her mate, Paddy,
who places his pride above love . . .*

FLORENCE V. MAYBERRY
Woman Trouble

I never did like living in Reno. I'm a desert woman, born and
raised just outside Winnemucca, Nevada. Trees and buildings,
and all those crowds milling around day and night on the streets
get in my way. I like to see clear and far off. Horizons, moun-
tains. Even people stand out better in the open desert. You can
see them coming, all alone and separate instead of muffled up in
all that town stuff.

Have you ever smelled, real good, the sage coming in off the
desert after a rain? Clean, heady, sweet. Seems to scour out the
lungs and makes your brain fresh. You can remember you've got
a heart, even a soul. Well, that's what I wanted for Paddy.

Paddy belongs to the desert. Wyoming country, he was born
there. Up where buttes are swept by winds and you have to
struggle a little to fill your lungs with oxygen, it's so high in the

sky, you know. Couple of years after we were married Paddy took me back to his old home ranch. Well, it wasn't his any longer— he'd lost it fooling around in Nevada's gambling clubs. But the people who bought it from the bank were nice folks, old friends of the family, and they pretended the ranch was still Paddy's.

Paddy and I rode alongside the buttes, sometimes stopping the horses and edging them together so we could kiss. "Paddy," I told him, "let's save up and buy back your ranch. Town's no good for us, we're open-country people." Especially town's no good for Paddy, I was thinking, and he knew it.

He grinned and said, "You're right, girl. No dice tables out here on the open range." He patted my arm and added, "First big killing I make, and I sure ought to be due for one soon, we'll buy us a spread. Build us a brand-new house on it with all the fixings, good as back in Reno."

Good as! My God. A two-room-with-kitchenette apartment. A stove with an oven which baked lopsided. A dwarf-sized refriger-ator. And all the gambling tables in the world, it seemed, just down the street.

"Paddy, I don't need fine things, I'm not used to them. It would be fun to camp out in a cabin, cook on a wood stove— nothing bakes good like a wood range. It would be like when I was a kid. Home-baked bread—my mother always did her own baking and she taught me. And we could have a little garden, Paddy. You'd be outdoors a lot—indoors don't suit you, Paddy, staying in that warehouse all the time, lifting those heavy loads."

"Lifting loads, woman?" His face took on that remote expres-sion he always got when he decided I had gone too far interfering in men's ways. "You mean pushing so hard on those little levers that do all the lifting? With a hundred-eighty-pounds, six-one of a man to do the pushing? Well, Angie, I sure got a hard life."

I wanted to say it was lifting the dice, shaking them, tossing them out that was too much for a hundred-eighty-pounds, six-one of a man. But when he got that look Paddy scared me. No, no, I don't mean he ever hit me or roughed me up. He never did.

Why, Paddy would just spit on the ground when he heard about men who hit women. Said only feisty little men did that who were too scared to tackle a man. But once, after that look, Paddy had walked out of our apartment and didn't come back. It took me a week to find him. Down in Vegas. And another week to beg him back.

That time I wished he had hit me instead. All the money we had in our joint savings account, $715, went that time. To the last penny. It takes a lot of standing on your feet and waiting on customers in a department store to get that much put away above what it costs to live these days.

Paddy didn't believe in savings accounts, even though I had his name on the bank book. Said it was for men who didn't have the guts to take a chance, or for women. That's why it didn't bother him when he drew it out. Grinned, patted me on the back, and said he'd pay it back one of these days with interest.

Me, I didn't care if he ever paid it back. All I wanted back was Paddy.

Like that evening later on when I was snuggling my face against his, whispering I wouldn't trade him for the whole world tied in ribbons.

He kissed me and whispered back, "You're a good kid." Then he scooted me off his lap, stood up, gave me a little smack on the bottom, and said, "Think I'll hit the clubs a while. Think I'll begin my first million tonight. So I can get you that little ranch you're always talking about. Only it'll be a big one. Maybe I'll try for two million, so's I can fence it in with those ribbons you're always talking about."

"Oh, Paddy, please! Don't go, Paddy. I don't want to be rich. I don't even need the ranch. Paddy, you know it's just you I need. And you've been away so much lately. Every night, Paddy, the last few weeks."

"Maybe there'll be a few more nights, too," he said easily. "Stick with it, one of these nights I'll strike it rich."

"I'll go with you, Paddy."

His face set. "No. You bug me at the tables."

No use arguing with Paddy. Unless I wanted to set out on another search all over Nevada.

I remember it rained that night in Reno. A good steady rain. Once I thought, I'll just go along Virginia Street, down the alley by the clubs, find out which one Paddy's in, say it was raining hard and that I'd brought him an umbrella. But it scared me to think of the way his face would look—*I'm a man, Angie, don't wet-nurse me. You bug me at the tables, Angie.* Or maybe he wouldn't say anything. Just never come home.

I'd rather he hit me every day, honest I would.

I woke up in the morning and felt for him next to me. The sheet was cool, untouched. All around me, all through the apartment, was the sweet sage smell that rises off the desert after a rain. But it wouldn't make the ache in my head go away. I perked some coffee, waited a while to eat, and hoped he would show up before he had to go to work. And I said to myself, *Damn the gambling and the gamblers, damn Reno to hell.*

Reno could have been a nice place, you know. A sweet hometown with the Truckee River running through, willows all along it. Over to the west, Mount Rose with snow still on it in summer. Old brown fat Peavine Mountain squatting toward the north. And the clean lovely desert spread to the east. My God, it could have been nice to live in with the man you love. Only it wasn't.

I left a place set at the table in case he showed up. Then I went down on Virginia Street, making like I was window shopping. At 6:30 in the morning, yet! Hoping I'd see him, but that he wouldn't see me: *Angie, you trying to make a woman out of me? I thought you married me because I was a man.* At 6:30 he could be grabbing a bite to eat at one of the club lunch counters, because he had to be at work by seven.

Then I saw him. Coming out of a club with a tall red-blonde holding onto his arm, almost head-high with him. Laughing, throwing her head back, tossing her long shiny hair. She had on a long black dress and it fit her like she was the model on which all women ought to be patterned. I noticed that especially because I'm short and stocky-built. Not fat or anything, just short and stocky-built, the strong kind. I used to help my Dad chop wood—Mother and Dad never had any boys.

I wanted to walk over and sock the girl in the nose. But I always have a sense to be fair about things. It was Paddy who needed the sock in the nose. How would the girl know Paddy belonged to me if he didn't tell her?

I speeded up and came even with them just as she leaned toward him and kissed his cheek. Paddy had his arm up hailing a taxi. I said, "Hi, Paddy, won't you be late for work?"

Paddy was a gambler. His face stayed cool and easy, and it was like hoods dropped over his eyes so I couldn't see into them. "Hi, Angie," he said with his mouth. But I could feel the inside of him saying, *Get the hell out of here.* That wasn't fair. He was the one on the spot, not me. Besides, this was woman trouble. I'd never had woman trouble with Paddy before. Far as I knew. A wife can't buckle under when it's woman trouble.

"I laid out your breakfast on the table—you shouldn't go to work on an empty stomach. Paddy, I don't think I've met your friend."

I was talking to Paddy, but I was looking square at this woman. Woman she was, somewhere between 25 and 30, not much younger than me. She had the skin and the looks of an 18-year-old, only young kids don't get that confident look on them. This woman looked strong and sure of herself, like maybe she'd fought her way up.

She was beautiful, I'll say that. Her eyes were so blue their color almost hurt you to look at. Big, too. Only thing, they stared at me bold as brass, shrewd too. Had me figured first look, and it was striking her funny. She took on a little half smile like she was holding back a laugh.

She knew how to put on makeup, just enough to turn her skin to honey and rose. Or maybe the Lord shot the works on her, maybe she was born that way. Makeup on her eyes, though, and lashes that almost brushed her cheeks. And like a halo, all that red-blonde hair.

"Is this your wife?" she asked Paddy.

He nodded and said, easy, "Sure is. Angie meet Molly."

She looked him level in the eye, laughed, and said, "You're a cool one, I'll say that for you." She turned to me. "Chin up, lady, so he can take a poke at it for good measure." She laughed again, climbed in the taxi and drove off.

What she said shook Paddy. He whipped his face away from the taxi like he'd been slapped, and he didn't give me that goodbye look like he had just before he'd hopped off for Vegas. He said, "I'm sorry, Angie. But you shouldn't have come looking for me. And I'm not going to lie to you, tell you I was just coming out to put her in the taxi. I was going with her."

Well, I couldn't hardly jump on him after that. I mean, he'd come square with me. So I said, "I'm sorry too, Paddy. See you tonight. I've fixed up a good roast for dinner." *Last night while you made up to this Molly with her bold, laughing, beautiful face, I was home cooking for you. I'm not ugly, Paddy. I got big brown eyes, nice features—you told me it's brown eyes you like, not blue like yours. You said brown eyes always got you.*

He let a deep breath sigh out and said, "Okay. See you tonight."

"You've never hit me, Paddy. Not once. She shouldn't have said that."

Kind of like it hurt as the words came out he said, "She's seen 'em hit." Then he turned and walked off.

What do you do when you love a man and as far as you know he's never two-timed you before, and then you find out he did— or was going to? And you begin thinking maybe all those gambling nights and the money gone, that $715 out of the savings account—maybe it wasn't all for gambling?

You brood on it, if you're like me.

All day long while I was selling girdles, pantyhose, and things, I couldn't stop thinking about that tall bold Molly. The way she laughed and told off Paddy, and him standing there looking like he could eat her. And the contempt she'd had for his little dumb wife.

Paddy was there when I got home. He didn't say anything, just pulled me down on his lap and kissed my forehead and my eyes. "You got nice eyes, Angie," he said. "They never did see nothing bad about me. You got nice lovin' eyes."

That's all. What I wanted to say was such a big lump in me that I was afraid to let it out. So I just kissed him.

But after dinner I said, "Paddy, let's pull out and go on up to Wyoming. We could save for our own place up there as well— maybe better—as here in Reno. I could find a job and maybe you could get us a little house on a ranch where you'd work. There's an old cabin on your home place, maybe they'd rent it to us and we could fix it up. Get our roots in."

"One of these days," he said. "Maybe."

He helped me with the dishes that night—usually he didn't do that, said he felt silly lifting teacups and a rag in his hand. But that night he helped me. And he kissed me sweet. Tender, it was. Never once mentioning going to the clubs. It was wonderful.

But sometime in the night—well, it was two o'clock when I turned on the light—I found myself alone in the bed. Paddy was nowhere in the apartment.

Molly, her name was. *Angie, meet Molly.* That's all, no last name. How do you find a Molly in a place as big as Reno?

You get up and dress and go down to the gambling clubs and start looking for Paddy. Or Molly.

But I didn't go. Paddy needed some kind of honor, even if it was the kind I made up myself.

Around four o'clock I laid out some potatoes, ready to fry the way Paddy likes them. Set the table pretty. Listened for the creak of the elevator which meant somebody was coming up. Went to the bathroom to do what I could about my face. Bluish circles under my eyes smudged the upper part of my face. Face puffy from worry and lack of sleep—or like a puff adder getting mad, ready to strike. I was only in my early thirties, but this morning I looked 40 or more. Little dumpy woman. Why wouldn't Paddy, eyes blue as heaven, six-one of muscle, a sidewise grin, why wouldn't——

"Stop it!" I told myself in the mirror. "Stop it!"

Paddy loved me. He told me so lots of times. And Paddy never lied, no matter what else he did.

I put the potatoes away in the refrigerator, drank a cup of coffee, and walked to work. It wasn't fair, and besides we didn't have a car any more. Used to, but Paddy hit a winning streak a year or so back and wanted to raise his bets. So I signed the car over—it was in my name—and Paddy sold it. Oh, well, it costs money for gas.

It's tough to stand on your feet all day, straightening up counters that customers are always messing up the minute you've folded things. It's tough smiling, when you ache all over from wondering where Paddy's gone to. I thought once I'd call him at work. But if he was there he'd be mad. And if he wasn't there his boss would be mad knowing Paddy's wife was hunting for him again.

I tried to eat a sandwich at lunch, but it just wouldn't go down. So I asked my boss could I go home, I didn't feel good. He was real nice, told me not to come back till I felt completely okay. They like me at work. Steady, always on time. Just a dumb, steady, day-after-day salesclerk that redheaded Molly wouldn't be caught dead being.

I went home and took a couple of aspirins. Tried to lie down and relax. Got up and mopped the kitchen and bathroom. Took a shower. Put on my new coral pants suit. Took it off. Broad as a barn door from the rear. Put on a long straight jersey dress. Looked like a Japanese wrestler in a nightgown. Finally put back on the dark dress I had worn to work. And it was past five o'clock and no Paddy.

Well, Reno's free and open—anybody can go in the clubs and play a few nickels and dimes in the slot machines. That's what

I'd tell Paddy if I saw him. But maybe he wouldn't see me. I could hide behind the machines, leave once I knew where—no. Not if he was with Molly.

I walked my legs off that night. Tried to eat a hamburger. Couldn't make it. Got to bed around three in the morning. Alone.

Next morning I called at work and said I was still sick. It was no lie. I was sick. The boss was nice, said to take care of myself. So I was ashamed to walk the streets, running in and out of clubs. I stayed in the apartment. Which was good because Paddy's boss telephoned and asked what happened to him the last two days. "We're sick," I said. What kind of sick? "We must have eaten something funny. Sick to our stomachs."

"Yeah," his boss said. "Not down in Vegas again, is he, Angie, and you packing to go find him?"

"Listen, Pete, you got no right to say that—my God, can't a man have a stomachache without——"

"Okay, okay, Angie, cool it. Take care of yourselves. Tell Paddy to forget about tomorrow, it's Saturday, he might as well get a good start on Monday."

"Thanks, Pete, I'll tell him."

If Paddy was in the clubs he was like a ghost slipping in and out, because I hit them all. And that wasn't Paddy's style. Even losing, he'd stick at one table, waiting for the odds to break his way. And Paddy hadn't left for Vegas, he was still in Reno. My insides told me so.

They kept telling me something else. Paddy was with Molly.

So I concentrated on how I could find Molly.

You ever looked over the list of attorneys in the phone-book yellow pages? In Reno? You wonder how they all eat, except Reno's built on divorce as well as gambling—some fine recommendation for your hometown, huh? I started calling attorneys' offices and ran smack into, "Molly? The last name, please? You say you saw this lady drop her purse in one of the clubs and there's no identification in it, so how do you know the name is

Molly? Oh. One of the dealers. Well, my suggestion would be to ask that dealer about her, or turn over the purse to the cashier or the police." A long pause. "May I ask why you didn't just give it to the lady?" Or, "I'm sorry but we never give out clients' names. Why don't you try the police?"

Well, it was a dumb try anyway.

I thought, why not go down to that club where I first saw Paddy with her and ask around.

Down to the club. Jangling, brassy sound of slot machines, busy, busy. Everybody pulling handles like it was a job doing some good, like cleaning up the world or something every time a coin dropped in. Most of the time nothing was coming out, no loaf of bread or can of beans, nothing. Once in a while a little money to be stuffed back into the machine.

"Say, do you know a pretty redhead named Molly? Tall girl, dressed good. She was here the other night. I—I've got something I think may belong to her. I got to find her."

The dealer at the blackjack table grinned sidewise and said, "Honey, I hope it's something nice you got for her. If it is, you might try the office. Something different, you better take it home. No, I don't know any tall redhead named Molly."

I tried a couple of other dealers. Then the lunch counter. A waitress there said, "Say, aren't you Paddy Finley's wife?"

I nodded and she said, "I thought so. See, I used to live in your same apartment house, couple of floors below, but I used to see you come in together."

"I've got something may be this Molly's," I said again. "The other day down here I saw her with—something like it. But I don't know where to find her. I just thought someone here might know her."

She gave me a quirky smile. "I don't know her, honey, but I do know Paddy, he's here a lot. Hard to miss Paddy, looks like kids used to think cowboy heroes ought to look. Eastern divorcees still think that. You know what I'd do, Mrs. Finley—I'd go home, take two-three aspirins, and have yourself a nice rest. Then when

Paddy came home you'd be in shape to flatten him. Wanta cup of coffee, I'll throw in the aspirin?"

It's peculiar, how when your mind's upset it's the middle of your stomach that hurts. Like a knot tied in it. But all the time the real hurt is in your mind where you can't touch it.

Out on the street, up a way, I got this queer feeling. Like I wanted to shake all over but was too frozen to do it. I felt something either pulling on me or breathing on me. I mean, it was screwy, like I was a Geiger Counter and had run into what I was looking for. I turned.

Across Second Street, headed towards the alley that leads into the clubs, was Molly. Wearing a long bright-green skirt and a white turtleneck sweater. With all that pretty reddish hair in a big topknot, like she was deliberately making herself taller than she already was. Conspicuous, you know?

Paddy wasn't with her.

I was so relieved I felt like I ought to walk over and apologize to her. Instead I went close to the store windows, turned, and watched her swing along the street. Like she'd owned Reno so long she'd even forgotten it belonged to her.

Then I saw him, Paddy. Walking fast behind her, his long legs giving at the knee in that little bend that cowpunchers never quite lose. He came up to her, grabbed her arm, flung her face to face with him. She wasn't surprised. Just took on a strong bold look. Said something. Laughed. He grabbed her throat and shook her back and forth. Her long legs kicked at him, her fingers raked his cheeks. Her knee came up hard. Paddy staggered back, bent over. Even from across the street I could see he was pale, sick.

Molly turned away, cool as you please, not even touching her throat though it was bound to be hurting. Bold as brass. Still owning the town, she was.

I cut across the traffic to Paddy. He was leaning against a building, while people clustered around staring, eyes thrilled like they were watching a movie being shot.

"Paddy, let's go home."

Somebody snickered.

Flames shot through me. Like a chimney long unused and then too much paper is put in the firepot and the soot blazes and sets the house on fire. I plunged into the ring of gawkers, punching, slapping, screaming for them to mind their own business, to leave my Paddy alone.

I felt hands on my shoulders. Paddy's hands. "Angie, that's enough. Let's get out of here."

The crowd parted and we walked through it, turned towards the river. Paddy hailed a taxi and we got in it. Paddy wasn't walking too good.

"That Molly—that Molly, why did you——" I began after we shut the door of our apartment.

"I don't want to talk about it," Paddy said, his face white and drawn. He went in the bathroom and closed the door.

I made some coffee, then stood by the stove wondering whether he'd rather have steak or soup. Or if either of us ever wanted to eat again.

It's hard for a wife of twelve years not to ask her man why he chokes a girl he's just met. If he just met her. Especially with Paddy always spitting on the ground at the mention of men who hit women. Said they ought to take out their mad on wrangling horses or find a man their size or bigger. Now he was choking Molly. Like she had set him crazy.

And then she bested him, right in the middle of Reno with his wife and a crowd watching. *Damn you, Paddy, how'd that look in the papers if a cop had been around and taken you both to the station and me, too? The papers saying your girl friend beat you up and your wife beat up the crowd for snickering. Like you were some ragdoll for women to toss around. Damn you, Paddy, how'd you like that?*

Paddy was a long time in the bathroom. I heard the bath water running. When he came out he was shaved and had on clean underthings I kept in a bureau for him in the bathroom. "I got soup hot and steak ready to broil," I said as he went through the living room to the bedroom, that's the screwy way our apartment was.

"I don't want anything."

I heard him moving around the bedroom. Pretty soon he came out, dressed up, and his suitcase in his hand. "So long, Angie," he said.

"You can't go like this, Paddy. It's not right, it's not fair to me. We got to talk. Listen, Paddy, I can overlook what happened. Just tell me why, then we won't talk about it any more."

"This time don't come looking for me," he said, staring straight ahead at the outside door.

"Paddy, you don't want her after what she done—she don't want you, you don't want a woman don't want you. But I want you."

"So long, Angie."

"Paddy, let's pack up and head for Wyoming, get out of this damn state with its no-good life, gambling, and loose women like——"

He wheeled on me, his eyes blue fire. "Don't say her name!"

He opened the door and went out. I just followed him, like a puppy dog that's been kicked but won't stay home. Down the hall after him. He took the stairs instead of the elevator, his long legs going fast. I kept up. Outside on the sidewalk, down to the corner, me with no purse or anything.

He turned and said, "Angie, I don't want you no more." He started walking again, with me right behind.

He began running. I'm stubby-built, but I've got lasting power. I ran behind him, down almost to Virginia Street. Paddy stopped and I stood beside him.

"You want to go along and hear me tell her I love her before I kill her?"

"You're not going to kill anybody."

"Okay, just keep hanging onto my tail." He started walking, and I did too. We crossed the Truckee Bridge, over by the old Post Office, past the Holiday Hotel. Turned back again, the opposite direction, with him trying to lose me, up the hill above the river, then we turned again.

"You got no pride, Angie," he said over his shoulder.

What's pride? It don't fill emptiness. I kept walking.

Finally he stopped in front of a fine old house above the river, not far from downtown, that was split into apartments. "She lives here," Paddy said, "I'm going in. And if she's not there I'll wait for her. Because she's mine, she's not going to change her mind just because she's got her divorce and is tired of playing around. Angie, you go get you a divorce. I'm taking Molly. One way or another."

He went up the porch steps, through the entrance, up the stairs. Me back of him. At the top of the stairs he turned and said, "You're asking for it, Angie," and hauled back his arm. I stood, waiting for it. If he hit me, maybe he'd think of me the way he did Molly. But his hand dropped.

He knocked on a door, with a number 3 on it. Inside were footsteps and a woman asked, "Who is it?" Molly.

"You know who," Paddy said.

She laughed. "You want to get messed up again?" She slid a bolt fast on the other side and walked away.

Paddy stepped back and kicked the door. Ordinarily a kick that hard would have gone on through. But this was an old-fashioned house with heavy oak doors. Nothing happened except a big deep scar on the finish.

Paddy kicked again. Then he went crazy. Kept kicking that door like a bronco with a cactus under its saddle, his face a sick-gray and his eyes blazing. I pulled at him. He shook me off and kept kicking. Nobody came out of the apartment across the hall—the folks must have been gone. Downstairs a woman was yelling. The landlady, it turned out, who went back inside and called the police.

Suddenly the cops were there, no sirens or anything, and they were manhandling Paddy. It took the two of them to handcuff him and drag him downstairs. I stood there, frozen. One cop came back, knocked on Molly's door, asked her to open up and tell him what the trouble was. "No trouble of mine," she said through the door. "I didn't call you. Nobody came in my apartment. Just some stupid idiot kicking my door. Go talk to the one who called you."

"It's the police. We need information."

She didn't answer. He turned to me, "You in on this, lady? You trying to get inside, too?"

I shook my head. "I'm his wife. I never touched the door. He just wanted to talk to her. She wouldn't talk to him and he got mad. There wasn't any more to it than that, he just lost his temper."

"Some temper the way the door's beat up. You better come down to the station and tell the Chief about it."

"I'm his wife. I've got no complaint. And if I did, you can't make me say anything against Paddy, I'm his wife. I've got no complaint."

"Well, I have!" the landlady yelled behind us. "Breaking up my door, disturbing my tenants, you bet I'll complain, I'll follow you down to the station in my car."

"I'll pay for all the damage," I said. "You tell the Chief that."

The policeman and the landlady left and I sat down on the top stairstep, shaking like a Washoe Zephyr had struck me. After a bit the bolt slid on Molly's door and the door slowly opened.

She saw me. "Oh," she said.

I didn't say anything.

"You're his wife, aren't you?" I nodded.

"Listen, I'll be straight with you. When I first hit this town I bumped into Paddy. In one of the clubs. I was just getting my bearings, had no place to go or anyone to see. And Paddy—well, he has a way with him. Anyway, I didn't know he was married, so we played around. Then you showed up, talking about breakfast. So I split. But he looked me up after that and said he'd left you. Kept hanging around. But frankly, lady, I run on a different track than Paddy. With bosses, not hired help. So I said bye-bye and he wouldn't listen. So he tried muscling me around." She laughed, high and hard. "Shows how stupid a good-looking guy can be. I was trained by pros, and he's an amateur."

"Paddy never once raised his hand to me."

She looked at me wise, and a little sad. "Maybe it would have worked out better if he had. Honest to God. Women!" She went back inside and closed the door.

I'd been trying to hate her. But I couldn't. I couldn't even hate Paddy. I felt nothing but sick, sitting there in a strange place like a cast-off ragdoll with its stuffing out.

I got up and went outdoors.

Like I said, it was an old-fashioned house turned into apartments. Whoever had changed it had made kind of a thing out of it being old-fashioned. They'd kept the old veranda, shaped like an L, and put up an old-time hanging porch swing around the corner from the house front. I felt so done in that I went and rested in the swing.

After a while a car drove up. It was the landlady looking like she'd bit into a chunk of iron. She stomped inside, never saw me. It got dark, but I just kept sitting there.

Maybe I had a hunch what would happen.

Molly came out of the house. She went down the steps to the sidewalk, her hair shimmering under the porch light and her long black dress swirled with embroidery that matched the color of her hair. When she reached the sidewalk, she turned towards town.

I heard footsteps, running from a clump of trees across the street. I stood up, my heart feeling like it filled my whole chest. Molly stopped, tall and defiant, turning towards the man who rushed at her. Paddy. I knew it would be Paddy. She laughed, never a flinch out of her. "Did that poor fool woman bail you out?"

"They didn't hold me. I paid for the door."

"Well, scram! You can't pay for me. The price is too high."

He called her a name. Then pleading like, his hands reaching out almost as if he was trying to climb up some slick and muddy riverbank, "Please, Molly. Please! I'm begging, Molly. I never felt this way before about anybody. I've got to have you, Molly!"

"Go to hell," she said. "I'm no horse you can break. So lay off the big he-man Wild West stuff with me."

Paddy swung. She dodged but the blow glanced her head. She staggered back. He came at her again, both his hands grabbing. She must have reached in her purse. I couldn't see. I only heard a sharp crack, the sound reverberating in my ears until it made me dizzy. Paddy was on the ground, crawling around like he was trying to find something.

I floated down the steps, no feet, out to the sidewalk. Then Molly was on the pavement and I was pounding her head onto the concrete.

See Paddy out there? Gentlest man in the world. Sweet and quiet, just rocking on the porch. Hums to himself and rocks. Oh, now and again he walks out to the little corral I built and pets the mare I bought after I moved us up here to Wyoming. But Paddy just stays gentle and quiet, that's his real nature. That Molly had no right to stir him up, make fun of him. Then try to kill him. She turned him crazy, her face and her bigtime ways.

Right after the trial I brought Paddy back to Wyoming.

Yes, the trial scared me. Not so much for myself as for Paddy. Because if I got sent to the penitentiary, who'd look after him? That shot of Molly's addled him. Struck his head. Made him like a child. Sometimes he cries at night, gets on the floor and crawls around. Just like he did that night. Like he's looking for something he'll never find.

Molly didn't die right away. Not for almost two weeks after that night. But that didn't get me off. Manslaughter it was. In the heat of passion. And my lawyer brought out that I was protecting my husband. So they gave me a suspended sentence. On probation for three years. I have to check in every month.

So I rent this little house on Paddy's old home place from the folks who own it now. Family friends. They keep an eye on Paddy while I'm at work. Except for some nights Paddy's happy. Thinks the mare is a whole string of horses, calls her a lot of different names.

Me?

Well, I'm kind of happy, too. Kind of. No more worry about Paddy running off to the clubs. And by now I'm used to it.

Used to what?

Oh, like with the mare, Paddy calls me by a different name. Just one. Molly. So it hurts a little, but I just figure it's me who answers. Me, Angie.

*The story that follows, the Edgar winner in the short story
classification, I do not recommend for the faint of heart or the
timid of spirit. It's a tale that cuts and slashes through bland
exteriors and superficial human benevolence . . . to expose—
what? A pattern for survival that is more horrible than what is
survived?*

HARLAN ELLISON
The Whimper of Whipped Dogs

On the night after the day she had stained the louvered window
shutters of her new apartment of East 52nd Street, Beth saw a
woman slowly and hideously knifed to death in the courtyard of
her building. She was one of twenty-six witnesses to the ghoulish
scene and, like them, she did nothing to stop it.

She saw it all, every moment of it, without break and with no
impediment to her view. Quite madly, the thought crossed her
mind as she watched in horrified fascination, that she had the
sort of marvelous line of observation Napoleon had sought when
he caused to have constructed, at the Comédie Française theaters,
a curtained box at the rear, so he could watch the audience as
well as the stage. The night was clear, the moon was full, she had
just turned off the 11:30 movie on channel 2 after the second

commercial break, realizing she had already seen Robert Taylor in *Westward the Women,* and had disliked it the first time; and the apartment was quite dark.

She went to the window, to raise it six inches for the night's sleep, and she saw the woman stumble into the courtyard. She was sliding along the wall, clutching her left arm and her right hand. Con Ed had installed mercury vapor lamps on the poles; there had been sixteen assaults in seven months; the courtyard was illuminated with a chill purple glow that made the blood streaming down the woman's left arm look black and shiny. Beth saw every detail with utter clarity, as though magnified a thousand power under a microscope, solarized as if it had been a television commercial.

The woman threw back her head, as if she was trying to scream, but there was no sound. Only the traffic on First Avenue, late cabs foraging for singles paired for the night at Maxwell's Plum and Friday's and Adam's Apple. But that was over there, beyond. Where *she* was, down the seven floors below, in the courtyard, everything seemed silently suspended in an invisible force-field.

Beth stood in the darkness of her apartment, and realized she had raised the window completely. A tiny balcony lay just over the low sill; now not even glass separated her from the sight; just the wrought iron balcony railing and seven floors to the courtyard below.

The woman staggered away from the wall, her head still thrown back, and Beth could see she was in her mid-thirties, with dark hair cut in a shag; it was impossible to tell if she was pretty: terror had contorted her features and her mouth was a twisted black slash, opened but emitting no sound. Cords stood out in her neck. She had lost one shoe, and her steps were uneven, threatening to dump her to the pavement.

The man came around the corner of the building, into the courtyard. The knife he held was enormous—or perhaps it only seemed so: Beth remembered a bone-handled fish knife her father had used one summer at the lake in Maine: it folded back on itself and locked, revealing eight inches of serrated blade. The knife in the hand of the dark man in the courtyard seemed to be similar.

The woman saw him and tried to run, but he leaped across the distance between them and grabbed her by the hair and pulled her head back as though he would slash her throat in the next reaper-motion.

Then the woman screamed.

The sound skirled up into the courtyard like bats trapped in an echo chamber, unable to find a way out, driven mad. It went on and on . . .

The man struggled with her and she drove her elbows into his sides and he tried to protect himself, spinning her around by her hair, the terrible scream going up and up and never stopping. She came loose and he was left with a fistful of hair torn out by the roots. As she spun out, he slashed straight across and opened her up just below the breasts. Blood sprayed through her clothing and the man was soaked; it seemed to drive him even more berserk. He went at her again, as she tried to hold herself together, the blood pouring down over her arms.

She tried to run, teetered against the wall, slid sidewise, and the man struck the brick surface. She was away, stumbling over a flower bed, falling, getting to her knees as he threw himself on her again. The knife came up in a flashing arc that illuminated the blade strangely with purple light. And still she screamed.

Lights came on in dozens of apartments and people appeared at windows.

He drove the knife to the hilt into her back, high on the right shoulder. He used both hands.

Beth caught it all in jagged flashes—the man, the woman, the knife, the blood, the expressions on the faces of those watching from the windows. Then lights clicked off in the windows, but they still stood there, watching.

She wanted to yell, to scream, "What are you doing to that

woman?" But her throat was frozen, two iron hands that had been immersed in dry ice for ten thousand years clamped around her neck. She could feel the blade sliding into her own body.

Somehow—it seemed impossible but there it was down there, happening somehow—the woman struggled erect and *pulled* herself off the knife. Three steps, she took three steps and fell into the flower bed again. The man was howling now, like a great beast, the sounds inarticulate, bubbling up from his stomach. He fell on her and the knife went up and came down, then again, and again, and finally it was all a blur of motion, and her scream of lunatic bats went on till it faded off and was gone.

Beth stood in the darkness, trembling and crying, the sight filling her eyes with horror. And when she could no longer bear to look at what he was doing down there to the unmoving piece of meat over which he worked, she looked up and around at the windows of darkness where the others still stood—even as she stood—and somehow she could see their faces, bruise purple with the dim light from the mercury lamps, and there was a universal sameness to their expressions. The women stood with their nails biting into the upper arms of their men, their tongues edging from the corners of their mouths; the men were wild-eyed and smiling. They all looked as though they were at cockfights. Breathing deeply. Drawing some sustenance from the grisly scene below. An exhalation of sound, deep, deep, as though from caverns beneath the earth. Flesh pale and moist.

And it was then that she realized the courtyard had grown foggy, as though mist off the East River had rolled up 52nd Street in a veil that would obscure the details of what the knife and the man were still doing . . . endlessly doing it . . . long after there was any joy in it . . . still doing it . . . again and again . . .

But the fog was unnatural, thick and gray and filled with tiny scintillas of light. She stared at it, rising up in the empty space of the courtyard. Bach in the cathedral, stardust in a vacuum chamber.

Beth saw eyes.

There, up there, at the ninth floor and higher, two great eyes, as surely as night and the moon, there were *eyes*. And—a face? Was that a face, could she be sure, was she imagining it . . . a face? In the roiling vapors of chill fog something lived, something brooding and patient and utterly malevolent had been summoned up to witness what was happening down there in the flower bed. Beth tried to look away, but could not. The eyes, those primal burning eyes, filled with an abysmal antiquity yet frighteningly bright and anxious like the eyes of a child; eyes filled with tomb depths, ancient and new, chasm-filled, burning, gigantic and deep as an abyss, holding her, compelling her. The shadow play was being staged not only for the tenants in their windows, watching and drinking of the scene, but for some *other*. Not on frigid tundra or waste moors, not in subterranean caverns or on some faraway world circling a dying sun, but here, in the city, here the eyes of that *other* watched.

Shaking with the effort, Beth wrenched her eyes from those burning depths up there beyond the ninth floor, only to see again the horror that had brought that *other*. And she was struck for the first time by the awfulness of what she was witnessing, she was released from the immobility that had held her like a coelacanth in shale, she was filled with the blood thunder pounding against the membranes of her mind: she had *stood* there! She had done nothing, nothing! A woman had been butchered and she had said nothing, done nothing. Tears had been useless, tremblings had been pointless, she *had done nothing!*

Then she heard hysterical sounds midway between laughter and giggling, and as she stared up into that great face rising in the fog and chimneysmoke of the night, she heard *herself* making those deranged gibbon noises and from the man below a pathetic, trapped sound, like the whimper of whipped dogs.

She was staring up into that face again. She hadn't wanted to see it again—ever. But she was locked with those smoldering eyes, overcome with the feeling that they were childlike, though she *knew* they were incalculably ancient.

Then the butcher below did an unspeakable thing and Beth reeled with dizziness and caught the edge of the window before she could tumble out onto the balcony; she steadied herself and fought for breath.

She felt herself being looked at, and for a long moment of frozen terror she feared she might have caught the attention of that face up there in the fog. She clung to the window, feeling everything growing faraway and dim, and stared straight across the court. She *was* being watched. Intently. By the young man in the seventh floor window across from her own apartment. Steadily, he was looking at her. Through the strange fog with its burning eyes feasting on the sight below, he was staring at her.

As she felt herself blacking out, in the moment before unconsciousness, the thought flickered and fled that there was something terribly familiar about his face.

It rained the next day. East 52nd Street was slick and shining with the oil rainbows. The rain washed the dog turds into the gutters and nudged them down and down to the catch-basin openings. People bent against the slanting rain, hidden beneath umbrellas, looking like enormous, scurrying black mushrooms. Beth went out to get the newspapers after the police had come and gone.

The news reports dwelled with loving emphasis on the twenty-six tenants of the building who had watched in cold interest as Leona Ciarelli, 37, of 455 Fort Washington Avenue, Manhattan, had been systematically stabbed to death by Burton H. Wells, 41, an unemployed electrician, who had been subsequently shot to death by two off-duty police officers when he burst into Michael's Pub on 55th Street, covered with blood and brandishing a knife that authorities later identified as the murder weapon.

She had thrown up twice that day. Her stomach seemed incapable of retaining anything solid, and the taste of bile lay along the back of her tongue. She could not blot the scenes of the night before from her mind; she re-ran them again and again, every movement of that reaper arm playing over and over as though on a short loop of memory. The woman's head thrown back for silent screams. The blood. Those eyes in the fog.

She was drawn again and again to the window, to stare down into the courtyard and the street. She tried to superimpose over the bleak Manhattan concrete the view from her window in Swann House at Bennington: the little yard and another white, frame dormitory; the fantastic apple trees; and from the other window the rolling hills and gorgeous Vermont countryside; her memory skittered through the change of seasons. But there was always concrete and the rain-slick streets; the rain on the pavement was black and shiny as blood.

She tried to work, rolling up the tambour closure of the old rolltop desk she had bought on Lexington Avenue and hunching over the graph sheets of choreographer's charts. But Labanotation was merely a Jackson Pollock jumble of arcane hieroglyphics to her today, instead of the careful representation of eurhythmics she had studied four years to perfect. And before that, Farmington.

The phone rang. It was the secretary from the Taylor Dance Company, asking when she would be free. She had to beg off. She looked at her hand, lying on the graph sheets of figures Laban had devised, and she saw her fingers trembling. She had to beg off. Then she called Guzman at the Downtown Ballet Company, to tell him she would be late with the charts.

"My God, lady, I have ten dancers sitting around in a rehearsal hall getting their leotards sweaty! What do you expect me to do?"

She explained what had happened the night before. And as she told him, she realized the newspapers had been justified in holding that tone against the twenty-six witnesses to the death of Leona Ciarelli. Paschal Guzman listened, and when he spoke again, his voice was several octaves lower, and he spoke more slowly. He said he understood and she could take a little longer to prepare the charts. But there was a distance in his voice, and he hung up while she was thanking him.

She dressed in an argyle sweater vest in shades of dark purple, and a pair of fitted khaki gabardine trousers. She had to go out, to walk around. To do what? To think about other things. As she pulled on the Fred Braun chunky heels, she idly wondered if that heavy silver bracelet was still in the window of Georg Jensen's. In the elevator, the young man from the window across the courtyard stared at her. Beth felt her body begin to tremble again. She went deep into the corner of the box when he entered behind her.

Between the fifth and fourth floors, he hit the *off* switch and the elevator jerked to a halt.

Beth stared at him and he smiled innocently.

"Hi. My name's Gleeson, Ray Gleeson, I'm in 714."

She wanted to demand he turn the elevator back on, by what right did he pre*sume* to do such a thing, what did he mean by this, turn it on at once or suffer the consequences. That was what she *wanted* to do. Instead, from the same place she had heard the gibbering laughter the night before, she heard her voice, much smaller and much less possessed than she had trained it to be, saying, "Beth O'Neill, I live in 701."

The thing about it, was that *the elevator was stopped*. And she was frightened. But he leaned against the paneled wall, very well-dressed, shoes polished, hair combed and probably blown dry with a hand drier, and he *talked* to her as if they were across a table at L'Argenteuil. "You just moved in, huh?"

"About two months ago."

"Where did you go to school? Bennington or Sarah Lawrence?"

"Bennington. How did you know?"

He laughed, and it was a nice laugh. "I'm an editor at a religious book publisher; every year we get half a dozen Bennington, Sarah Lawrence, Smith girls. They come hopping in like grasshoppers, ready to revolutionize the publishing industry."

"What's wrong with that? You sound like you don't care for them."

"Oh, I *love* them, they're marvelous. They think they know how to write better than the authors we publish. Had one darlin' little item who was given galleys of three books to proof, and she rewrote all three. I think she's working as a table-swabber in a Horn & Hardart's now."

She didn't reply to that. She would have pegged him as an anti-feminist, ordinarily; if it had been anyone else speaking. But the eyes. There was something terribly familiar about his face. She was enjoying the conversation; she rather liked him.

"What's the nearest big city to Bennington?"

"Albany, New York. About sixty miles."

"How long does it take to drive there?"

"From Bennington? About an hour and a half."

"Must be a nice drive, that Vermont country, really pretty. They just went coed, I understand. How's that working out?"

"I don't know really."

"You don't know?"

"It happened around the time I was graduating."

"What did you major in?"

"I was a dance major, specializing in Labanotation. That's the way you write choreography."

"It's all electives, I gather. You don't have to take anything required, like sciences, for example." He didn't change tone as he said, "That was a terrible thing last night. I saw you watching. I guess a lot of us were watching. It was really a terrible thing."

She nodded dumbly. Fear came back.

"I understand the cops got him. Some nut, they don't even know why he killed her, or why he went charging into that bar. It was really an awful thing. I'd very much like to have dinner with you one night soon, if you're not attached."

"That would be all right."

"Maybe Wednesday. There's an Argentinian place I know. You might like it."

"That would be all right."

"Why don't you turn on the elevator, and we can go," he said, and smiled again. She did it, wondering why it was he had stopped the elevator in the first place.

On her third date with him, they had their first fight. It was at a party thrown by a director of television commercials. He lived on the ninth floor of their building. He had just done a series of spots for *Sesame Street* (the letters "U" for Underpass, "T" for Tunnel, lower-case "b" for boats, "C" for cars; the numbers 1 to 6 and the numbers 1 to 20; the words *light* and *dark*) and was celebrating his move from the arena of commercial tawdriness and its attendant $75,000 a year to the sweet fields of educational programming and its accompanying descent into low-pay respectability. There was a logic in his joy Beth could not quite understand, and when she talked with him about it, in a far corner of the kitchen, his arguments didn't seem to parse. But he seemed happy, and his girlfriend, a long-legged ex-model from Philadelphia, continued to drift to him and away from him, like some exquisite undersea plant, touching his hair and kissing his neck, murmuring words of pride and barely-submerged sexuality. Beth found it bewildering, though the celebrants were all bright and lively.

In the living room, Ray was sitting on the arm of the sofa, hustling a stewardess named Luanne. Beth could tell he was hustling: he was trying to look casual. When he *wasn't* hustling, he was always intense, about everything. She decided to ignore it, and wandered around the apartment, sipping at a Tanqueray and tonic.

There were framed prints of abstract shapes clipped from a calendar printed in Germany. They were in metal Crosse frames.

In the dining room a huge door from a demolished building somewhere in the city had been handsomely stripped, teaked and refinished. It was now the dinner table.

A Lightolier fixture attached to the wall over the bed swung out, levered up and down, tipped, and its burnished globe-head revolved a full three hundred and sixty degrees.

She was standing in the bedroom looking out the window, when she realized this had been one of the rooms in which light had gone on, gone off, one of the rooms that had contained a silent watcher at the death of Leona Ciarelli.

When she returned to the living room, she looked around more carefully. With only three or four exceptions—the stewardess, a young married couple from the second floor, a stockbroker from Hemphill, Noyes—everyone at the party had been a witness to the slaying.

"I'd like to go," she told him.

"Why, aren't you having a good time?" asked the stewardess, a mocking smile crossing her perfect little face.

"Like all Bennington ladies," Ray said, answering for Beth, "she is enjoying herself most by not enjoying herself at all. It's a trait of the anal retentive. Being here in someone else's apartment, she can't empty ashtrays or rewind the toilet paper roll so it doesn't hang a tongue, and being tightassed, her nature demands we go.

"All right, Beth, let's say our goodbyes and take off. The Phantom Rectum strikes again."

She slapped him and the stewardess's eyes widened. But the smile stayed frozen where it had appeared.

He grabbed her wrist before she could do it again. "Garbanzo beans, baby," he said, holding her wrist tighter than necessary.

They went back to her apartment, and after sparring silently with kitchen cabinet doors slammed and the television being tuned too loud, they got to her bed, and he tried to perpetuate the metaphor by fucking her in the ass. He had her on elbows and knees before she realized what he was doing; she struggled to turn over and he rode her bucking and tossing without a sound. And when it was clear to him that she would never permit it, he grabbed her breast from underneath and squeezed so hard she howled in pain. He dumped her on her back, rubbed himself between her legs a dozen times, and came on her stomach.

Beth lay with her eyes closed and an arm thrown across her face. She wanted to cry, but found she could not. Ray lay on her and said nothing. She wanted to rush to the bathroom and shower, but he did not move, till long after his semen had dried on their bodies.

"Who did you date at college?" he asked.

"I didn't date anyone very much."

"No heavy makeouts with wealthy lads from Williams and Dartmouth . . . no Rensselaer intellectuals begging you to save them from creeping faggotry by permitting them to stick their carrots in your sticky little slit?"

"Stop it!"

"Come on, baby, it couldn't all have been knee socks and little round circlepins. You don't expect me to believe you didn't get a little mouthful of cock from time to time. It's only, what? about fifteen miles to Williamstown? I'm sure the Williams werewolves were down burning the highway to your cunt on weekends, you can level with old Uncle Ray. . . ."

"Why are you like this?!" She started to move, to get away from him, and he grabbed her by the shoulder, forced her to lie down again. Then he rose up over her and said, "I'm like this because I'm a New Yorker, baby. Because I live in this fucking city every day. Because I have to play patty-cake with the ministers and other sanctified holy-joe assholes who want their goodness and lightness tracts published by the Blessed Sacrament Publishing and Storm Window Company of 277 Park Avenue, when what I *really* want to do is toss the stupid psalm-suckers out the thirty-seventh floor window and listen to them quote chapter-and-worse all the way down. Because I've lived in this great big snapping dog of a city all my life and I'm mad as a mudfly, for chrissakes!"

She lay unable to move, breathing shallowly, filled with a sudden pity and affection for him. His face was white and strained, and she knew he was saying things to her that only a bit too much Almadén and exact timing would have let him say.

"What do you expect from me," he said, his voice softer now, but no less intense, "do you expect kindness and gentility and understanding and a hand on *your* hand when the smog burns your eyes? I can't do it, I haven't got it. No one has it in this cesspool of a city. Look around you; what do you think is happening here? They take rats and they put them in boxes and when there are too many of them, some of the little fuckers go out of their minds and start gnawing the rest to death. *It ain't no different here, baby!* It's rat time for everybody in this madhouse. You can't expect to jam as many people into this stone thing as we do, with buses and taxis and dogs shitting themselves scrawny and noise night and day and no money and not enough places to live and no place to go have a decent think . . . you can't do it without making the time right for some god-forsaken other kind of thing to be born! You can't hate everyone around you, and kick every beggar and nigger and *mestizo* shithead, you can't have cabbies stealing from you and taking tips they don't deserve, and then cursing you, you can't walk in the soot till your collar turns black, and your body stinks with the smell of flaking brick and decaying brains, you can't do it without calling up some kind of awful——"

He stopped.

His face bore the expression of a man who has just received brutal word of the death of a loved one. He suddenly lay down, rolled over, and turned off.

She lay beside him, trembling, trying desperately to remember where she had seen his face before.

He didn't call her again, after the night of the party. And when they met in the hall, he pointedly turned away, as though he had given her some obscure chance and she had refused to take it. Beth thought she understood: though Ray Gleeson had not been her first affair, he had been the first to reject her so completely. The first to put her not only out of his bed and his life, but even out of his world. It was as though she were invisible, not even beneath contempt, simply not there.

She busied herself with other things.

She took on three new charting jobs for Guzman and a new group that had formed on Staten Island, of all places. She worked furiously and they gave her new assignments; they even paid her.

She tried to decorate the apartment with a less precise touch. Huge poster blowups of Merce Cunningham and Martha Graham replaced the Brueghel prints that had reminded her of the view looking down the hill from Williams. The tiny balcony outside her window, the balcony she had steadfastly refused to stand upon since the night of the slaughter, the night of the fog with eyes, that balcony she swept and set about with little flower boxes in which she planted geraniums, petunias, dwarf zinnias and other hardy perennials. Then, closing the window, she went to give herself, to involve herself in this city to which she had brought her ordered life.

And the city responded to her overtures:

Seeing off an old friend from Bennington, at Kennedy International, she stopped at the terminal coffee shop to have a sandwich. The counter circled like a moat, a center service island that had hung advertising cubes rising above it on burnished poles. The cubes proclaimed the delights of Fun City. *New York Is a Summer Festival* they said, and *Joseph Papp presents Shakespeare in Central Park* and *Visit the Bronx Zoo* and *You'll Adore our Contentious but Lovable Cabbies.* The food emerged from a window far down the service area and moved slowly on a conveyor belt through the hordes of screaming waitresses who slathered the counter with redolent washcloths. The lunchroom had all the charm and dignity of a steel rolling mill, and approximately the same noise-level. Beth ordered a cheeseburger that cost a dollar and a quarter, and a glass of milk.

When it came, it was cold, the cheese unmelted, and the patty of meat resembling nothing so much as a dirty scouring pad. The bun was cold and untoasted. There was no lettuce under the patty.

Beth managed to catch the waitress's eye. The girl approached with an annoyed look. "Please toast the bun and may I have a piece of lettuce?" Beth said.

"We dun' do that," the waitress said, turned half away as though she would walk in a moment.

"You don't do what?"

"We dun' toass the bun here."

"Yes, but I *want* the bun toasted," Beth said, firmly.

"An' you got to pay for extra lettuce."

"If I was asking for *extra* lettuce," Beth said, getting annoyed, "I would pay for it, but since there's *no* lettuce here, I don't think I should be charged extra for the first piece."

"We dun' do that."

The waitress started to walk away. "Hold it," Beth said, raising her voice just enough so the assembly-line eaters on either side stared at her. "You mean to tell me I have to pay a dollar and a quarter and I can't get a piece of lettuce or even get the bun toasted?"

"Ef you dun' like it. . . ."

"Take it back."

"You gotta pay for it, you order it."

"I said take it back, I don't want the fucking thing!"

The waitress scratched it off the check. The milk cost 27¢ and tasted going-sour. It was the first time in her life that Beth had said that word aloud.

At the cashier's stand, Beth said to the sweating man with the felt-tip pens in his shirt pocket, "Just out of curiosity, are you interested in complaints?"

"No!" he said, snarling, quite literally snarling. He did not look up as he punched out 73¢ and it came rolling down the chute.

The city responded to her overtures:

It was raining again. She was trying to cross Second Avenue, with the light. She stepped off the curb and a car came sliding through the red and splashed her. "Hey!" she yelled.

"Eat shit, sister!" the driver yelled back, turning the corner.

Her boots, her legs and her overcoat were splattered with mud. She stood trembling on the curb.

The city responded to her overtures:

She emerged from the building at One Astor Place with her big briefcase full of Laban charts; she was adjusting her rain scarf about her head. A well-dressed man with an attaché case trust the handle of his umbrella up between her legs from the rear. She gasped and dropped her case.

The city responded and responded and responded.

Her overtures altered quickly.

The old drunk with the stippled cheeks extended his hand and mumbled words. She cursed him and walked on up Broadway past the beaver film houses.

She crossed against the lights on Park Avenue, making hackies slam their brakes to avoid hitting her; she used that word frequently now.

When she found herself having a drink with a man who had elbowed up beside her in the singles' bar, she felt faint and knew she should go home.

But Vermont was so far away.

Nights later. She had come home from the Lincoln Center ballet, and gone straight to bed. She heard a sound in the bedroom. One room away, in the living room, in the dark, there was a sound. She slipped out of bed and went to the door between the rooms. She fumbled silently for the switch on the lamp just inside the living room, and found it, and clicked it on. A black man in a leather car coat was trying to get *out* of the apartment. In that first flash of light filling the room she noticed the television set beside him on the floor as he struggled with the door, she noticed the police lock and bar had been broken in a new and clever manner *New York* magazine had not yet reported in a feature article on apartment ripoffs, she noticed that he had gotten his foot tangled in the telephone cord that she had requested be extra-long so she could carry the instrument into the bathroom, I don't want to miss any business calls when the shower is running; she noticed all things in perspective and one thing with sharpest clarity: the expression on the burglar's face.

There was something familiar in that expression.

He almost had the door open, but now he closed it, and slipped the police lock. He took a step toward her.

Beth went back, into the darkened bedroom.

The city responded to her overtures.

She backed against the wall at the head of the bed. Her hand fumbled in the shadows for the telephone. His shape filled the doorway, light, all light behind him.

In silhouette it should not have been possible to tell, but somehow she knew he was wearing gloves and the only marks he would leave would be deep bruises, very blue, almost black, with the tinge under them of blood that had been stopped in its course.

He came for her, arms hanging casually at his sides. She tried to climb over the bed, and he grabbed her from behind, ripping her nightgown. Then he had a hand around her neck and he pulled her backward. She fell off the bed, landed at his feet and his hold was broken. She scuttled across the floor and for a moment she had the respite to feel terror. She was going to die, and she was frightened.

He trapped her in the corner between the closet and the bureau and kicked her. His foot caught her in the thigh as she folded tighter, smaller, drawing her legs up. She was cold.

Then he reached down with both hands and pulled her erect by her hair. He slammed her head against the wall. Everything slid up in her sight as though running off the edge of the world. He slammed her head against the wall again, and she felt something go soft over her right ear.

When he tried to slam her a third time she reached out blindly for his face and ripped down with her nails. He howled in pain and she hurled herself forward, arms wrapping themselves around his waist. He stumbled backward and in a tangle of thrashing arms and legs they fell out onto the little balcony.

Beth landed on the bottom, feeling the window boxes jammed up against her spine and legs. She fought to get to her feet, and her nails hooked into his shirt under the open jacket, ripping. Then she was on her feet again and they struggled silently.

He whirled her around, bent her backward across the wrought iron railing. Her face was turned outward.

They were standing in their windows, watching.

Through the fog she could see them watching. Through the fog she recognized their expressions. Through the fog she heard them breathing in unison, bellows breathing of expectation and wonder. Through the fog.

And the black man punched her in the throat. She gagged and started to black out and could not draw air into her lungs. Back, back, he bent her further back and she was looking up, straight up, toward the ninth floor and higher . . .

Up there: eyes.

The words Ray Gleeson had said in a moment filled with what he had become, with the utter hopelessness and finality of the choice the city had forced on him, the words came back. *You can't live in this city and survive unless you have protection . . . you can't live this way, like rats driven mad, without making the time right for some god-forsaken other kind of thing to be born . . . you can't do it without calling up some kind of awful. . . .*

God! A new God, an ancient God come again with the eyes and hunger of a child, a deranged blood God of fog and street violence. A God who needed worshippers and offered the choices of death as a victim of life as an eternal witness to the deaths of *other* chosen victims. A God to fit the times, a God of streets and people.

She tried to shriek, to appeal to Ray, to the director in the bedroom window of his ninth floor apartment with his long-legged Philadelphia model beside him and his fingers inside her as they worshipped in their holiest of ways, to the others who had been at the party that had been Ray's offer of a chance to join their congregation. She wanted to be saved from having to make that choice.

But the black man had punched her in the throat, and now his hands were on her, one on her chest, the other in her face, the smell of leather filling her where the nausea could not. And she understood Ray had *cared,* had wanted her to take the chance offered; but she had come from a world of little white dormitories and Vermont countryside; it was not a real world. *This* was the real world and up there was the God who ruled this world, and she had rejected him, had said no to one of his priests and servitors. *Save me! Don't make me do it!*

She knew she had to call out, to make appeal, to try and win the approbation of that God. *I can't . . . save me!*

She struggled and made terrible little mewling sounds trying to summon the words to cry out, and suddenly she crossed the line, and screamed up into the echoing courtyard with a voice Leona Ciarelli had never known enough to use.

"Him! Take him! Not me! I'm yours, I love you, I'm yours! Take him, not me, please not me, take him, take him, I'm yours!"

And the black man was suddenly lifted away, wrenched off her, and off the balcony, whirled straight up into the fogthick air in the courtyard, as Beth sank to her knees on the ruined flower boxes.

She was half-conscious, and could not be sure she saw it just that way, but up he went, end over end, whirling and spinning like a charred leaf.

And the form took firmer shape. Enormous paws with claws and shapes that no animal she had ever seen had ever possessed, and the burglar, black, poor, terrified, whimpering like a whipped dog, was stripped of his flesh. His body was opened with a thin incision, and there was a rush as all the blood poured from him like a sudden cloudburst, and yet he was still alive, twitching with the involuntary horror of a frog's leg shocked with an electric current. Twitched, and twitched again as he was torn

piece by piece to shreds. Pieces of flesh and bone and half a face
with an eye blinking furiously, cascaded down past Beth, and hit
the cement below with sodden thuds. And still he was alive, as
his organs were squeezed and musculature and bile and shit and
skin were rubbed, sandpapered together and let fall. It went on
and on, as the death of Leona Ciarelli had gone on and on, and
she understood with the blood-knowledge of survivors *at any cost*
that the reason the witnesses to the death of Leona Ciarelli had
done nothing was not that they had been frozen with horror, that
they didn't want to get involved, or that they were inured to
death by years of television slaughter.

They were worshippers at a black mass the city had demanded
be staged, not once, but a thousand times a day in the insane
asylum of steel and stone.

Now she was on her feet, standing half-naked in her ripped
nightgown, her hands tightening on the wrought iron railing,
begging to see more, to drink deeper.

Now she was one of them, as the pieces of the night's sacrifice
fell past her, bleeding and screaming.

Tomorrow the police would come again, and they would question her, and she would say how terrible it had been, that
burglar, and how she had fought, afraid he would rape her and
kill her, and how he had fallen, and she had no idea how he had
been so hideously mangled and ripped apart, but a seven-story
fall, after all . . .

Tomorrow she would not have to worry about walking in the
streets, because no harm could come to her. Tomorrow she could
even remove the police lock. Nothing in the city could do her
any further evil, because she had made the only choice. She was
now a dweller in the city, now wholly and richly a part of it.
Now she was taken to the bosom of her God.

She felt Ray beside her, standing beside her, holding her, protecting her, his hand on her naked backside, and she watched the
fog swirl up and fill the courtyard, fill the city, fill her eyes and
her soul and her heart with its power. As Ray's naked body

pressed tightly in to her, she drank deeply of the night, knowing whatever voices she heard from this moment forward, they would be the voices not of whipped dogs, but those of strong, meat-eating beasts.

At last she was unafraid, and it was so good, so very good not to be afraid.

You've encountered James Powell in this series before, and here's another of his distinctive tales. He adds an admirable new wrinkle onto the theme of the convicted man wreaking vengeance on the jurist who sentenced him.

JAMES POWELL
A Murder Coming

Fog is always over there and never here. When the man in the fur-collared overcoat and homburg reached the CNR tracks, the fog had moved to the edge of the lake. When he reached the lake and the sagging wharf, the fog stood a bit off from shore.

For a moment the man stared fretfully out across the water. Then he noticed someone on the edge of the fog at the end of the wharf and quickly picked his way out to him. "Did Alcott send you for me?" he asked. "My name is Watford."

The other man was staring down into a rowboat. He looked up slowly. His face was broad and stubbled with white. "No," he said. His breath smelled of alcohol.

"Damn!" Muttered Watford and hurled a ball of paper off into the fog. ("Would you mind delivering this, Judge?" the stationmaster had asked, handing Watford his own telegram in which he had answered Alcott's curious wife and announced his arrival time.) The fine, drifting rain had started up again. "Five dollars to row me out there," said Watford. The man looked at him with soft unblinking eyes. Watford drew a banknote from his wallet and held it under the man's nose. "If you don't know where Alcott's place is, I can show you," he said.

"Not many people on the islands this time of year," said the man.

"Five dollars," said Watford, who didn't care to discuss the comings and goings of a future provincial minister of justice with a local inhabitant.

The man shrugged and tucked the money in a pocket of his mackinaw. He stepped down into the boat and drew it up tight against the pilings. With a strong hand under Watford's elbow, he helped—almost lifted—him down. Then, as his passenger arranged himself in the bow, the man untied the boat and pushed off. Before the oars were in their locks the fog had closed in and the wharf had disappeared.

Now nothing was visible beyond the boat except a dark rim of water tufted with mist. At intervals shapes emerged from the fog and then slipped back into it. Watford, who felt the cold off the water almost at once, hunched inside his coat and thought of crocodiles and Loch Ness. "Your boat's taking water," he said suddenly, noticing the water lapping around his dapper little feet.

The man at the oars had been watching him with an expression as placid as a cow's. Now he shook his head.

"Don't tell me all this is from the rain," insisted Watford.

The man shook his head. "The boat's taking water."

"That's what I said," snapped Watford.

The man shook his head again. "It's not my boat."

Watford frowned. "Well, we could still use a can or something to bail with," he said uneasily.

"Try your hat," the man suggested.

As he groped for a cutting reply, it occurred to Watford that the man wasn't staring as much as offering his face to be recognized. "Have you and I met before?" he asked.

"You once sentenced me to be hanged, Judge," said the man. "If you call that a meeting."

Watford leaned forward curiously, searching the slack cheeks, the pitted skin, the water-blue eyes. The man grinned shyly. Then, holding the oars in his armpits, he took a drink from a bottle in a brown paper bag. Watford refused the bottle with a disdainful shake of the head. Then he shook his head again, perplexed.

The man started to row again. "Edward McSorley," he said.

"Ah, yes," said Watford. In the late forties McSorley, a small-town hardware-store owner, had been convicted of the murder of his wife. In the course of the trial it was also revealed that the McSorleys were The Shouting Bandits, bank robbers whose brief career had made them the darlings of the southern Ontario press. In fact, McSorley claimed his wife wasn't dead but had run off with their accumulated loot.

Abruptly Watford gave a dry laugh. "McSorley, do you remember the witness, the neighbor who saw you through the window come up behind your wife that night and choke her with your arm? Do you remember how you answered him when you took the stand? You said——"

"My wife is a judo expert," repeated McSorley gravely. "I often let her practice on me after dinner."

Watford forced a frown. "Not that I approve the commuting of your sentence, McSorley," he said. "The death penalty is a last bastion of the grand style in this all too colorless world. In his heart even the simplest of murderers sees the justice of an eye for an eye. Isn't that so?"

"Don't look at me. I didn't kill my wife," said McSorley.

"I had hoped we could speak frankly," said Watford. "After all, you've served your time." He paused. "You have, haven't you?"

"Twenty-five years," said McSorley, peering over his shoulder into the fog.

"Good for you," said Watford. "But now that the time has

come to rehabilitate yourself, here's a tip: talk about the bloody deed at the drop of a hat. I mean it. If you ask me, our prisons should emphasize the teaching of communications skills—public speaking, first-person narrative, dramatic reading with gestures, and all. You see, so few of us actually get to kill in white heat. The man on the street thirsts to know what it's like. I confess to a certain curiosity myself."

McSorley rested on his oars. "Maudie's still alive," he said. "And the only thing I learned in prison was this." He lunged forward, a hunting knife in his upraised hand. Wide-eyed with fear, Watford fell backward across the bow. The knife arced down and stopped just short of his throat. "I learned you don't do it like that," said McSorley. With one hand he pulled Watford back into his seat. "You come up like this." He arced the knife up from the bottom of the boat and pressed it against Watford's stomach. "Want me to go through that one more time?" he asked earnestly. "Are you sure you got it?"

"I got it," said Watford.

McSorley looked at him doubtfully. After a moment he said, "I guess you'd better do some bailing." Watford crushed his homburg into a scoop and started throwing water over the side. McSorley watched, mildly interested, lounging back on his seat, legs crossed and an elbow on the gunwale. He took a drink, then another.

Watford bailed. "You have to admit you had a fair trial," he said hurriedly, regretting the squeak in his voice. "Eminently fair, as I recall. The evidence was all there. Oh, perhaps Brownish could have made more of prosecution's failure to positively identify those bone fragments in the incinerator as your wife's."

"He giggled a lot," observed McSorley.

"Yes," panted Watford as he bailed, "Brownish was famous for his little giggling fits in the courtroom. But he came from a fine family. We all forgave him a lot for that. Poor Brownish. He died several years ago, or perhaps you hadn't heard. Walked into an open manhole in broad daylight."

The boat was now bailed out. Watford's fingers were like sticks from the cold. The icy water had set his wrists aching. He started to throw the sodden wreckage of his hat over the side.

But McSorley wagged the knife. "Why don't you put it on?" he said.

Watford did. The leather sweatband made him shiver. Water trickled down his face and the back of his neck. He had the sudden urge to cry.

"Here's to Brownish," said McSorley, raising the bottle to his lips. "We're having a wonderful time and wish he was here." Then he handed the bottle to the unhappy Watford.

Watford braced himself, tilted the bottle, and choked in surprise. "Cognac?" he asked hoarsely, pulling down the bag to read the label.

"Special occasion," said McSorley.

As he handed the bottle back, Watford remembered with a start that it was Alcott who had prosecuted McSorley's case. He cleared his throat nervously and said, "Say, is this what you read about in books where the released murderer hunts down the person he's supposed to have killed and then murders him before the very eyes of the judge and prosecutor who convicted him? The ironic part, you see, is that he can't be tried twice for the same crime." He added almost hopefully, "Is that what all this is about?"

"I couldn't kill anybody," said McSorley. "I'm just not a violent person. Now, Maudie is a violent person. Once I saw her break a man's nose with her forearm." McSorley looked at the knife as though seeing it for the first time. He offered it to Watford. "Here," he said sheepishly, handing the judge the knife.

Watford's heart pounded. Was it a trick? He had to force himself to take the knife. Had McSorley just wanted to humiliate him? Clenching the knife, Watford looked the man in the eye defiantly and swept the wet homburg off his head and over the side. McSorley grinned meekly.

Breathing easier now, Watford said, "All right, let's get going. We can't sit here all afternoon." Watford had never ordered anyone to do something at knifepoint before. He found it strangely exhilarating. Frightened, he pushed the knife deep in his pocket and folded his arms. "What is it you want, McSorley?" he demanded.

McSorley rowed in silence. Finally he said, "At the trial nobody asked why we were called The Shouting Bandits."

"It was hardly relevant," said Watford. A small island with a single pine tree slid by in the fog. Alcott's island wasn't far now. "Proceed," said Watford. "Consider yourself asked."

"I guess the first time I met my wife is the best place to begin," said McSorley. "She was the new bank teller just arrived in town that day, a big-boned, broad-shouldered woman with this hard-of-hearing problem and a voice like a bugle. But too vain to wear a hearing aid. Funny, because she was plain as a post. Kicked out of the School of Library Science at the University of Western Ontario because of it—her hearing, not her looks." He faltered. "I'm not telling it right again," he said helplessly. "I guess maybe prisons should teach those communications skills you talked about."

McSorley pulled on the oars thoughtfully, as though ordering things in his mind. "Hardware stores smell of things with weight to them," he began again. "But banks smell like courtrooms, all paper and dried-up ink."

"More matter and less art, McSorley," said Watford.

"When my turn came at the teller's window that first day, Maudie blared right out, 'Speak up there, Mr. Man. You're not in church,'" said McSorley in a rush. "Everybody turned. The bank manager stuck his head out of his cubbyhole. But what really hit me like a load of bricks was that she was right. I mean I had been whispering in the bank all my life and so had my father before me.

"The next day, Sunday, I spent walking the few streets of the town trying to figure out what to do after two generations of whispering to put things right and become my own man again. All of a sudden there was Maudie coming out of Fallows Tourist Rooms carrying a fiber suitcase. The bank had fired her and she was going home to Sarnia.

"Well, there weren't any buses on Sundays, so I offered to drive her. It was in the car that I laughed and shouted and guessed the only way for me to get my own back was to rob the bank. Maudie punched my arm and shouted that was the best damn idea she'd ever heard and to count her in. She felt banks had given her a raw deal. And libraries, too. But we both agreed there was more money in robbing banks.

"The next thing I knew I was visiting Maudie regularly in Sarnia where we'd sit around and shout about robbing banks. You wouldn't really think that could lead to wedding bells, but it did. On our honeymoon we sneaked back to town in masks and robbed the bank. That's when she broke the bank manager's nose. He didn't jump when she shouted 'Jump!' A violent person, Maudie.

"For the next few months, Mondays meant close up the hardware store and rob a bank. But I'd had my fill. Nothing makes you speak right up in a bank like knowing you've robbed it. Besides, I was elected captain of the Northside-River Street-Merchants hockey team with Monday practises and a good chance that year of beating our Southside rivals. So I said, 'Hold the phone, Maudie.'

"She didn't like that a bit. I could hear it in her voice after dinner when she'd get me in a full nelson, snap my neck, and say, 'Tomorrow we're going to rob a bank. One and done.' 'No, now Maudie,' I'd say, 'enough's enough.' But love curdles fast when you've built a marriage on robbing banks."

"So you say she took all the money and ran," said Watford. "But why make it look as if you'd killed her?"

"Because I'm somebody to be reckoned with," insisted Mc-Sorley. "I rob banks just because I whispered in them. She had to be afraid of what a guy like that would do if she stole his share. So you were supposed to kill me. But you didn't."

"God knows I tried," said Watford. "I wasn't the one who commuted your sentence."

"Anyway, the big question now in her mind is what a guy like me is going to do to make up for those twenty-five long years I spent in jail," said McSorley.

"So you've really found her then," said Watford.

"I put a private detective on that," said McSorley. "She owns a place called Echo Lake Lodge about forty miles from here—just a couple of ratty cabins for fishermen and a three-stool lunch counter." He smiled. "Tell you what I did: when I got out I bought an old car and paid her a visit, just a wave and a smile and hanging around outside, just giving her the jumps."

A dark shelf loomed ahead of them in the fog. Alcott's landing. "If that's what this is all about, I wouldn't advise you trying to harass Mr. Alcott and myself," warned Watford. "We have friends with the police who'd be happy to extend themselves on our behalf."

"I'm not going to bother you any more, Judge. Honest," promised McSorley. "Just let me finish what I was telling you. You see, I knew she couldn't take much of the waiting, and wondering what I was going to do. She'd have to come after me. And so there she was, padlocking the lunch-counter door behind her and there I was driving off in a cloud of dust. I let her chase me until I caught her, Judge. Now I've got her where she can't get away."

"Why tell me all this?" demanded Watford.

McSorley edged the boat up against the landing. "Because you're a judge," he said. "Because you say when people have the right to kill and when they don't."

"I've already told you you've got a murder coming, so to speak," said Watford, standing up.

McSorley helped him out of the boat and onto the landing. "The trouble is I'm just not a violent person," he said. "But I let her chase me until she could taste my blood and then I put her where she couldn't get away. When the police come looking they'll find her. Or her body."

Watford looked down at him. "Her body?" he asked.

McSorley grinned. "Well, you see, Judge, I told her a lie. I told her I'd hired a couple of guys to kill her."

"Figuring on scaring her to death?" asked Watford contemptuously. He stuffed his hands in his pockets and started to walk away. Then he stopped and pulled out the knife. "Here. This is yours," he said.

But McSorley had already pushed off. "That's all right," McSorley said gravely. "You just remember what I told you." He arced his fist down. "Not like that." He arced his fist up. "Like this. Mr. Alcott never did get that straight."

Watford gave a puzzled frown. Then something moved in the fog. Someone was coming down the landing toward him. "Alcott?" he called doubtfully, for Alcott was a small man with a quick step.

"Alcott?" he called again.

McSorley rested his oars and sat there on the edge of the fog. He held up the bottle in a little salute and before putting it to his lips said, "You'll have to shout louder than that, Judge. A lot louder than that."

Jerry Jacobson is a relative newcomer to mystery fiction, and this is his first appearance in these anthologies. His story, sensitive, poignant, immensely evocative, will linger long in your memory.

JERRY JACOBSON
Morning Watch

Patrolmen Alonzo Trippy and Garth Morgan were moving into the last half of the morning watch and fighting to stay awake. Their shift began at one a.m. and extended an hour past the morning rush hour, but between five a.m. and the time freeway and city street traffic began to build at seven, their district was dead.

Duck Lake district's furtive night people had closed up their dubious shops. The hippies and wandering street people who had not been arrested for loitering, smoking pot, or caught selling or buying it, were coming down hard with the real world of dawn staring them in their vague, beleaguered faces. The world of garbage trucks, street cleaners, newsboys and produce vans began seeping into their drug-floating world and they scurried from that world to crash-pads to escape this reverse plague. Coffee shops began opening their doors to Duck Lake district's few prostitutes who were grabbing a cup of coffee before calling it a night. Also out on the streets were the anonymous wanderers, wayward troubled people neither Trippy nor Morgan had identified as criminals or potential suicides, sex maniacs or just plain kooks with a few vital nuts loose in their heads.

Old men came out during these dull hours to walk their dogs, or to sit on a bench at Duck Lake and reflect, or merely to put behind them with each step, troubles too heavy to bear on their stooped shoulders. Of all the flotsam and near-flotsam afloat in a half-sleeping, just-waking world, it was this group that troubled Garth Morgan most. Often he thought it would be a helpful gesture to tell these aging men, for whom the world no longer had work, that their leisure was a golden reward for the years of thankless, repetitive toil, that they should not feel shame because of it, that they should not be so preoccupied with their next reward—the heavenly reward—that they failed to enjoy the rewards now in their hands. Morgan knew, however, that he would never draw up the courage to tell this even to one old man.

The morning was chilly, but the squad car's heater had been spewing warmth on them all night. Officer Morgan cracked open the wing window to stir the heavy heat inside the car and the indolence inside his brain. Before heading over to the freeway for their two hours of roving patrol at six-thirty, they had only a few routine checks to make; but first on their list of routine business was their fifth and final crusing tour of Duck Lake.

Besides its perimeter, they were responsible for the surveillance of the West Duck Lake and East Duck Lake bathing beaches, bathhouses, indoor pools, cul-de-sac parking lots, boathouses, and bicycle houses. Vandalism in the Duck Lake district was not the highest in the city, but it could break out at the most unexpected times nonetheless. The task did not exactly have Officer Garth Morgan crawling with anticipation of action, but it was part of the routine and the routine had to be done.

Behind the wheel, Officer Alonzo Trippy worked off a monstrous yawn and sneaked a look at his watch. "Do the lake again?" he said. "It's about time, unless you want to grab a cup of coffee."

"I can wait if you can," Morgan told him. "Let's hit the lake, Jeeves."

It was while they cruised past an open patch of rolling grass fronting the lake that Officer Morgan spotted them in the near darkness—a man and a woman, it appeared, sitting together on a stone bench before the asphalt bicycle path about fifty yards away. Their backs were to the squad car and the man had his arm draped across the woman's shoulders as they looked out at the moonlit lake.

Morgan reached across and tapped his partner on the shoulder lightly, a signal to slow down. "A couple down at the lake. On one of the benches."

"Young lovers," Trippy said.

"At five a.m.?"

"Then they're getting an early start or a late finish. You want to check them out?"

"Wouldn't hurt," Morgan said. "Maybe the two weren't together originally. Know what I mean?"

"Morgan, you've got a dirty mind."

"I've got a suspicious mind. You want to come along? Stretch your legs? Skip a few rocks?"

"If it were warmer," Trippy said. "And we may get a call. I'll wait here."

"Suit yourself," Morgan told him and got out of the car. The grass beneath his shoes still held a shimmering coat of predawn dew and the freshly mowed blades stuck to the soles and toes as he walked. The breeze off the lake was fresh and wholesome and for a moment he forgot he was a city patrolman and that he was on duty.

That had been, and still was, a sore point between Morgan and his wife. He was always on duty, she often said. He fretted and stewed and worried as though he owned the entire department, she sometimes told him. If he kept taking his job so personally, she'd admonish, he would have a big, throbbing ulcer long before he even came up for his examinations for sergeant.

He never argued with her on the point, because he knew

Glenna had only his interests at heart. She didn't want him taking it all too seriously, was all. She didn't want him sick inside at thirty, she didn't want to see him eating himself away because of crime and criminals and because he couldn't singlehandedly wipe them both from the face of the globe.

Perhaps she was right about that, about his becoming so involved in his work in a personal way. Perhaps his makeup, the crazy, complex way that he was deep inside, made him powerless to change, helpless to be any other way. He did not hate crime or criminals, not the way many of the older officers did. He could not rage against them, or curse them for the way they were or for the crimes they committed. Instead, he felt deep empathy for criminals, understood in some cases the forces which had driven them into their dark lives. *You cannot hope to begin to forgive until you understand,* his father had once told him when he was a young boy of eight or nine. *And you cannot begin to understand until you have worn another man's skin, lived another man's sorrows, felt another man's hatred and cried another man's tears.* That was how he had been brought up, with a belief that there was worth in every human being and that there was a reason behind every transgression.

As he approached the stone bench from behind, Garth Morgan could now see the couple was not yet man and woman, but boy and girl. They were both perhaps no more than seventeen or eighteen at the most, but intelligent enough to have dressed warmly for the morning's chill breeze moving in off the lake. They didn't seem to hear him.

When Morgan had come within ten or fifteen yards of the bench he called out, "Good morning," in a pleasant voice, not to startle them, and from that distance so they could turn and identify him. The girl's face was healthy-looking, peachy and fresh, though not from the chill wind. It was the way it looked for another reason, but for the moment Morgan could not put his finger on the reason it glowed with such serenity. The boy's face held a mildly guarded look until he recognized the uniform

Morgan was wearing and then it, too, became relaxed and pleasant like the girl's.

"Is something wrong, Officer?" the girl said. "We haven't done anything wrong. We just came out to look at the lake."

Morgan continued walking until he was between the bench and the lake. Then he turned slowly and smiled. "No, nothing's wrong," he said evenly. "It's just that it strikes me as a little early to be out looking at the lake." He now identified the reason for the young girl's serene glow. She was going to have a baby. Even the bulky, wool coat she wore could not hide the fact. Seven or eight months, Morgan judged.

"It does seem awfully early," the girl said, "but George catches the bus for work in a little while and we thought how nice it would be to spend some time here together while he's waiting. This is my husband, George, by the way."

Perhaps because he had been mentioned as an afterthought, George grimaced mildly, though he did not remove his arm from around her shoulder. Neither wore a wedding ring, Morgan noticed, but that was not unusual in this age of trial marriages, and living-in, and shacking, and whatever else the young kids used as a euphemistic substitute for the cold finality of marriage these days.

"Where do you work, George?" Morgan asked.

"Down at the gypsum plant on Industrial Avenue," George said, with mild distaste. "I crush hydrous calcium sulfate. Sounds like some chemical big deal, but I'm just a common laborer."

"We all did a little of that when we were young," Morgan told him. "Come to think of it, I'm doing a lot of that right now."

"Yeah, I might give being a cop a whirl," George said, with careless disdain. "You have to take a civil service test, right? And you gotta be a high school graduate, too, right?"

"Or get your high school diploma. Lot of night study and classes involved, but it's worth it. You can't be too far behind your graduating class."

"Last September," George said. "I had to drop out, because my father got crushed in a plant accident and we didn't have any money coming in. He died in April, anyway, so it wasn't any big deal."

"I'm sorry to hear that," Morgan said.

"Yeah, well, it wasn't any big deal," George said.

Somehow they had slipped into a mood of mild morbidity. Morgan made an attempt to break it. "I see you two are going to have a baby."

Again George grimaced mildly. The girl's slender hands seemed to tense in her lap without actually clenching. "She's having the baby," he said.

"And you're having the worries and the bills," Morgan said, suddenly realizing he had opened his big mouth again and mentioned two more negative thoughts. "What's it going to be? Boy or girl?"

"Oh, we don't care," the girl said. "One or the other is all right with us."

"A boy, maybe," said George, in a brief moment of wistfulness. Then the implacability in his expression and voice returned, and he added, "Whatever."

"Well, whatever it is, I hope it is a healthy, brilliant child," Morgan said.

"Thank you, Officer," the girl said and smiled at him briefly.

The breeze off the lake blew up suddenly and the girl fought through a shiver. George instinctively hugged his wife closer with his protective arm.

"Do you live with your parents?" Morgan asked, not defining whose parents.

"We used to live with hers," George said, "but we moved out about three months ago."

"We have a small apartment back there." The girl gestured behind her with her arm. "On Duck Lake Avenue. It's only three rooms, but it's very nice and close to the lake. I come down here sometimes while George is at work, when the weather's nice."

"I met Lucinda at this lake," George put in, with modest

pride. "She was going with this other guy, Mike. Big muscleman, with a tan like a roast chicken. Very big deal beach-bum type. I sure put out his fire in a hurry, didn't I, Lu?"

Lucinda nodded with a blush and seemed to push closer to his side.

"I didn't put it out soon enough, though," George said suddenly.

"How do you mean?" Morgan asked.

"Aw, it's no big deal. I put it out, that's all that counts. I got Lucinda, and all he's got now is his crummy suntan lotion and sand crabs all over him. I really think guys like that are queer, if you want my opinion. What do you call it? Narcissism, or something like that? I wouldn't be surprised if the guy runs around his house with dresses on, and queer garbage like that."

"*George,*" Lucinda said, in soft but stern censure.

"Yeah, well anyway, it's no big deal."

Lucinda smiled again, and George gave her waist a possessive little squeeze.

Morgan glanced swiftly at his watch and saw they were running behind on their patrol rounds. They would have to skip the supermarkets if they were going to put in an honest bit of traffic control on the freeway.

"It's been nice meeting you two," he told them, smiling warmly. "You have a good baby, both of you. And George, you start thinking seriously about going after that high school diploma. And Lucinda, you make a nice home for the three of you."

Both smiled up at him but did not answer.

"And I'd suggest you not come down to the lake until it begins to get light. This can be a dangerous place at times, especially in the early-morning hours. You never can tell about the kind of people who are out and about this time of morning."

"We'll be all right, Officer," Lucinda told him.

"It's no big deal, but thanks for the warning anyway, Officer," George said.

"Well, have a nice morning. Don't miss your bus."

"I won't. Thanks."

"Good-bye, Officer," Lucinda said, in a tone Morgan could not read precisely, a mixture of sadness and fondness, of cordiality and barren emptiness; of something other than what Morgan supposed a goody-bye should be.

He left them then, returning up the slope to the squad car idling in the near distance. Two young married people out gazing at a lake in the predawn wasn't the gloomiest thing in the world, Morgan decided. In a strange way, the act contained an element of pure beauty, a basis of simple love. They'd had it rough in their lives, with an early (and very possibly forced) marriage, the abrupt discontinuance of education and early entry into the labor market, the tragic death of a father in a senseless industrial accident. Yet they would prevail somehow, Morgan was sure of it.

"How did they check out?" Alonzo Trippy asked, as Morgan slipped back into their patrol car. "Runaways?"

"Nothing like that," Morgan said. "Just a young married couple out looking at the lake."

"They high on something?" Trippy was just a little more suspicious and cynical about people than Morgan.

"Just each other," Morgan told him. "Girl's going to have a baby and the husband works at the gypsum plant on Industrial Avenue. They were just spending a few private minutes together before he caught his bus for work."

"One of those *modern* marriages?" asked Trippy. "Reciting poetry to each other in a forest, with an owl for a minister and a flock of doves for wedding guests?"

"Something like that," Morgan said.

"You check their identification?"

Morgan gave Alonzo Trippy a brief scowl. "I asked them their names. Lucinda and George were good enough for me."

"You're the investigating officer, Officer."

"Let's start checking those schools before the freeways get so clogged we have to go downtown and watch traffic on a video relay unit," Morgan said gruffly.

He wasn't worried about Lucinda and George and the baby they were about to have. They would weather it all and survive and have a fairly good life. They would never again cross Morgan's path, except by accident or chance meeting, would never cross his path the way most humans he met did: in the process of robbery or burglary, in the midst of an act of physical violence, or in the commission of an act against private or public property. He felt equally certain he would not meet them as participants in any of the sad phases of the drug experience. Basically they were good kids, a little confused and frustrated by the vagaries and pressures and injustices of life perhaps, but strong enough to surmount them, or accept them philosophically. They would live within the law, with respect for the law and would not turn out to be the kind of people over whom Morgan mourned, by whom he was perplexed and puzzled, and for whom he felt, deep inside him, tremendous sadness and personal guilt.

"Hey, cheer up, partner," Alonzo said, as he drove them in the direction of Carmen Gatzert Grade School. "We've got this shift made now, and you look like we just ran over your dog."

"Just thinking," Morgan said.

"And I was just thinking that kid George has got a long hike to his bus."

"What?"

"His bus. He's gotta walk at least ten blocks. There aren't any bus lines on Duck Lake Avenue."

"So he has a long walk to his bus," Morgan said, in an anxious voice. "So what does that prove? Trippy, I swear you're the most suspicious cop I ever met. I'll bet you even suspect that old Blind Charlie, the newspaper vendor on Lux Avenue, has been able to see all along."

"You never know what goes on behind those black lenses."

Morgan slumped down into his seat and said no more. He had faith in people, tremendous faith, and Lucinda and George would be all right. They, like thousands of others, would grin and bear through it all and land on their feet.

What appeared to be a family of ducks had waddled up from the lake bank beyond the stone bench and the asphalt bicycle path. There were six in the family: a mother, a father and four baby ducklings churning their tiny webbed feet into the sand and desperately trying to keep up with their parents.

"A family of ducks, George," Lucinda said, tugging his arm.

"Yeah. Big deal. I wonder if the old man knows they're all his. Or if he thinks there's a stud duck named Mike hanging around in the bushes."

For a moment they were quiet. They listened to the ducklings' squeaky quacks, the breeze moving through the trees around them and the lake waters lapping on the shore.

"You could get your job back," Lucinda said. "If you really wanted it back, you could get it back. Talk to Mr. Molling about it."

"I beat him up, remember?" George said. "I warned him twice to quit leaning on me, to quit yelling at me, to quit hanging over my shoulder while I was crushing his damned hydrous calcium sulfate. He got fair warning."

Lucinda tried to change the subject. "I thought the policeman was nice. Didn't you?"

"Cops are all the same," George said. "Always trying to pry, always trying to learn about the private things in your life, trying to get something on you."

"I liked him."

"Cops are all alike. What do you know about anything, anyway? You're no big deal, I'm no big deal, cops are no big deal. Nothing is no big deal."

The family of ducks passed the stone bench in single file and disappeared into a hamlet of thick bushes behind them. Their quacking ceased but the water continued its soft lapping and the breeze kept singing into the trees.

"Well, it's about time now," George said, without turning his head toward Lucinda, who was beginning to sob very softly. He removed his arm from around her shoulder and put it into a pocket of his Windbreaker. When he extracted his hand, it was gripped around the handle of a small, black pistol. He let it rest in his palm and stared down at it as though it were a small, black bird he was nursing back to health.

"It's no big deal, Lucinda," he said, and then without speaking another word to her, without even uttering a good-bye, he placed the pistol's barrel against her right temple and pulled the trigger.

He watched Lucinda as her body tumbled from the stone bench and onto the hard sand beneath his feet. Then he placed the pistol's barrel against his own temple.

"You see, Lucinda? It's no big deal, just like I promised," he whispered, and then pulled the trigger the second and final time.

Jeff Sweet's first story appeared in EQMM *in 1971, and he's been a rewarding contributor to the field since then. He offers here a sober vignette of our society, concerning what may happen when the reality of day to day existence becomes unbearable.*

JEFF SWEET
Over the Borderline

"Don't you see? He had to be stopped."

"Stopped, Mrs. Sutherland? Stopped from doing what?"

"If I hadn't acted she would have died. He would have killed her."

"Who, Mrs. Sutherland? Who would he have killed?"

"You're looking at me like you don't believe me, Lieutenant Foley. You think I'm just a batty old lady, don't you? An old lady who's lost her marbles."

"No, I don't. Really, I don't."

"Like crazy Mrs. Jessup who's always calling the police or the F.B.I. about enemy agents hiding under her bed. I'm right, aren't I? That's what you think."

"I swear, Mrs. Sutherland, I don't think that at all."

"Then why don't you believe me?"

"Well, I'll tell you, Mrs. Sutherland, it isn't that I don't believe you. It's just that I—well, I guess I really don't *understand*. I mean, I don't have the full picture."

her himself. 'I love you,' he said. 'You give my life purpose. If you don't say yes, I don't know what I'll do.' To make a long story short, she did say yes and they were married soon after. He even delivered the baby."

"Mrs. Sutherland, what has this got to do with——"

"Lieutenant, please!"

"Sorry, Mrs. Sutherland."

"As I said, they were married and were so happy, and the baby didn't look a bit like Harrington. But I could tell they weren't over the worst of it. I knew in my bones that tragedy was going to strike, but for the longest time I didn't know how.

"To tell you the truth, I was having an awful time sleeping. I finally had to go to Dr. Sumroy and get a prescription for sleeping pills. I'd never used them before because I've heard so many stories of old people accidentally taking an overdose. And not just old people. Young people, too. It's supposed to be especially bad if you take them when you've been drinking, though in my case that was no problem. But I was having so much trouble sleeping because of all my worrying about Cora and Jim that I just *knew* something tragic was going to happen even though I didn't know what.

"Then, suddenly, it came to me. I can't tell you how it came to me because I honestly don't know how to explain such things. Call it woman's intuition, if you like, but I knew what was going to happen. *Harrington was going to kill Cora in an automobile accident!* It was inevitable. He'd just bought a new sports car— one of those fancy foreign things that makes a lot of noise, and it was common knowledge he was speeding recklessly all over town. So you see, it was logical.

"Of course, I couldn't let it happen. I remember how heart-broken I was when Mr. Sutherland died in an accident, only he wasn't killed by a foreign car. I was so miserable, I nearly died. So what was I supposed to do? I knew what would happen if something weren't done, and I couldn't just sit quiet and *let* it happen. I had to do something. But what?

"Then, today, an amazing coincidence brought me the answer.

I came into the city to shop on Fifth Avenue for my nephew's birthday, and I stopped into a restaurant on Forty-Seventh Street. Not too far away from Radio City and Rockefeller Center, you know the area? And who was in the restaurant but young Harrington!

"I went up to him, and I said, 'Mr. Furth?' He smiled. I'll say that for him, he had a nice smile. 'Mr. Furth,' I said, 'I want to talk to you.' He stood up, a little woozy from all the liquor he'd been drinking, and offered me a seat, which I accepted. 'Mr. Furth,' I said, 'I'm going to speak plain. I know what's going to happen.' 'What's going to happen?' he said, still smiling. 'I know you're going to kill Cora Franklin with that fancy foreign car,' I answered.

" 'How did you find out?' he asked, obviously surprised. 'Never you mind how I found out,' I said. 'What I'm saying is so, isn't it? You're going to kill her with your sports car, aren't you?'

" 'Yes,' he said, 'that's so.'

"He admitted it! With a smile! There wasn't a trace of regret anywhere on his devilish face. He actually seemed happy about it! I knew I was in the presence of great evil.

"He excused himself and went to the men's room. I suddenly knew what I had to do. I opened my handbag and took out the sleeping pills I had got from Dr. Sumroy, and I dropped something like two dozen of them into his coffee. I left, waited until I was sure it was all over, then came here to turn myself in. And that, Lieutenant, is my confession."

"I see."

"Do you believe me?"

"Yes, I believe you, Mrs. Sutherland."

"One thing you have to know—I did this for them. Lieutenant. For Jim and Cora and the baby. You have to realize that it was the only way. You do understand, don't you?"

"Yes, Mrs. Sutherland, I think I do."

A few minutes later, after Mrs. Sutherland had been led away, Lieutenant Foley turned to Sergeant Warren, who was standing a few feet away. "Well, that settles that," he said.

"Lieutenant, maybe I'm some kind of an idiot," said the sergeant, "but I don't see that it settles anything. Her story about the overdose in Maxwell's coffee jibes, and she matches the waiter's description, but I'll be damned if I can figure out why she kept calling Taylor Maxwell by the name Harrington Furth."

"Sergeant, Taylor Maxwell was an actor."

"I still don't get it, sir."

"I've just been looking at his résumé. For the past few years he's been a regular on an afternoon TV soap opera called *The Will To Live*," explained the lieutenant. "The name of the character he played was Harrington Furth."

The Yearbook of the Detective Story

Abbreviations: *EQMM*—Ellery Queen's Mystery Magazine
AHMM—Alfred Hitchcock's Mystery Magazine
MSMM—Mike Shayne Mystery Magazine

BIBLIOGRAPHY: 1973

I. Collections

1. Allen, Grant: *The Reluctant Hangman and other stories of crime.* Boulder, Colorado (Box 4119): The Aspen Press. A chapbook containing two tales from *Ivan Greet's Masterpiece* (1893) and the title story (1891), apparently heretofore uncollected, along with the original illustrations from *The Strand Magazine.*

2. Allingham, Margery: *The Allingham Minibus.* New York: William Morrow & Co. Eighteen stories, including three about Albert Campion.

3. Andrews, Charlton: *The Resources of Mycroft Holmes.* Boulder, Colorado (Box 4119): The Aspen Press. Three slight parodies from 1903 reprinted in this chapbook, with useful commentary and bibliographic material.

4. Bangs, John Kendrick: *Shylock Homes: His Posthumous Memoirs.* Arlington, Virginia (Box 203, 1621 North Ode Street): The Dispatch-Box Press. Ten minor Sherlockian pastiches collected for the first time here from 1903 newspapers.

5. Brennan, Joseph Payne: *The Casebook of Lucius Leffing.* New Haven, Connecticut: Macabre House. Sixteen stories from *AHMM* and *MSMM,* plus one heretofore unpublished, all about psychic investigator Lucius Leffing.

6. Collins, Wilkie: *Tales of Terror and the Supernatural.* New York: Dover Publications. Twelve stories in a softcover collection.

241

7. Derleth, August: *The Chronicles of Solar Pons.* Sauk City, Wisconsin: Mycroft & Moran. The last collection, comprising ten stories, of the late August Derleth's pastiches.

8. Freeman, R. Austin: *The Best Dr. Thorndyke Detective Stories.* New York: Dover Publications. Seven stories from early collections, plus a shorter, earlier and heretofore uncollected version of the novel *The Mystery of 31 New Inn* which went unnoticed for decades and may represent Freeman's first writing about Thorndyke.

9. Futrelle, Jacques: *Best "Thinking Machine" Detective Stories.* New York: Dover Publications. Twelve stories, including two not previously collected in book form.

10. Gilbert, Michael: *Amateur in Violence.* New York: Davis Publications. A softcover collection containing a short novel and ten short stories.

11. Jaffee, Mary and Irving: *Beyond Baker Street.* Culver City, California (Box 261): The Pontine Press. A chapbook containing five Sherlockian pastiches.

12. Palmer, Stuart: *The Adventure of the Marked Man and one other.* Boulder, Colorado (Box 4119): The Aspen Press. A chapbook containing two Sherlockian pastiches from the 1940s.

13. Post, Melville Davisson: *The Strange Schemes of Randolph Mason.* Philadelphia (P.O. Box 1891): Oswald Train. A collection of seven stories first published in 1896 and out of print for half a century or more.

II. Anthologies

1. Dickensheet, Dean, editor: *Men & Malice.* Garden City, N.Y.: Doubleday & Co. Seventeen stories, thirteen appearing for the first time, by West Coast writers.

2. Greene, Sir Hugh, editor: *The Further Rivals of Sherlock Holmes.* New York: Pantheon Books. Thirteen stories from the Holmes years in this the third in Greene's series of anthologies.

3. Hitchcock, Alfred, editor: *Alfred Hitchcock Presents: Stories to be Read With the Lights On.* New York: Random House. Thirty-seven stories, reprinted largely from magazine sources.

4. Hitchcock, Alfred, editor: *Death-Mate.* New York: Dell. Fourteen stories from *AHMM,* 1961–1970.

5. Hitchcock, Alfred, editor: *Let It All Bleed Out.* New York: Dell. Fourteen stories from *AHMM,* 1960–1970.

6. Hubin, Allen J., editor: *Best Detective Stories of the Year—1973:* 27th Annual Collection. New York: E. P. Dutton & Co. Seventeen of the best crime stories published in the U.S. in 1972.

7. Kahn, Joan, editor: *Trial and Terror.* Boston: Houghton Mifflin Co. Nineteen stories and six true crime articles from a wide diversity of sources.

8. Manley, Seon and Lewis, Gogo, editors: *Grande Dames of Detection: Two Centuries of Sleuthing Stories by the Gentle Sex.* New York: Lothrop, Lee & Shepard. Nine stories.

9. Manley, Seon and Lewis, Gogo, editors: *Mistresses of Mystery: Two Centuries of Suspense Stories by the Gentle Sex.* New York: Lothrop, Lee & Shepard. Eight stories and a play.

10. Queen, Ellery, editor: *Ellery Queen's Anthology:* Spring–Summer 1973. New York: Davis Publications. A semi-annual softcover anthology from *EQMM,* including ten from the magazine and five heretofore unpublished.

11. Queen, Ellery, editor: *Ellery Queen's Anthology:* Fall–Winter 1973. New York: Davis Publications. Seven short novels in a semi-annual softcover anthology from *EQMM.*

12. Reno, Marie, editor: *A Treasury of Modern Mysteries.* Two Volumes. Garden City, N.Y.: Doubleday & Co. Four novels and fifteen shorter stories, largely from the 1960s.

13. Santesson, Hans Stefan, editor: *Mirror, Mirror, Fatal Mirror.* Garden City, N.Y.: Doubleday & Co. Twenty-two stories, five heretofore unpublished, in the annual anthology from the Mystery Writers of America.

14. *The Times of London Anthology of Detective Stories.* New York: The John Day Company. Ten stories from the detective story competition sponsored by the *Times* of London in 1972.

III. Critique and Reference

1. Barker, Dudley: *G. K. Chesterton.* New York: Stein and Day. A new biography of Chesterton, giving brief and dismissive attention to his detective/crime fiction.

2. Briney, Robert E. and Nevins, Francis M., Jr., editors: *Multiplying Villainies: Selected Mystery Criticism, 1942–1968,* by Anthony Boucher. Salem, Massachusetts (4 Forest Avenue): A Bouchercon Book. A rich sampling of the peerless American critic of mystery fiction, including his annual year-end summaries from the *New York Times Book Review.*

3. Bruccoli, Matthew J., editor: *Chandler Before Marlowe*. Columbia, South Carolina: University of South Carolina Press. A selection of twenty-nine poems, eight essays and sketches, and four reviews written by Chandler before he turned to detective fiction.

4. Farmer, Philip Jose: *Doc Savage: His Apocalyptic Life*. Garden City, N.Y.: Doubleday & Co. An imaginative "biography" of the pulp magazine hero, tracing his lineage to several famous sleuths of history.

5. Lovecraft, Howard Phillips: *Supernatural Horror in Literature*. New York: Dover Publications. A new edition of Lovecraft's notable critical work, out of print since the 1940s.

6. Norris, Luther, editor: *The Pontine Dossier—1973*. Culver City, California (P.O. Box 261): The Pontine Press. Articles and commentary on August Derleth and his Solar Pons stories.

7. Pearson, John: *James Bond: the authorized biography of 007*. New York: William Morrow & Co. A fictional account of the life of Ian Fleming's superspy.

8. Stout, Rex: *The Nero Wolfe Cook Book*. New York: The Viking Press. 225 original recipes, flavored by numerous appropriate excerpts from the Wolfian canon.

AWARDS

Mystery Writers of America

Best novel—Tony Hillerman, *Dance Hall of the Dead* (Harper & Row)

Best American first novel—Paul E. Erdman, *The Billion Dollar Sure Thing* (Charles Scribner's Sons)

Best short story—Harlan Ellison, *The Whimper of Whipped Dogs* (*Gallery* Magazine)

Crime Writers Association

1972: Gold Dagger: *The Levanter,* by Eric Ambler (Weidenfeld)
Silver Dagger: *The Rainbird Pattern,* by Victor Canning (Heinemann)

1973: Gold Dagger: *The Defection of A. J. Lewinter,* by Robert Littell (Hodder & Stoughton)
Silver Dagger: *A Coffin for Pandora,* by Gwendoline Butler (Macmillan)

John Creasey Memorial Award (for best first crime novel) : *Don't Point That Thing at Me,* by Kyril Bonfiglioni (Weidenfeld and Nicholson) .

NECROLOGY

(the assistance of George Wuyek in compiling this section is once more gratefully acknowledged)

1. Alexander, David (1907–1973). Newspaperman, turf writer, and author of sixteen volumes of mystery fiction, 1951–1961; editor of the 14th Mystery Writers of America anthology, *Tales for a Rainy Night* (1961).

2. Barlow, James (1921–1973). Mainstream British novelist whose works verge closely on crime fiction in several instances.

3. Bayer, Eleanor (?–1973). Collaborated with her husband, Leo G. Bayer, to produce four mystery novels in the 1940s under the pseudonym Oliver Weld Bayer.

4. Bishop, Morris (1893–1973). Scholar, biographer, poet, and, as "W. Bolingbroke Johnson," author of the detective novel *The Widening Stain* (1942).

5. Brean, Herbert J. (1907–1973). Author of fiction and non-fiction, including seven fine mystery/detective novels, 1949–1966; editor of *The Mystery Writer's Handbook* (1956) ; past president of the Mystery Writers of America.

6. Conly, Robert L. (1918–1973). As "Robert C. O'Brien," author of the intrigue novel *A Report from Group 17* (1972).

7. Coppel, Alec (1909–1972). Australian playwright and screenwriter; wrote several mystery novels, including *Over the Line* (1947) and *Mr. Denning Drives North* (1951) ; collaborated on the screenplay of Hitchcock's *Vertigo*.

8. Creasey, John (1908–1973). The most prolific mystery novelist in history; author of some 560 books under more than 20 bylines; Edgar Winner for *Gideon's Fire* (1961; as by J. J. Marric) ; founder of Britain's Crime Writers Association; member and past president of the Mystery Writers of America; editor of the annual *Mystery Bedside Book* (London, 1960–1965), of *John Creasey Mystery Magazine* (London, 1960s), and of the 19th *MWA* anthology, *Crimes Across the Sea* (1964).

9. Fetter, Elizabeth Head (1904–1973). As "Hannah Lees," mainstream

author of novels and short stories as well as three mysteries, *Prescription for Murder* (1941), *Death in the Doll's House* (with Lawrence P. Bachmann; 1943), and *The Dark Device* (1947).

10. Helú, Antonio (1902–1972). Foremost Mexican detective story writer, whose short story collection *La Obligacion de Asesinar* (*The Compulsion to Kill;* Mexico City, 1946) about rogue-detective Máximo Roldán is enshrined as Number 102 in Ellery Queen's listing of the most important books in the detective-crime short story field (*Queen's Quorum,* 1969).

11. Hostovsky, Egon (1908–1973). Czechoslavakia-born mainstream novelist whose works (such as *Missing,* 1951) contain elements in common with suspense fiction.

12. Howes, Royce (1901–1973). Detroit newsman and Pulitzer Prize winner (1955) for editorial work; author of numerous mystery stories, including eight novels (1935–1945).

13. Malleson, Lucy Beatrice (1889–1973). As "Anthony Gilbert," author of more than 60 detective novels, nearly 50 of them celebrating the exploits of Arthur Crook, wily and unconventional lawyer-cum-sleuth.

14. Maloney, Ralph L. (1927–1973). Novelist whose works included a humorous crime tale, *The Nixon Recession Caper* (1972).

15. Muir, Jean (1906–1973). Active for many years as a magazine writer, she turned latterly to books, including two novels of romantic suspense, *The Smiling Medusa* (1969) and *Stranger, Tread Light* (1971).

16. Procter, Maurice (1906–1973). British policeman turned author who produced a notable series of police procedural novels among some two dozen books.

17. Snow, Walter (1907–1973). Newspaperman and author, whose works included many mystery short stories and novels, among the latter *The Golden Nightmare* (1952).

18. Stevenson, D(orothy) E(mily) (1892–1973). Prolific author of romantic novels, among whose works was included the espionage novel *Crooked Adam* (1942).

19. Tessier, Ernest Maurice (1885–1973). As "Maurice Dekobra" a highly successful French novelist, who numbered many volumes of crime/mystery/detection among his works.

20. Thayer, Lee (1874–1973). Author of 60 detective novels, from *The Mystery of the Thirteenth Floor* (1919) to *Dusty Death* (1966), published when she was a nonagenarian. All but one of her books (*Doctor S.O.S.,* 1925) featured her sleuth Peter Clancy.

21. Tregaskis, Richard (1916–1973). War correspondent and author of nonfiction works as well as the intrigue-suspense novel, *China Bomb* (1967).
22. Wilson, Mitchell (1913–1973). Science writer and novelist, who produced four suspense novels, *Footsteps Behind Her* (1942), *Stalk the Hunter* (1943), *None So Blind* (1945) and *The Panic-Stricken* (1946), as well as the detective story, *The Goose is Cooked* (1940), under the by-line Emmett Hogarth, a joint pseudonym with Abraham Polonsky.

HONOR ROLL

(Starred stories are included in this volume.)

Asimov, Isaac: "Light Verse," *Saturday Evening Post*, September/October.

————: "The Obvious Factor," *EQMM*, May.

*Antonich, George: "Late, Late Call," *MSMM*, November.

Arthur, Ellen: "The Scene of the Crime," *EQMM*, August.

Bankier, William: "A Bad Scene," *EQMM*, July.

————: "My Brother's Killer," *EQMM*, April.

————: "Policeman's Lot," *EQMM*, October.

Bentley, Phyllis: "Miss Phipps on the Telephone," *EQMM*, July.

Blau, Kelly H.: "What Have You Been Doing All Day," *EQMM*, October.

Bloch, Robert: "See How They Run," *EQMM*, April.

Boeckman, Charles: "Class Reunion," *AHMM*, June.

Boylan, Eleanor: "The Hardest Part of All," *EQMM*, November.

Breen, Jon L.: "Champoux Versus Joshua," *EQMM*, July.

————: "Old Timers' Game," *EQMM*, April.

Brittain, William: "The Man Who Read G. K. Chesterton," *EQMM*, April.

————: "A State of Preparedness," *AHMM*, September.

Brown, Margaret E.: "To Hide a Tree," *AHMM*, May.

Carleton, Don: "The Tale of Sir Jeremy Fisher," *The Times of London Anthology of Detective Stories*.

Chesbro, George C.: "Country for Sale," *MSMM*, June.

————: "Rage," *AHMM*, February.

Christie, Agatha: "The Harlequin Tea Set," *EQMM*, June.

*DiGioia, Marie: "The Last Contract," *EQMM*, January.

Duke, Jim: "Bloody Oasis," *MSMM*, July.

Eckels, Robert Edward: "Bread Upon the Waters," *EQMM*, March.

Edwards, Tom: "A Winning Combination," *AHMM*, April.

Ellin, Stanley: "The Corruption of Officer Avakadian," *EQMM*, December.

*Ellison, Harlan: "The Whimper of Whipped Dogs," *Gallery*, June.

Enos, Ruth: "The Best of Accidents," *EQMM*, February.

Fish, Robert L.: "In the Bag," *Playboy*, April.

————: "Muldoon and the Numbers Game," *Saturday Evening Post*, July/August.

————: "No Rough Stuff," *EQMM*, September.

————: "The Wager," *Playboy*, July.

*Forsyth, Frederick: "No Comebacks," *Playboy*, May.

Francis, Dick: "Carrot for a Chestnut," *EQMM*, February.

Freeling, Nicolas: "Van der Valk and the Train Watcher," *EQMM*, April.

Freeman, Michael: "The Scapegoat," *The Times of London Anthology of Detective Stories*.

Fremlin, Celia: "Waiting for the Police," *EQMM*, February.

Garforth, John: "A Quite Conventional Death," *The Times of London Anthology of Detective Stories*.

Garrett, Randall: "A Stretch of the Imagination," *Men & Malice*.

Gilbert, Anthony: "Fifty Years After," *EQMM*, March.

Gilbert, Elliot L.: "The Sins of the Father," *EQMM*, June.

Gilbert, Michael: "The Death of Mrs. Key," *EQMM*, December.

————: "Of Suspicious Origin," *EQMM*, October.

Godwin, Tom: "She Was a Child," *MSMM*, April.

*Gores, Joe: "The O'Bannon Blarney File," *Men & Malice*.

Goulart, Ron: "Down There," *MSMM*, February.

————: "The Laughing Chef," *EQMM*, September.

Harrison, Michael: "The Jewel of Childeric," *EQMM*, April.

Hay, Jacob: "In an Outpost of Empire," *EQMM*, June.

Highsmith, Patricia: "Variations on a Game," *AHMM*, February.

————: "Who Dies, Who Lives?" *EQMM*, August.

Hoch, Edward D.: "Captain Leopold Plays a Hunch," *EQMM*, July.

————: "The Case of the Third Apostle," *EQMM*, February.

————: "The Gold Buddha Caper," *EQMM*, December.

————: "The Man Who Came Back," *AHMM*, May.

————: "The Theft of the Cuckoo Clock," *EQMM*, September.

————: "Two Days in Organville," *AHMM*, February.

Hocking, Mary: "Mr. Joslin's Journey," *EQMM*, May.

Holding, James: "The Photographer and the Artist," *EQMM*, May.

————: "The Photographer and the Butcher," *EQMM*, July.

Howard, Clark: "The Best Hideout," *AHMM*, March.

————: "Deadly August," *AHMM*, August.

————: "Next in Line," *AHMM*, June.

————: "The Seven Strangers," *MSMM*, November.

Irvine, R. R.: "Lobster Shift," *EQMM*, March.

Jacobson, Jerry: "From Tinker to Evers to Jail," *MSMM*, October.

*———: "Morning Watch," *AHMM*, March.

James, Vincent: "When Tomorrow Comes," *EQMM*, September.

Josey, Alex: "Oriental Justice," *The Times of London Anthology of Detective Stories*.

Kipp, George Grover: "Metamorphosis," *AHMM*, November.

Knowles, John: "Neville," *Cosmopolitan*, April.

Law, Warner: "The Alarming Letters from Scottsdale," *Fantasy & Science Fiction*, April.

Lee, William M.: "A Paris Symposium," *MSMM*, October.

Long, Virginia: "Always on Saturday," *AHMM*, October.

———: "A Fine and Private Place," *AHMM*, September.

———: "Neighbors," *AHMM*, December.

Lutz, John: "The Shooting of Curly Dan," *EQMM*, August.

Lyon, Dana: "Silence!", *Men & Malice*.

Marric, J. J.: "Gideon and the Inside Job," *EQMM*, April.

Marsh, Ngaio: "Chapter and Verse," *EQMM*, March.

Masur, Harold Q.: "The Graft is Green," *AHMM*, May.

Mathieson, Theodore: "Thomas Wolfe and the Tombstone Mystery," *EQMM*, March.

———: "White Sheep," *MSMM*, August.

Matthews, Clayton: "The Legend," *MSMM*, August.

Mayberry, Florence V.: "In the Secret Hollow," *EQMM*, December.

———: "Monkey-Face," *EQMM*, June.

*———: "Woman Trouble," *EQMM*, October.

*McBain, Ed: "Sadie When She Died," *AHMM*, January.

McConnor, Vincent: "First Guest of the Season," *AHMM*, December.

McHale, Tom: "A Society of Friends," *Playboy*, July.

*McKibbon, Mollie Pearce: "Beyond the Last House," *EQMM*, November.

McKimmey, James: "Wronged Cop," *AHMM*, April.

*McNear, Robert: "Neighbors," *Playboy*, June.

Miller, William: "Green Ink," *EQMM*, December.

Moore, Arthur: "The Green Monster," *AHMM*, September.

Nevins, Francis M., Jr.: "Murder of a Male Chauvinist," *EQMM*, May.

Newman, Aubrey S.: "Turnabout," *MSMM*, January.

Nolan, William F.: "Coincidence," *The Berserkers*.

———: "Violation," *Future City*.

Nielsen, Helen: "What Shall We Do About Angela," *AHMM*, December.

Nussbaum, Al: "An Easy Score," *AHMM*, January.

Oates, Joyce Carol: "Do With Me What You Will," *Playboy,* June.
Olson, Donald: "Green Thumbs and Trigger Fingers," *AHMM,* August.
————: "More Than a Home," *AHMM,* July.
————: "They Sent You," *AHMM,* October.
Pachter, Josh: "Take One," *AHMM,* November.
*Parry, Henry T.: "Homage to John Keats," *EQMM,* October.
Peirce, J. F.: "The Double Death of Nell Quigley," *EQMM,* December.
Pentecost, Hugh: "Chambrun Plays It Cool," *EQMM,* July.
————: "Jericho Plays It Cool," *EQMM,* July.
Perowne, Barry: "Raffles and the Point of Morality," *EQMM,* August.
Podrug, Junius T.: "Vendetta," *EQMM,* October.
Porges, Irwin: "The Stores That Come and Go," *MSMM,* September.
Powell, James: "The Ascent of the Grimselhorn," *EQMM,* April.
————: "The Bee on the Finger," *Playboy,* September.
*————: "A Murder Coming," *EQMM,* September.
————: "The Theft of the Fabulous Hen," *EQMM,* November.
Pronzini, Bill: "Proof of Guilt," *EQMM,* December.
————: "The Scales of Justice," *AHMM,* July.
Rafferty, S. S.: "Murder by Scalping," *EQMM,* July.
Rendell, Ruth: "Trapped," *EQMM,* September.
Ritchie, Jack: "But Don't Tell Your Mother," *AHMM,* August.
*————: "The Magnum," *Debonair.*
Rudin, John: "Sellin' Some Wood," *EQMM,* November.
Russell, Ray: "Quoth the Raven," *Men & Malice.*
Schmitz, James H.: "Crime Buff," *AHMM,* August.
Scortia, Thomas N.: "The Goddess of the Cats," *Men & Malice.*
Scott, Jeffry: "Trip Up on a Ripple," *EQMM,* February.
Sheppard, Madelyn: "The Lucky Stone," *EQMM,* December.
Sisk, Frank: "The Case of Dr. Caxton," *AHMM,* October.
————: "The Good Provider," *AHMM,* December.
————: "The Hogarth Plates," *Penthouse,* January.
————: "Morning Simplifies Everything," *AHMM,* June.
Sladek, John: "By an Unknown Hand," *The Times of London Anthology of Detective Stories.*
Smith, Pauline C.: "Linda is Gone," *AHMM,* November.
————: "A Motto for Murder," *AHMM,* June.
————: "No Imagination," *AHMM,* April.
————: "Petition for Justice," *MSMM,* January.
————: "Where Have You Been, Ross Ivy?", *AHMM,* January.
Stevens, R. L.: "The Most Dangerous Man," *EQMM,* February.

Stiles, Sean: "Occam's Razor," *The Times of London Anthology of Detective Stories.*

Strongman, Kenneth: "The Speculator," *The Times of London Anthology of Detective Stories.*

Sweet, Jeff: "The Discussion is Over," *EQMM*, January.

*———: "Over the Borderline," *EQMM*, May.

Symons, Julian: "How to Trap a Crook," *EQMM*, March.

Talbot, Michael: "Oddity Imports," *EQMM*, April.

Treat, Lawrence: "Give the Devil His Due," *EQMM*, February.

*Treat, Lawrence and Plotz, Charles M.: "The Good Lord Will Provide," *EQMM*, June.

Twohy, Robert: "Vengeance," *EQMM*, October.

Tyre, Nedra: "Locks Won't Keep You Out," *EQMM*, February.

Ullman, James Michael: "Light at the End of the Tunnel," *AHMM*, July.

———: "Lost and Found," *AHMM*, August.

Van Derveer, Max: "The Missing Priest," *AHMM*, March.

Walton, Bryce: "The Man on the Stair," *AHMM*, October.

Wasylyk, Stephen: "Funeral in a Small Town," *AHMM*, February.

———: "Lesson for a Pro," *AHMM*, July.

Weales, Gerald: "The Country of Silence," *EQMM*, May.

Webb, Jack: "This Man Must Die," *MSMM*, February.

*Weber, Thomasina: "Loaded Quest," *AHMM*, August.

Wellen, Edward: "I Kid You Not," *AHMM*, May.

Westphal, Roger: "Summer Job," *EQMM*, January.

Whitney, O. G. and Proctor, Lisa: "In the Land of the Great Spirit," *EQMM*, August.

Wolf, Luna: "The Kind and Considerate Murderer," *EQMM*, July.

*Yarbro, Chelsea Quinn: "The Ghosts at Iron River," *Men & Malice.*

Young, Alan K.: "To See Death Coming," *EQMM*, April.

Zuroy, Michael: "The Extortionists," *MSMM*, December.

———: "The Reckoning," *AHMM*, March.

———: "The Testing," *MSMM*, June.

ABOUT THE EDITOR

Allen J. Hubin is editor-publisher of *The Armchair Detective,* a periodical devoted to news about books and writers of detective fact and fiction. He lives with his family in White Bear Lake, Minnesota.